Slapton Sands

Inspired by a true story

by

RICHARD BLADE

Copyright © 2024 Richard Blade

Bladerocker Books

All Rights Reserved

ISBN: 9798322040644

Library of Congress Control Number 1-899075681

This novel is a work of fiction. Any reference to real events, dates, institutions, businesses, government agencies, organizations, or locales, are intended only to give the fiction a sense of reality and authenticity. Any resemblance to any actual persons, living or dead, is entirely coincidental.

No part of this book may be reproduced or transmitted in any form or by any means, electronic or mechanical, including photocopying, recording, or by any information storage or retrieval systems, without the written permission of the author.

Photographs in this book used by permission from the United States National Archives

Cover by 100 Covers

Also by Richard Blade

"You will devour Richard Blade's every word." *Jimmy Kimmel*

"Part Gladiator, part Pocahontas, 100% must-read." *Jim Amos, Forbes*

"Thrilling! Mystery, suspense, and genius twists." *Tony Potts, Access Hollywood*

"An incredible read that makes me want to time-travel and join these boys on stage." *Travis Knox, Executive Producer, The Bucket List.*

"Richard is the voice of the second British Invasion, and now he's written about it." *John Taylor, Duran Duran*

"A must-read action-packed adventure, beating with the pulse of a political thriller." *Robert Kinsler, Desert Star*

"Richard, your knowledge about the music and your caring for the artists is unmatched." *Ian Astbury, The Cult*

ACKNOWLEDGEMENTS

To Ken Small, thank you for your incredible efforts in bringing this story to light.

To all the heroes who fought to end the threat of fascism and stamp out the evil of the Nazi party, your sacrifice should never be forgotten.

To my beloved Krista. Thank you for always being there for me.

To Chloe and Tashi. Every time I write, I know you will both be there, cuddled by my feet.

To Mum and Dad, without you taking me to Slapton Sands, this book wouldn't have been written, Just another one of a million reasons I can never forget all you did for me.

INTRODUCTION

This book is deeply personal to me, as I grew up just a few miles away from Slapton Sands. Situated in the county of Devon, the heart of England's West Country, this coastal region has a great seafaring heritage spanning from one of the world's most prestigious naval colleges, BRNC, Dartmouth, to the city and port of Plymouth, from which Sir Francis Drake sailed to defeat the Spanish Armada of 1588, and where the Pilgrim Fathers departed to colonize the New World on the other side of the Atlantic Ocean.

As a child, my parents would take my brother and I to Slapton Sands to play on the two-mile-long beach and to check out the wildlife and colonies of migrating birds taking refuge in Slapton Ley, a marshy lagoon right behind the beach itself.

The village of Torcross at Slapton Sands is tiny, and we would stop at the one pub there for lunch, usually fish'n'chips with a shandy to drink. But as welcome as those delights were, the thing that fascinated me most about Slapton Sands were the signs posted all the way along the beach. They read, in deliberately scary wording, *If you see anything that looks like military ordinance washed up onto the shore, DO NOT GO NEAR IT. Dial 999 to report what you have found, and leave the area at once.*

Being a young boy, this seemed very exciting, and my brother and I would scour the shingle-covered beach looking for anything we could find. Over the years, we retrieved several bullet casings, and one time, our biggest treasure, the base of a large shell. Dad, who had served in the Royal Artillery, explained it had been fired and it was what remained in the big gun that shot it, and then jettisoned so a new round could be loaded. Stephen and I kept the brass casing, polished it, and for years it sat in pride of place by our fireplace in our house.

What we didn't know, is why so many army artifacts kept washing up, many of them still live and dangerous, twenty years after the end of the war. It was common knowledge the Americans had used Slapton Sands and the thirty thousand acres around it in the area called the South Hams, for training exercises prior to D-Day, but surely that didn't explain why so much ordinance was still being found. It was a mystery to all of us, and little did we know, a mystery to the entire world, because the reason for all the used ammunition and live charges still being found, was being deliberately concealed.

It was the summer of 1984 when I got the call from England explaining what had happened. I was living in America, in Los Angeles, when mum phoned. We talked at least three times a week, so it was no surprise hearing her voice on the line. What was a shock was how excited she was, and eager to share the news. I remember it as if it was yesterday.

"Richard, you won't believe what's happened."

"What? Are you okay, Mum?"

"I'm fine, my love. It's what's happened at Slapton."

"Did the bomb disposal squad blow up some more live ammo?"

"No, my love. They found a tank. An American tank."

"An American tank? Was it in the woods?"

"No, it was underwater. They found it out at sea."

"Underwater? How did it get there?"

"That's the big story. It's everywhere in the newspapers and radio. It's all they're talking about."

"Finding the tank?"

"No, but what happened after they found the tank."

"What happened?"

"Apparently, there was a big cover-up, my love. A huge battle was fought at Slapton Sands with the Germans, and hundreds of men were killed, but it's been kept secret all these years."

"Secret? Why?"

"We don't know yet, that's what all the reporters are asking and trying to find out who was responsible and why so many young men died. I'll send you some of the press cuttings from the Daily Mail and the Herald Express. It's a really big story over here."

A few months later I flew over to visit mum, and we went together to Slapton Sands. By now, a lot of the information was coming out; how it was one of America's biggest military disasters of World War II, and how it had been hushed up so that not even the families of the heroic GIs who died fighting knew what really happened to them. The cover-up went so deep that not a single one of the soldiers even received a purple heart, despite the hundreds of fatalities and the thousands of injuries caused during the battle.

Many times over the following years, I walked the area used as the training ground for one of America's two targets during D-Day, Utah Beach. Slapton Sands was an almost perfect match for that American landing spot in Normandy, France. The beach there was long and exposed, and behind it, the Germans had flooded the fields, creating a marsh to slow down an invading army. If the Americans practiced on Slapton Sands, and marshy Slapton Ley behind it, they would be prepared for the French beach designated, *Utah*.

I loved hiking the steep trail up to the cliffs framing the sprawling beach, cliffs the Rangers practiced on to prepare for their assault on the deadly gun emplacements overlooking the beaches. As I stared down from that vantage point, I knew this was a story that had to be told. But I wanted to write it as a novel, not as a non-fiction account as had been done, including in Ken Small's great book, *The Forgotten Dead*, which recounts the finding of the tank and the struggles to bring it up.

I wanted to go back and tell the story of those brave young soldiers, most of whom had never seen combat before. Kids, who were outside of America for the first time, and the intense training they were put through to get them ready to face the waiting German guns and Hitler's feared Atlantic Wall. And most of all, I wanted to write about the battle itself, the terrible night of April 28th, 1944, when seven hundred and forty nine heroic Americans died fighting, but were never acknowledged, not even by their own government, in perhaps the biggest military cover-up of WWII; one that was labelled Top Secret and concealed for more than forty years.

I have worked factual events into a fictional story and have made a few changes for dramatic purposes as we revisit the world through the eyes of two starcrossed lovers, a young sergeant from California and a beautiful English girl doing her part in the war effort, during those perilous days when the Nazis were Europe's brutal overlords, and the fate of freedom and democracy hung in the balance.

A very special thank you to the United States National Archives who granted me access to their files to research and use in this book, including formerly Top Secret dispatches and hundreds of photographs and still-frames from their film footage shot by combat photographers of the training at Slapton Sands from December 1943 to April 1944.

SLAPTON SANDS

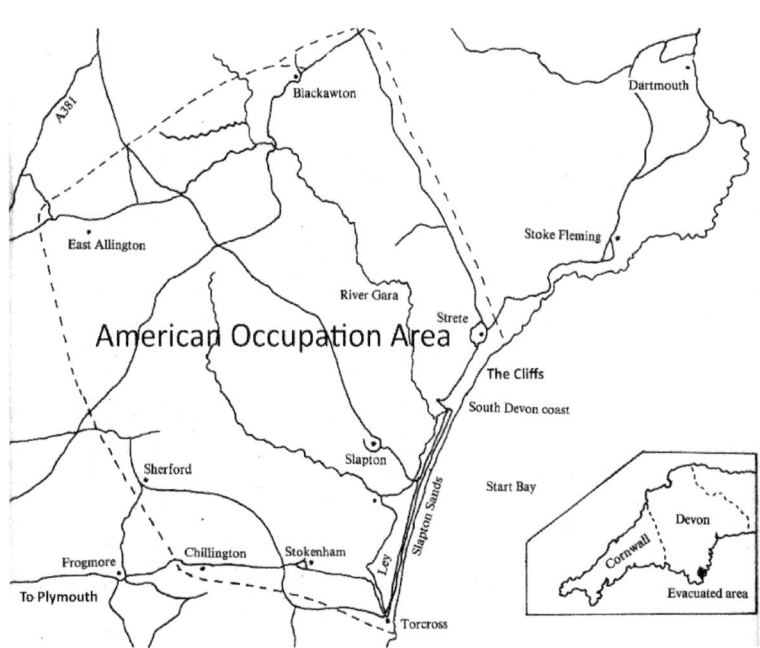

The village of Torcross at Slapton Sands

CHAPTERS

1	The Unwelcome Catch	1
2	Evacuation	23
3	Occupation	35
4	The Exercises Begin	45
5	Meeting	58
6	Chocolate	83
7	Live Fire	98
8	City In Flames	107
9	The Brook	133
10	The Old Soldier	142
11	Support	150
12	LST 289	164
13	Three Gifts	172
14	Exercise Tiger	181

CHAPTER ONE
The Unwelcome Catch

April 17th, 1979

Countless diamonds sparkled and danced on the empty ocean as the early rays of the springtime sun played upon the water's silky surface. A thirty-foot trawler, minutes out from its safe berth in Dartmouth Harbor, began a southwest cruise across the wide expanse of Start Bay, its weathered wooden bow cutting through the cold, calm sea.

Onboard the fishing vessel, the two crew members stood shoulder to shoulder in the cramped wheelhouse, the younger one lighting his third cigarette of the morning. The captain wrinkled his brow in disapproval. "How old are you, Peter?"

"Nearly twenty-two, sir."

"It's not *sir*, it's Fred. And if you want to see thirty, you'll give up that disgusting habit. I haven't smoked since sixty-three, what is that, sixteen years now, and I'll tell you, quitting was the best thing I ever did. I breathe easier and food tastes better too. And don't let me catch you throwing your butts in the water; if you have to smoke, put them with the rest of the rubbish."

"But that's not safe, si...Fred. It's a fire risk. On every boat I've ever worked, the captain always had me chuck them over the side."

"Well, not on this boat. Make sure they're out and we'll be fine." Fred Hunter turned his attention to the coastline slipping past. "Is that Slapton?" he asked.

"Almost. The cliffs there mark the beginning of it. That's Stoke Fleming; Slapton Sands comes right after; it'll be the really long beach stretching all the way down to Torcross."

"I think we should start running out the nets now. We can get some extra time in, and trawl all the way to Start Point-"

Peter cut him off. "Can't do that, sir. No one fishes off Slapton. That's the reason we're the only boat out here this morning."

"Why not? These aren't restricted waters."

"No, they're not. It's 'cause of what's down there. If we put the nets out now, we'll lose them. Something takes 'em."

"What do you mean, something takes them? When I moved here and bought this boat, no one said anything about the legend of a net-hungry monster." He stared hard at his first mate. "You sure those are cigarettes you're smoking?"

"Just tobaccy, Fred." He held up his pack of Woodbines. "I didn't say nothing 'bout a monster, but there is something out there snagging nets off the beach. Word is, it was good fishing here in the old days, lots of mullet and bass, and on the bottom, plaice and all kinds of flat fish, but unless you've got a rod and line, they're staying down there. No one's used a net off Slapton in years. The fisherfolk learned their lesson the hard way."

"That makes no sense. If there's fish in this area and we're the first boat in ..." he paused, "years-" Peter nodded in agreement. "Then there should be a fair bounty waiting for us. Look, boy, I may not have run a trawler in Devon before, but my first job at age twelve was fishing out of Hull, and then from Whitby when I was a teenager, and it wasn't often we came home without a decent haul." He swung his gaze across the flat surface of the English Channel. "From what I've been told, it's rare to get these quiet conditions this time of year so I say we take advantage of it before the springtime rains come and the winds make trawling out here cold and miserable. We'll run our nets out now." Fred's final words left no doubt of his decision.

Peter said nothing and stepped from the tiny wheelhouse, walking carefully across the wooden deck made slippery by the early morning damp air, and reached the stern where the nets were spooled around a large cylindrical winch stretching the entire ten-foot beam of the boat. He grasped the lever releasing the lock and freeing the nets, hesitating and looking back at Fred on the off-chance he'd reconsidered.

Fred understood the boy's silent apprehension and confirmed his decision. "Do it. Let them go."

Peter pulled hard and moved away quickly to avoid any entanglement as the weighted nets spun on the reel and unwound, beginning their descent below the waters. In less than a minute the winch was empty and all that remained and continued to unwind was the four hundred feet of heavy marine rope tethering the nets to the vessel.

With the winch's motor stopped, the boat fell quiet except for the low thump-thump-thump of the old diesel engine below deck. Neither spoke as they waited to see what would happen. Fred broke the awkward silence with a laugh. "I guess the Slap Ness monster or Neptune or Godzilla, or whatever's down there, is sleeping today. Nets are out and everything's good, and if I'm correct with my bearings, we should be off Slapton Sands."

"Just passed the cliffs, so you're right, and at our trawling speed of four knots, we'll be sailing past the beach for about forty-five minutes to an hour."

"Then let's make ourselves comfortable. We've done our job, now it's up to the nets to do theirs-" The winch screamed and the boat shuddered and slowed, the old timbers issuing a warning groan as the fastening bolts felt the unexpected pull. In seconds the boat began swinging against the sudden restraint.

"Told you, sir, we're caught. We 'ave to stop the engines or they'll burn out."

"Damn it." Fred Hunter slammed the boat into *'all stop'* and twisted the key, killing the diesels. "Alright, let's bring in the nets."

"Won't be able to do that if she's caught like the others were."

"We won't know until we try," Fred barked as he restarted the engines. "I'm going to turn her around and work our way back. If we winch them up from behind, they should come free."

"*Should* is a big word right now, sir. Make sure we don't catch the line in the propellers or we'll find ourselves in a right pickle."

"I know that." Fred heard the tone of his voice and tried dialing back his anger. "I'm going to go slow. We have about two hundred feet of line deployed; when we get behind whatever has snagged us, we'll bring it in, put pressure on the nets and free them." He could see the look on the boy's face was not hopeful. "We've got to try."

The old trawler began its slow circle, the hawser running down to the nets going limp as the tension on it eased. The captain waited impatiently for the boat to reach a position behind whatever had caught the nets dragging on the bottom, and finally, feeling they were in the optimum spot, again hit *'all stop.'* "Okay, Peter, bring them up, but do it half speed, just in case."

Peter's expression had not changed, and Fred thought he saw an almost imperceptible shrug as he engaged the motorized winch. With nothing pulling on it, the long cylinder turned and the two-inch-thick marine rope began to emerge from the green water. At half speed it seemed to take forever as the cable wound itself on to the spool.

"What do you think, another hundred feet?" asked Fred.

"'bout that. And the water's around sixty foot here so-" The howl of the motor sticking cut him off. Instantly Peter threw the winch back into neutral, relieving the pressure and saving the gears and engine. "Still stuck."

"I know!"

"We have to cut them loose."

"Not a chance. That's not going to happen."

"Then what do you want to do now?"

"I need to think." Fred turned from glaring at the winch, and stormed to the bow.

Peter rolled his eyes as he muttered to himself. "Got plenty of time to do that. This boat ain't going nowhere 'til we cut ourselves free." He stayed at the stern and lit another cigarette. He was about to start his second when Fred reappeared.

"You decide on anything?"

"Yes. We'll cut the cable, fix a buoy on it, and then we can find the nets when we come back."

"Isn't that a bit pointless? They'll still be stuck whenever it is we return here."

"There's no way in hell I'm losing five hundred quid's worth of nets on my first day out. I'd be a laughingstock. I'm going to come back and free them."

"Free them? How?"

"I'll rent some SCUBA gear, dive down and get them untangled with my bare hands if I have to. After that, we'll splice the cable and it'll be like it never happened."

"You'll need a license to rent an air tank for diving."

"I got one with BSAC. When I started in the service with the RAF at Brize Norton, they gave us the option to get certified in case we were forced to make a water landing; figured it would give us more confidence if we came down in the sea. I just need a place to rent the gear."

"Jack's Sports rents air tanks and all the stuff you'll need; they're not far, over in Preston. Better get a good rubber suit too. The water's fucking freezing this time of year, go in without one and you'll freeze your crown jewels in a minute."

"I'll get everything there-"

"And a speargun as well, in case it is a monster."

Fred shook his head. "If there's a monster down there big enough to snag my nets, seize the winch and stop the boat, I don't think a speargun would be much help. Come on, get me a buoy and a knife. We've got work to do so we can find this spot when we come back."

Fred splashed hard as he back-rolled from the boat. He tensed as the icy water entered his wetsuit; it must only be forty degrees he thought, as cold or maybe colder than on his search and rescue dive training in Oxford reservoir. He shivered as he kicked his way downward, wishing the water trapped between his skin and the tight neoprene wetsuit would warm up quickly.

It had been years since his last dive, and he moved slowly to let everything he'd been taught come back to him. Long, deep breaths, a relaxed kick, and keep one hand on the line leading from the buoy floating above on the surface. That was essential if he wanted to find the nets. The water was so murky he could barely see a yard in front of him, it would be easy to become disorientated in this green world. Following the line for reference would stop that from happening.

The gear he'd rented was basic, he hadn't bothered with any extras like a depth gauge or compass. Just two tanks in case he needed to go back down, a regulator and pressure gauge, wetsuit and weight belt, plus mask, flippers and a life jacket. At the last moment, he paid an extra thirty pence for a dive knife which he strapped to his right leg. He didn't want to use it. Cutting the nets would mean a lot of time repairing them, he was hoping to get them loose using only his gloved hands, but if he did need to cut them, he wanted to be prepared.

He felt he was getting close to the bottom, Peter had said the depth here was around sixty feet, and judging by the lengths of his breaths and the pressure on his ears, he guessed he was nearing that now. He instinctively tightened his grip on the rope to make sure he didn't overshoot the target and slowed his descent still more.

Through the sediment-filled water he could make out an enormous, shadowy shape waiting for him. The visibility was poor and little sun penetrated through to this depth to light up his goal, but whatever was below, it was big. He was right above it and all sides of the dark mass disappeared out into the gloom. He inched closer and saw most of its shape and size was obscured by nets, many encrusted with barnacles, showing how long they'd been underwater. He tugged the rope slightly and was rewarded by movement on the top and right side of the huge mound. Those had to be his nets; not only were they the most recent, covering the others, but the descent line was tied off to them. If they could be cleared away from the rest and what was holding them down here, he could winch them to the surface and they should be as good as they were when he'd lowered them, two days before.

Moving carefully, to avoid being caught in the wild tangle rising from the sea floor, he pulled on his weighted nets to see what was anchoring them to the bottom. Each batch he tested seemed to move freely and he could lift them several feet with no problem. Fred paused for a moment, remembering his diving course, and checked his pressure gauge. Eleven hundred pounds remained; he'd used two thirds of his air already. He cursed, and forced himself to slow down and control his breathing. That was what his sergeant-major stressed during his military training; no matter what was going on, try to concentrate on long, regular inhalation, it was the best way to extend time underwater.

He tugged a large section of net, knowing from how new it looked it had to be his. It didn't budge. This must be the part that had become caught. Maybe there was a rock protruding up from beneath the pile of discarded nets, a rock with crags or rough edges trapping the lines down there. He checked his gauge again; nine hundred pounds. With the safety stop he knew he needed to make at fifteen feet, he had only a few more minutes at this depth.

Instead of lifting upward, he tried sliding the net forward, hoping to get it loose from whatever was holding it. It began to move, confirming he was right, it was looped around something, but he couldn't see what it was. As he tugged on it, several of the older nets moved also, seemingly caught on the same outcropping. He had to be careful now, if they all suddenly came free they could entangle him, and with so little air left... He didn't want to think of the consequences.

His net, the last hooked, was almost off. He knew his excitement was mounting and tried controlling the feeling, knowing it would only burn through more of his precious air, but it was hard to do as he was so close now. He pushed the older nets back with his left hand and wrenched his net forward. It slipped off, leaving only one loop remaining tight around the object. Get that free and he could winch his net up intact, saving both his bank account and his reputation. He finned to the last loop to pull it clear and recoiled in shock. A giant gun barrel loomed out of the dark water, pointing at his face.

Fred tried stifling a gasp, but the regulator fell from his mouth and bubbles exploded around him. He kicked desperately upward while reaching down and sweeping with his right hand to find the regulator and put it back in his mouth. Without whatever air he had left in the tank, he'd never make it to the surface.

He grabbed the regulator and shoved the mouthpiece between his lips, first clearing it of water then breathing in the life-giving air. The sound of it flowing into his lungs helped calm him and he slowed his kicks. He wasn't sure where he was; in his wild ascent he'd lost sight of the rope, but he knew salvation waited above. But not right away; he had to do the planned safety stop first for five minutes. If he didn't, he risked the bends, which could mean a spell in hospital or perhaps much worse.

With less that one hundred pounds of air left, he finally broke the surface. He spat out his regulator, gripped the life jacket's manual tube between his teeth, bit down on the one-way valve to open it and blew four deep breaths inside, fully inflating it. With no danger of sinking now, he bobbed in the small waves, orientating himself, and caught sight of his boat fifty yards away. He rolled onto his back and kicked toward it, being careful not to overstretch his legs and trigger a cramped calf in these freezing waters.

He handed his weight belt and fins up to Peter and clambered back onboard. The boy couldn't contain his eagerness to learn what his captain had found down there. "So?"

"I got the nets free."

"Yes!" There was finally excitement in Peter's tone. "Should I winch them up now?"

"No, not yet. Make me a hot cup of tea while I change tanks and find some spare line. I'm going back down."

"Why?"

"Because we were caught on something strange, I'm not sure what, but I want to be able to find it again after we bring the nets up, so I'm going to tie a rope on it and make sure we leave a marker buoy above."

"But if we get the nets back, what's the point? There's always weird stuff on the bottom somewhere. The whole Spanish Armada went down around here."

"It's not some old wooden galleon, it's a lot more modern than that, and I'm pretty certain it's military gear. I can't let this go without knowing what it is. I'll tell you more after I get a good look, but right now I need a hot cuppa before I dive again; I'm chilled to the bone even in this wetsuit."

The sun was setting as the little fishing boat returned to its berth in Dartmouth Harbor. Peter jumped onto the old stone dock and tied the boat securely to the rusted iron cleats that had been doing their job for over four centuries. "Are we going out tomorrow?"

"No. Help me with these." He passed the heavy dive tanks, one at a time, to his deck hand who stood them on the pier. "We'll wait until Thursday. I need to get the cylinders filled and rent some other things from Jack's Sports."

"You're diving again so soon? What about fishing?"

"Fishing can wait. I told you; I want to find out what's down there and how it ended up on the sea floor." He forced a smile. "It's what I did for two decades with the RAF. I guess that kind of curiosity never goes away."

"I'll still get paid, right?"

"Right. You'll be my surface support; I can't do this without you."

Peter beamed. "Makes a nice change from being told I'm in the way. What time Thursday?"

"Six. Sunrise should be around seven. That'll give us time to prepare the boat for a full day of diving."

"Okay, see you then." Peter waved a quick farewell to his boss and turned to head for the harborside pub, eager to share stories about his crazy captain. As he walked, a cloud of nicotine-laden smoke marked his departure.

Deep underwater, Fred worked systematically around the tangled mound, and with his own nets gone and safely surfaced, he cut from the top, discarding the sliced webbing onto the sea floor. Twice he had to move his descent line and find another spot to retie the rope securing the marking buoy floating on the surface sixty feet above him. As he cut through the obscuring netting, the object began to appear. Even in the low visibility he could make out the barrel was attached to a turret. Was it a ship's gun? He used the serrated side of his dive knife to saw through the tougher sections. It was then he caught glimpse of the articulated track. There was no doubt anymore, it was a tank. He checked his pressure gauge – eight hundred pounds – time to start ascending, make his required safety stop, surface, change cylinders and do one more dive today.

"How can it be a tank? We're near two miles offshore, how did it get out here?" Peter's tone echoed his puzzlement.

"That's what I want to know. It's mostly clear of the nets now, and I found a serial number on the side, but it's too long to remember. I'll buy a slate, come back tomorrow, write it down, and use that to figure out where it came from and how it ended up off of Slapton Sands."

"Where do you find that kind of information?"

"I'll try researching the library first. If they don't have what I need, I'll have to make some phone calls."

Fred Hunter sat in his small front room, its window looking out across Dartmouth's picturesque port, the phone pressed tightly to his ear, making sure he wouldn't miss the person he had been trying to reach for three days. Finally, after what seemed to be an interminable hold, a voice crackled down the line.

"This is Colonel McDonald. I understand you've called several times."

"Yes, I have. You're a hard man to get through to."

The voice sighed at the comment. "We do tend to be a little busy here at the Ministry of Defense. Normally I don't take outside calls but I've been led to understand you were a lieutenant in the Royal Air Force and had quite a distinguished career in Search and Rescue. My son is a fly boy himself and he's based out of Brize Norton like you were. He's there while he waits on an overseas posting, so I thought I'd make an exception. How can I help you, Lieutenant Hunter?"

Fred smiled at the friendly, if pretentious, tone. "I found something, Colonel McDonald, and I think you may be interested in getting it back."

"And what is it you've found?"

"A tank, sir."

"A tank! I haven't heard anything about us missing a tank. Where did you find it?"

"Sixty feet underwater, off the south coast of Devon."

"Underwater? Are you sure?"

"I'm sure, colonel."

"How on earth did it get there?"

"That's why I'm calling you; I have no idea what it's doing on the sea bottom. I wanted to ask if you knew why it ended up there."

There was silence as the high-ranking officer thought through his reply. "Lost submarines, mermaids, seahorses, and underwater tanks are not something I deal with on a regular basis – or ever for that matter. And without a report of a tank going missing, how on earth could I answer your question?"

"Would it help if I gave you the tank's serial number? I wrote it down after I found it."

"Yes, that would be of great assistance, old chap. Give it to me and I'll look it up. It might tell us why a tank went swimming off of Devonshire."

"I was hoping you'd say that, sir." Fred checked his notes. At the top of the hand-written sheet of paper containing a dozen phone numbers he'd used to track down the colonel, were three letters and a five-digit number. "I'll read it to you. AAF179-"

Colonel McDonald spoke up, cutting off Fred's numerology. "Let me stop you there, lieutenant. I can tell you it's definitely not one of our tanks. Whatever it is you found, it's not British military equipment. The number you gave me started with three letters, AAF, correct?"

"Correct, sir."

"That was a World War Two designation given to American military vehicles operating in the European theatre. AAF – it stands for American Armed Forces. You've found yourself a Yankee tank."

It was Fred's turn to fall silent. He had not expected this.

"You still there, lieutenant?"

"Yes." Fred stumbled over his words. "If it's not ours-"

"It's certainly not."

"Then what was an American tank doing over a mile offshore from a beach in the south of England?"

"I have no idea. And judging from the number, it was a long time ago, at least thirty-five years."

"What can I do to find out how it ended up down there?"

Colonel McDonald was getting tired of this questioning and his tone reflected it. "Well, I'm frightfully sorry, but I'm not the man to answer that question. And being as it's not one of ours, I won't be able to help you any further. I'm going to have to go."

"Wait. What should I do now? Someone has to know about this."

"Someone probably does. Lost tanks are pretty rare."

"So, who do I ask next? Is there anyone you can suggest?"

"Suggest? I suggest you make another phone call, lieutenant. But this time, call the Yanks."

The sun blazed down across Washington, D.C. as the hint of an early summer approached. Air conditioners blew welcome cooling into the offices of the Defense Department as the staff returned from lunch to carry out their work protecting the nation. A young secretary scurried down the corridor and knocked hesitantly on the door of her boss, her apprehension driven by previous rebukes from the four-star general who was rapidly approaching retirement age.

"Come in." It was not a welcoming greeting.

The secretary meekly entered. "Sorry to bother you, sir, but it's the Englishman I told you about. He's calling again."

"Again! How many times is this?"

"Seven, sir. He said he's going to keep calling until he can talk to you."

"Damn it. What was it he wanted?" The general tried to remember.

"He says he found something of ours we might want back."

"Then tell him to mail it to us. It would be a lot cheaper for him than making all these annoying long-distance calls, I'm sure."

"I suggested exactly that, but he said it's too big."

"Too big? What is it?"

"He won't tell me. He said he could only tell the officer in charge, and that would be you, sir."

"Carol, I am well aware of my position and rank. Does he know how busy my office is? With all the greedy senators pushing for increased funding in their states, and the appropriations committee up my ass, I barely have time to breathe."

"I explained that too, but he said he would keep calling until he got to you; it was too important to give up. He has a military background; he's a former officer with Britain's Airforce and seems very determined."

General Frasier shook his head. "Okay, let's get rid of him. Is he on one of my lines?" He gestured to his phone bank which showed three of the five lines blinking.

"Yes. Line two."

"I'll take it now. You can go back to your desk." The general waited until Carol left before punching the button and picking up the phone. "Yes?"

Two thousand three hundred and forty miles away, Fred heard the abrupt tone of the voice on the phone and despite the man's obvious irritation, he momentarily closed his eyes in satisfaction. Finally, I've gotten through, he thought to himself. "Is this General Frasier?"

"It is. I understand you've been calling about having something of ours, am I correct?"

"That's right. I didn't think you would take my call."

"Then why did you keep trying?"

"You don't win a battle by giving up, general."

"And you're in a battle with me?"

"No, sir. To the contrary. I come from a military family. I like to do things right."

"That's a good way to be." General Frasier didn't want to waste any more time with small talk. "I understand you have a military souvenir of ours you want to return. What is it? An old helmet or a medal you bought at a swap meet?"

"No, it's a tank."

"A what?"

"A tank. A World War Two Sherman tank."

"That's impossible. How did you get it?"

"I found it."

"You found a Sherman tank? Did someone leave it parked on the side of the street? Or was it on display at some kind of military exhibition and you stole it? You got in, started it up and drove it off?"

"Sir, I don't think this tank could drive anywhere. It's sixty feet underwater in the English Channel."

The voice on the other end of the line paused, and when General Frasier continued, the sarcasm in his words changed to a questioning tone. "How is that possible?"

"Exactly what I asked myself, and that's why I'm calling you. I have the tank's serial number."

"And what is it?"

"AAF17924."

He scribbled the numbers down. "Let me check on that. Give me a minute." The general put the phone on hold and rose from his seat. He stepped to the large bookcase at the back of his office and retrieved two thick volumes, carrying them to his desk. He switched the phone to speaker as he opened the first big book. "You still there?"

"Still here, general."

"I'm looking through our records of armored vehicles, particularly those listed as missing in action or destroyed during WWII, hold on." He shut the first book and opened the second. These were the ones he was looking for. He flipped through the numbers quickly until he came to the ones starting with AAF. He ran his finger down the long list before stopping suddenly. He double checked the numbers and the color drained from his face. He sat rigid in his chair, stunned.

"General, are you there?"

The old military man tried to gather himself. "Where did you say you found this tank?"

"In the English Channel."

"That's a big body of water. Can you be more exact?"

"Off the coast of Devonshire, in the south-west of England. There's an area called the South Hams. The tank is underwater and located between one and two miles out, on the eastern side of Slapton Sands. It's a beach about two miles long."

The General glanced at the serial number on the page of his record book. Next to it was written *Slapton Sands*. And following, in block letters, *BIGOT*. He exhaled long and hard, then spoke clearly into the phone. "I'm sorry to tell you, we have no record of any such tank ever existing. The number doesn't match any vehicle of ours."

It was Fred's turn to be shocked. "But I've seen it. The tank is down there, underwater."

"What you saw was definitely not a tank. Probably some wrecked boat that over the years has rotted away and looks different. Perhaps the mast collapsed and is sticking out horizontally, resembling a tank's gun barrel."

"No, it's nothing like that. I was down there and saw it; it has a turret, an articulated track, everything. It's definitely a tank."

"I appreciate your interest and enthusiasm, but I'm telling you, no matter what you think it is, I can assure you it's not a tank. That number has never been used for an American military vehicle and never will be. Best if you leave the thing underwater and move on."

"But-"

"I have to go. Thank you for your concern, but whatever you think you've found is not a tank and is nothing of any importance to anyone." The general slammed down the receiver, ending the call. He stared at the phone for several seconds before shaking his head and getting to his feet. He stormed to the window as fury burned across his face, and screamed two words. "Jesus Christ!"

The Slapton Arms was busy for a Wednesday evening. The little village's sole public house, dating back more than two centuries, was filled with locals enjoying their first pint of the night to the accompaniment of ABBA blaring from the jukebox, letting everyone inside know that Napolean had met his Waterloo.

Fred Hunter, bundled up against the cold wind blowing outside, made his way across the cracked tile floor to the curving wooden bar and waited among the bustling crowd for his turn to get a drink. After only a couple of minutes the young bartender asked to take his order.

"A pint of bitter, please," said Fred.

"Coming right up. Any crisps or maybe a hot pastie to warm you?" offered the bartender.

"The beer is fine."

The young man poured it expertly from the tap, leaving a quarter inch of foam to cap the bitter with an enticing head. "There you go. You timed it right coming in here now. We were slammed a little earlier; it's just starting to slow down a bit."

Fred grasped the beer and raised it up, hesitating before taking a sip. "You're a local, right?"

The bartender nodded. "Yup. I was born and raised here. Been my home for all my life, over thirty years."

Fred continued. "If you've got a second, can I ask something? I was walking the beach today and saw signs everywhere about not going near any military ordinance that might have washed up. Does that happen a lot?"

"Oh yes, that's why they have the signs. They're every hundred yards or so, the whole length of Slapton. Sometimes, after a big storm, people find bullets or hand grenades along the tide line. We call them in to the local police and they send their army or navy experts from Devonport dockyard to take care of it. A few weeks ago, they came here and blew up an unexploded bomb. Made a hell of a racket, it did. It was better than Guy Fawkes night."

"Where does all this stuff come from?"

"Out there." The bartender pointed to the window and the dark sea beyond. "Left over from the military exercises they did here during the war. I guess the Yanks didn't clean everything up when they left."

"When was that, exactly?"

"I'm not sure of the date. I was born when the war was finishing up, so I was too young to see anything that went on here." The bartender paused. "You're not from Devon, are you?"

"No," admitted Fred. "I'm originally from Yorkshire. I came to Slapton Sands today see what the beach was like and if I could find anything out."

"Yorkshire? You must be the fisherman who's been doing all the diving. The whole village has been talking about you."

"They have? I'm surprised anyone knows about my diving."

"Oh, yes. Us locals love to talk, and a bit of gossip spreads quick in a little village, particularly if there are crazy things going on."

"I wouldn't say it was crazy."

"You might not, but all of us think it's plain daft going into the water this time of year. You must have skin like a walrus.

The sea's so bloody cold now it could freeze you in a minute, and it won't start getting tolerable for even a quick dip until midsummer."

"It's certainly not warm; I can't imagine what it would be like without a wetsuit." Fred wanted to get back to digging up a lead on his underwater find. "If you don't know about the American exercises here, is there anyone who does, someone I could talk too?"

"Yeah. See the lady over there? She was here right through the war. Saw everything. She owns this pub as well." He pointed to a well-dressed woman in her late fifties sitting alone at a small window table sipping a Babycham.

"Would she mind?"

"Go and ask her. She won't bite your head off, I promise." He flashed a wide grin.

Fred nodded a thank you, took his beer and approached the lady. He stopped a respectful yard from her table. "Excuse me, I hope I'm not bothering you. The bartender suggested I should talk to you."

She looked up at him, puzzled. "Is there a problem?"

Fred shook his head. "No, not in the slightest, the beer and the service is very good. He said you might have some stories for me from the war."

Her brow furrowed and she cut him off quickly. "I'm not into telling '*stories*' about that time. It's best put behind us. I'm not giving you any tales about fighting and glory you can tell your friends when you finish your holiday and go home."

"I'm not on holiday; I live down here, in Dartmouth."

Her manner changed instantly. "Dartmouth? I spent a lot of time there when I was younger. That makes you almost a local. Okay, you can sit down if you like. Find yourself a seat."

Fred took a vacant chair and slid it over. He sat down, putting his beer on the table.

"And you are...?" asked the lady.

"Fred Hunter."

"Nice to meet you, Mr. Fred Hunter. I'm Mary Sheppard. I've spent a lot of my life here, starting during the Blitz in the summer of nineteen-forty when I was evacuated to the South Hams from London."

"Did you see many American soldiers in Slapton during the war?"

Mary stiffened. "What is it with you and that question? Why are you asking about American soldiers? Are you with a newspaper? Or the army, because if so, it won't work."

"No, really, none of that. I have a fishing boat. I'm not a reporter."

"Then why is a fisherman interested in American soldiers?"

"Because something of theirs took my nets, and that started everything."

Mary took a few seconds before she spoke. "Started what?"

Fred scooted in closer and lowered his voice. "This is going to sound like I'm a looney bird, but I was out there trawling and my nets snagged. I rented some SCUBA gear and went down to see what it was."

"And what was it?"

He dropped his voice even more. "It was a Sherman tank."

Mary jerked in shock in her chair, knocking her drink, spilling the Babycham, the glass rolling off the table and smashing on the floor. In seconds, the bartender leaped over the bar and rushed to the table, his eyes glaring in accusation at Fred. "I heard a glass break. Are you alright? Is he bothering you?"

"No, no he's not. It was my fault; I was clumsy and dropped my drink. I'll get it cleaned up in a minute. You can leave us, I'm fine."

He nodded and stepped cautiously away, glancing back protectively before reaching the bar to make sure things really were okay with the pub's owner and this stranger.

Mary waited to speak until they wouldn't be overheard. "You found the tank." It was a statement not a question.

"*The* tank? You know about it?"

"I saw it go down."

Fred sucked in a long deep breath. "Thank God. I thought I was losing my mind. Everyone was telling me I shouldn't believe my own eyes. That the tank didn't exist."

"They told me the same thing. And when I insisted I'd seen everything happen that night, they threatened me."

"They threatened you?"

"Yes, with all kinds of things, including the Official Secrets Act and then something called BIGOT, which apparently is a category above Top Secret and carries all sorts of penalties. They said I could get life in prison if I talked about it. And they weren't nice about telling me. I was only a girl then, in my twenties, but the army sent their military police down here and put the fear of God in me."

"Why would they do that?"

Mary lowered her voice further. "Because so many men were killed that night, and it was the fault of a few big-wig officers on both sides, the English and the Americans. Those poor soldiers who died were heroes, but no one was told how it happened. Their relatives got letters saying they were killed in an accident on the base or fell off a ladder or caught the flu and passed away. The same letters went out to hundreds of grieving families."

"Hundreds? That many?" Fred was shocked as he tried to contemplate the number of dead soldiers.

"Yes, hundreds." She unconsciously raised her voice. "It was all damned lies. The boys died fighting, but not a one was acknowledged or given a medal and there's been no memorials put up. What happened at Slapton Sands was a huge cover-up and they've never told the truth about it."

"But that was so long ago, what, thirty-five years? Why would they keep it a secret even today?"

"To protect people at the top. It was their mistakes that caused the death so many of those boys. A lot of the officers responsible are still alive, and they don't want the blame and the retribution. All they care about is keeping their ranks and pensions." Mary realized how loud she was talking and tried to calm herself. "Fred, can you find the tank again?"

"Of course. I put a buoy on it."

"Good. Then we'll bring it up. Once we have the tank on dry land, they won't be able to deny it any longer."

"Mary, I've been doing my research since I found it, and the tank weighs at least forty tons, and if it's been underwater since the war ended it'll be full of mud and silt; so now it'll weigh twice that. It'll be almost impossible to get it to the surface."

"*Almost* impossible?"

Fred nodded. "Yes, almost."

"So, it could be done?"

"Perhaps. But it would take time and money."

Mary sighed. "Time is something I have. I've already waited so many years for proof about what happened that night and now you've found it for me. As for money, I own my house and this pub, free and clear. I can take a mortgage out and use it to pay the costs to raise the tank."

Fred was stunned. "Are you sure? It would be one hell of a project you'd be getting into."

"I'm sure."

"What about the Official Secrets Act and the BIGOT thing? You could be put away."

"If we get the tank to the surface, and it's sitting there, in broad daylight, let them try locking me in prison. It would only bring more attention to what they did to conceal everything." She leaned in close to Fred. "You've given me a chance to at last find peace after all this time. And maybe, we can also find justice for the hundreds of troubled souls who died fighting that dreadful night and the lies that were told so their deaths were forgotten by the rest of the world. Well, I haven't forgotten, not one thing, and I'll tell you, right here and right now, exactly what happened and how we can finally put an end to this unforgiveable cover-up."

CHAPTER TWO
Evacuation

December 2nd, 1943

The tiny village bustled with activity. The narrow, cobbled streets were packed with people, bundled in heavy coats, scarves, and wool sweaters in a futile attempt to ward off the cold and damp of the winter afternoon.

Seemingly oblivious to the chill air, perhaps warmed by their excitement, two children laughed and giggled as they maneuvered through the crowds, struggling to pull a small hand cart loaded with an oversized Christmas tree.

Unseen by the busy shoppers, three Jeeps and a large truck, all painted in military camouflage colors, their headlights obscured by strips of masking tape reducing the openings to narrow slits to dim any chance of them being spotted by enemy aircraft at night, came over the cliff road and headed down to the long, paved strip paralleling the sea and leading into Slapton Sands and Torcross.

At the edge of the village a uniformed local policeman stood waiting for the small convoy, his bicycle propped against a sign reading, *Beer and Fish'n'Chips at The Slapton Arms*. He spotted the vehicles approaching and directed them to a parking lot better designed for the occasional summer tourist than military personnel. As they pulled over and stopped, the passengers from the forward Jeeps stepped out, two American officers and a British major.

"I was told to expect you." The policeman checked his pocket watch. "You're an hour late."

"Sorry if we took you away from walking your beat in the village, but in case you didn't know, there's a war going on." The American captain smirked at his comment.

"There's no need for rudeness, the constable's only doing his job," interjected the major. He nodded to the Bobby, "We're going to need your help distributing these pamphlets. If there's anywhere special they should be put up, maybe the main square or town hall, it would be good to know."

"We don't have neither of those things 'ere in Torcross, we're a small little place. One on each door would be sufficient. Once word gets out, all the locals will be talking about it. Give me a minute to read it." The policeman scanned the flyer then looked up; his eyes wide. "You sure? This can't be right. That's less than two weeks from now."

"It's correct, constable. It comes directly from the War Office," stated the major.

"But it's not-"

"It is," cracked the American officer. "If you don't like it, you can send your objections to Ike or Churchill."

"I'm afraid he's right. Time is short for all of us, and this is from the very top." The major placed his hand sympathetically on the policeman's arm. "We'll take it from here. They'll be no blame falling on you." He turned to the other American officer and nodded.

Taking the cue, the lieutenant waved to the driver of the lead Jeep. "Unload the men."

The driver, his sergeant stripes glistening on his shoulder, jumped from the Jeep and knowing what was expected of him, ran to rear of the waiting truck, flinging open the back canvas cover and unhooking the tailgate. "All right, GIs, fall in."

On his command, twenty soldiers leaped from the truck, happy to stretch their legs after the bumps and rolls of the seventy-mile drive, and formed two tight lines.

The sergeant gestured to the second Jeep, and the driver reached behind him to the back seat, lifting out a large cardboard box. Loaded down with its weight, he walked toward the waiting soldiers.

The sergeant addressed his men. "I'm giving each of you a stack of these flyers. In the tool box on the truck, you'll find hammers, nails, tacks and rolls of tape, enough for everyone. Our officer is approaching. He'll take over from here."

The American captain strolled back to the squad, paused to get their attention, then spoke up. "Your orders are simple. You are to go into the village and post a flyer on every door you see. And not just doors. If there's a tree in the town, nail a flyer to it. If there's a lamppost, tape one on. Pretend you lost your beloved Fido and you're trying to get the word out because you want him back. I need every villager to see this. There can be no excuses they didn't know what's coming. Make this quick, and do not, I repeat, do not, engage in any conversation with the villagers, no matter how upset they are. Am I understood?"

"Yes, sir," came the synchronized reply with zero hesitation.

The officer turned to his NCO. "Carry on, sergeant."

"Sir." He spun to face his GIs. "You heard the captain. Get those flyers posted on the double."

On his words the men broke rank, ready to go, excited this wartime task didn't involve shells, bullets, or latrine duty. The soldiers sprinted toward the cottages, and for the first time in its seven-hundred-year history, the tiny hamlet facing Slapton Sands heard the thunder of military boots crashing over its cobbled streets.

As the uniformed squad disappeared between the small stone cottages, the senior US officer turned to his British counterpart. "After this is done and the locals get the word, do you really think it's feasible to have everybody gone from Torcross and Slapton within ten days?"

"That's the plan," answered the major. "We have temporary accommodations assigned for all five hundred and twenty-seven of the residents here, plus the eighteen hundred farm workers we'll be moving out of the South Hams. They'll be taken to billets in Torquay, Exeter, Bovey Tracy and Newton Abbott. The cattle and livestock will be loaded up and shipped off to either North Devon or Cornwall, while the sheep, because they are hardier, have pens waiting for them on Dartmoor. It won't be easy on the people though, losing their homes right before Christmas."

"This war isn't easy on anybody. The troops coming here will be living in tents and Quonset huts throughout the winter. But it has to be done to prepare them for what is coming. We need this area completely cleared for training."

"You'll have it. More than thirty thousand acres are being emptied for your men. This will be the largest American base outside of the United States. The only non-coms in the entire area will be ten members of the Coastal Watch. They'll work in shifts and come in daily from their homes in Salcombe, Stoke Fleming, and Dartmouth. The War Office has already prepared their papers."

The American captain took a half step back, staring at the British major in disbelief. "We were guaranteed there would be no limeys here. And what the hell is Coastal Watch?"

The major breathed deeply; he had expected this from the Americans. "Coastal Watch is made up of volunteers who form a human chain around Britain's southern coastline, stretching from Land's End to East Anglia. Their job is to watch for invaders or enemy boats."

"Jesus H. Christ!" The captain couldn't believe his ears. "What's a bunch of civilians going to do if they see the Nazis coming?"

"They would signal they'd spotted them and alert the appropriate authorities."

"What kind of signal?"

"These days they use radios and morse code. In the past, it was bonfires."

"That's fucking great. Bonfires. Look the Germans are coming. Let's invite them to a barbecue. We'll cook up some hot dogs and a burger."

Major Williams tensed at the American's tone; he would not have his country insulted this way. "You may think it's funny to mock us, but this is one of our great traditions. Ever since the sixteenth century when Britain was threatened by the Spanish Armada, whenever there is a danger of invasion, volunteers are recruited to watch the coast. It was done during both Napoleonic wars, Crimea, and the First World War." He left no doubt at his seriousness in the forceful way he uttered the next few words. "And they will continue to do so during this conflict."

"I noticed you didn't mention the Revolutionary War, major," gloated the American officer.

"No, sir, I didn't. We use Coastal Watch when there is the possibility of enemy landings happening in our country. Being an island, the only way for an opponent to get enough troops ashore is by coming in over the water. America had no navy in 1776, just a few rowing boats and a couple of skiffs. Hardly enough to get the rebels across the Atlantic."

"Yet we were still able to kick your asses." The captain was pleased to be able to drive that nail in.

"Indeed, you did. And you haven't let us forget the loss of our colonies. But when it comes to British soil and a valued institution such as Coastal Watch you must remember this is a Crown appointment and supersedes your rank and authority."

"Would it be so bad to leave the rest of your amateur watchers in place along the coast, but not have them here? That way they can light their little signal fires in case they see the Krauts coming, but they won't be around to bother us while we do the real work."

"That wouldn't be possible. Coastal Watch forms an unbroken chain two hundred miles long. I'm sure, even you, would understand how ineffective a chain is if you remove even a single link?"

The second American officer broke his silence and stepped forward to intercede in the hope of breaking the impasse. "It'll be fine, captain. We can spare a detail to make sure the Brits don't wander around our camp or get into trouble. We'll just let them know to have their papers with them at all times to show the guards and sentries." He shrugged, trying to make the best of it, "And who knows, maybe they'll see something we don't."

"Yeah, like more damned rain." The captain shook his head, frustrated. "Where would you put these looky-loos?'

"Their station will be on the high point overlooking Slapton Sands. From there they have a clear viewpoint across the bay and out into the channel."

"That won't work, major. Your high point is on top of the cliffs on the east side of the beach, right?"

The English officer nodded his agreement as the American continued.

"We're going to be using those cliffs for a big part of our training, and some of it will be live fire. If your civilians are up there, they could find themselves on the wrong end of a friendly bullet made in Evansville, Indiana."

"I appreciate your concern for their welfare, captain, but if you take the time to actually check out the top of the cliffs, you'll see they're capped with a relatively flat plain stretching back more than one hundred yards to a thick line of trees. When your men do their climbing exercises, we will have our people moved way back out of harm's way. That should allow your troops all the space they need to complete their tasks." He locked his eyes on the captain. "We do have this planned out, you know."

The captain fought to control his irritation, but couldn't stop from rolling his eyes. "Okay, your Coastal Watch stays.

But one thing, no radios. With the invasion coming, word about this military encampment is restricted for obvious reasons, and only authorized US military personnel have access to radios. We know the Germans are always listening, trying to find out what's going on. Your Brits can stand watch and do their morse code with flashing lights and bonfires, and all that crap, but if any of them are caught with a radio, they'll be a big problem." His tone showed the seriousness of his intent.

"Understood. I'll pass the word to the watch that radios are not permitted."

"Good. Let's hope they follow instructions. That way you can rely on their dot dot dot dash dash dash bullshit; we'll rely on our radar."

"Which, don't forget, you Yanks got from us. Radar is yet another great British invention." The English major smiled in satisfaction at finally getting a one up on the aggressive American, clicked his heels to attention, then turned and marched back to his waiting Jeep.

The American captain shook his head in frustration as he watched the proud officer walk away. "Damn Brits. We come all the way over here to save their butts; they could at least show a little gratitude."

The village was at a standstill. The inhabitants and shoppers froze in place as American GIs rushed along the narrow streets nailing and taping the flyers into place. A portly farmer, outfitted in tweed and a worn, flat hat, tried stopping two of the soldiers to ask what the devil was happening, but following their orders the Americans moved on, saying nothing, merely handing the inquisitive man one of the printed sheets.

The farmer stared down at the paper as he read the words in disbelief. It was almost too much for his brain to process, so to help him concentrate he pulled off his cap, stuffing it in his jacket pocket as he re-read the pamphlet, his index finger slowly tracing its way across each sentence to make sure he wasn't missing anything.

The Parish vicar stepped up to join him. "What is all this commotion, Charlie? I was inside working on my sermon when I heard the ruckus. I thought old lady Spencer had fallen down again."

"Worse than that, Father," said the farmer, waving the notice wildly. "Look at this madness. Some soldier boys are passing it out and putting it up all over the place. It makes no sense to me, but then, I've never been much good with words. Maybe you can make head or tail of it."

The vicar took the proffered paper and looked it over quickly. "This can't be."

"Can you explain it to me?"

"Yes, though I can see why you find it confusing. It says it comes from our people in Whitehall, but it looks like the Americans are the ones behind it." The vicar pulled himself together and read the words slowly in the voice he saved to address his small but devoted congregation every Sunday. "Under the Defense Act of 1939, the villages of Torcross and Slapton and the surrounding areas of the district known as the South Hams are hereby requisitioned –"

The farmer cut him off. "That's one of the words I didn't understand. Requi–"

"Requisitioned. It means taken over. Let me keep reading, Charlie. ...are hereby requisitioned by His Majesty's Government for the defense of the realm. All citizens and livestock shall be removed from the surrounding villages and farms within twelve miles of the coastal waters and resettled to other areas, by no later than December the twelfth, in the year of our Lord, nineteen hundred and forty-three. We wish you well in this time of war. God save The King."

"Cor, blimey."

"Exactly." The vicar stared at the big farmer. "And we've only got a short time before they move us all out, Charlie."

"That's impossible. I got so many animals on me farm. What are they going to do about all my sheep?"

The vicar turned his head and looked at the stunned villagers around him. "We both have a flock to worry about. Who will care for mine?" He straightened up. "I have to go."

The man of God nodded a farewell to Charlie and started back to his cottage attached to the tiny church. As he walked through the village, he turned onto a little lane taking him past a red brick house glowing from the lights on inside. In the front bay window, the two children who had been pushing the Christmas tree through the town had it up now and were happily putting decorations on the branches.

An elderly lady stood outside watching them, and beamed at their efforts, remembering her younger days and the excitement she had felt at this time of year. She saw the vicar and waved to him, her wide smile and lack of concern revealing she had not yet seen the proclamation.

"They're doing a good job with the tinsel and ornaments, don't you think, vicar? It's going to be a beautiful tree."

The holy man fell silent as he watched the children at work, then sighed. "Yes. But they won't be able to take it with them."

The lady stared at him, confused. "None of us can, Father. You, of all people, should know that."

Inside the brightly lit room, the children's mother stumbled in, grasping the flyer, her other hand across her mouth stifling the scream she fought to hold back. Her two daughters stopped draping the shiny garlands and spun around to their mum, but instead of the happy smile which always greeted them, they saw tears washing over their mother's rosy cheeks.

December 12th, 1943

The rain poured down, as if Nature was crying in sympathy with the residents of this coastal hamlet, as they bid their final farewells to the little village which had been home to them for most of their lives. A convoy of canvas-covered army trucks waited for the last few to board with their hastily packed belongings, before the order could be given to move out and take them to pastures unknown.

The local constable helped his remaining people onboard, then took a last look around the little village to make sure no one had been missed. He shook his head sadly as he turned to the four American soldiers standing with him. "That should be it, all of them." He passed the sergeant his clipboard containing the names of the passengers. "I've made a second copy for myself, in case anyone gets lost."

"Good." It was obvious the burly sergeant didn't really care how many copies the British bobby had. "Now if you could get on board, we'll move everyone out."

"All right." The policeman reached for his bike resting against the wall.

"What are you doing with that?"

"Bringing it with me. It's how I get around on my beat."

"Leave it. There's no room left on any of the trucks."

"Perhaps we could fit it in one of the Jeeps up front?"

"No. The bike stays. You'll have to find another when you get to where you're going."

The constable looked at his well-worn three-speed push bike. "Shame. This old bitty was special to me. Had it since I was a kid. Me dad gave it to me."

"I understand. Now will you get in the truck?" It was not a request.

The bobby climbed inside and the soldiers closed the back flap, unrolling the rear canvas cover to protect the passengers from the rainstorm.

The sergeant blew a whistle, and on his command the diesel engines of the line of GMC CCKW trucks, nicknamed '*Jimmys*', started up and began their exodus from Slapton Sands, leaving the formerly busy village to become a ghost town. As the roar of the motors faded and the clouds of choking exhaust fumes dissipated, the only sound drifting through the hamlet was that of the torrential downpour hammering against the windows of the empty homes and turning the cobbled streets into rivers of raging water racing down to the stony beach and into the cold sea.

Two pairs of eyes watched the desolate scene from the top of the towering cliffs framing the eastern side of Slapton's beach that stretched for two miles. Seated on folding chairs and huddled under an umbrella, an elderly man and his much younger female companion tried to stay warm and dry, an almost impossible task, even though they were outfitted in raincoats, heavy cardigans, hats, and wellington boots.

The man patted his long jacket to slide some of the pooled rain drops off before they could soak through and chill him even more. "This old coat's seen better days. I'll have to try and get me a new one next time I'm in Dartmouth. But that won't be for a while. It'll be crowded there with everyone being moved out from Slapton."

"Think they've all gone, Grandpa?"

"I do, Mary. Those trucks took the last of them. They've made sure the whole village is empty, along with the countryside and all the farms. There's not a light to be seen anywhere, not even inland at the old William's place, and that's normally lit up like Piccadilly Circus this time of year, except when the air raid sirens go off. They've all been loaded up and taken away, for sure. It's just you and me now, up here in the rain, looking for Germans."

"But it won't stay that way for long, just us, will it?"

"No, it won't, lass. They've been moved for a reason. We should have known something was up when you and me, and the rest of the watch, were issued those government papers. Haven't seen anything so official with me name on it since my days in the army."

"What do you think is going on?"

"Don't know, don't want to know, and neither do you. Not my business or yours. We're here to lookout for Jerry sneaking across from France and that's what we'll do. Though how we could ever see anything in this bloody awful weather, is beyond me."

With that he took out his binoculars and turned his attention from the deserted village and his granddaughter's curious questions to the storm-tossed waters of the English Channel.

The view from Coastal Watch, on top of the cliffs overlooking Slapton Sands

CHAPTER THREE
Occupation

December 24th, 1943

It had been less than two weeks, and Mother Nature had taken advantage of the short time Slapton Sands had been left bereft of people, to reclaim it as her own. Weeds pushed up through the dirt between the cobbles on the street, and rain pooled in deepening puddles in every depression and low point in the village. Though all the lights in the tiny town of Torcross were off, had anyone been passing by, they would have clearly seen through the window of one of the homes, the once green Christmas tree which had held the promise of being a holiday gathering spot for a happy family, was turning brown, its needles falling, the result of twelve days of sitting inside, unwatered and uncared for.

  A small puppy trembled in a doorway, trying to stay dry and find some semblance of warmth, as it wondered where its owners had gone and why there had been no food for so long. It lay down and started to curl up when a loud noise startled the abandoned dog and it ran for its life into the darkness.

The first of a long convoy of trucks roared into the village, led by six Jeeps painted olive green and bearing the markings of a white five-pointed star on the engine side panels and hood. They pulled to a halt between the stone cottages, with the line of two-and-a-half ton trucks stopping behind them and reaching back a hundred yards along the beach road.

A colonel stepped out of the lead Jeep and swept his gaze around the village. "Damn. It is small. I thought they were joking when they described it."

In seconds he was joined by his companion in the Jeep, a young major with a brutally short buzzcut. "We were warned, sir."

"I know, but hell, these buildings are about the size of my daughter's dollhouse."

"Two of our quartermasters came through last week to run an assessment, sir. They said there are enough houses for the officers. Some of the juniors, the lieutenants, might have to share, but there's enough rooms for captains and above."

"I understand. We'll make do. And the men will billet as planned?"

"Yes. This batch, the first two thousand, will camp along Slapton Ley tonight, then starting on Saturday, they'll begin putting up the Quonset huts. Engineering will truck in the parts, but it'll still take them a while; we've got another forty-two thousand men coming, sir."

"Why Saturday? Why can't they start building them tomorrow?"

The major paused before answering, surprised. "It's Christmas tomorrow, sir. The men should have the day off to celebrate."

"Let's hope the Germans make it a holiday too. Okay, Saturday it is. But don't forget, major, this place is about to become the largest American military base outside of the States. We don't have time for Santa or sentiment." He looked around, then back to the major. "Which house is assigned to me?"

The major pointed to a two-story, white painted building. "That one. It was the mayor's home. It has three bedrooms, one bathroom, and a room downstairs you can use for meetings. They figured it would be perfect for your officer briefings."

"Got it." He shook his head as he took in the cramped stone houses crammed tightly together. "This place had a mayor? It doesn't look big enough to have had a janitor. I'll check out my quarters, you have the men locate their campsites for tonight."

The soldiers packed inside the lead truck, safely shielded from the rain by the heavy, waxed canvas roof, looked back and forth at each other as the trucks rumbled forward again. A young, dark-haired soldier turned to his fellow sergeant sitting beside him. "I've got a feeling we're here, Ricky."

"Wanna bet? Nine hours on this truck, and we've had three stops already. Why do you think this one is different?"

"Because they didn't have us get out to pee or eat. I think they were checking the surroundings before unloading us. And I can hear waves and smell the salt air."

"You can smell the salt? You must have a better nose than my dog back home. And what's the big deal about salt air, Mac?"

"Come on, Ricky, you know we're part of the invasion force, so we have to be on the coast for our training." Mac lowered his voice. "Word is they've found a perfect match for the beaches we'll be landing on in France."

"Let's hope they've found a perfect match for the French girls I'm going to be landing on."

"Don't forget, to find the French girls you'll have to get through the Germans first."

"No problem. We did it in Sicily, Mac. We can do it in France."

"Sicily didn't have the defenses like they say Hitler's put up all along the French coast. And we weren't the first ashore in Sicily."

"And we're going to be in the first wave now?"

Before Mac could reply, the truck came to a halt and within seconds the rear flap was thrown open. A sergeant major stood there with two other soldiers as they lowered the tailgate, fully opening the back of the vehicle.

"All right ladies, we are here. We've got about an hour before we lose what's left of the light, so the quicker you get out the easier it's going to be putting up your tents. Your spaces have been outlined with chalk, but you might have to look hard to find them because all this damn rain has washed away a lot of the markings. I suggest you grab your bags and tents from under the benches and start right now, otherwise it'll be the coldest, wettest Christmas Eve you've experienced. Get to it."

With those words, fifty soldiers, cramped from their long drive, leaped from the truck to begin work on the biggest military campsite ever seen in the south of England.

As the sun set through the heavy clouds embracing the distant hills of Dartmoor, the snow-capped rocky peaks turned from white to amber, reminding the onlooker of the tight grip January held over England's West Country. Eight hundred tents and Quonset huts, erected in the hope of warding off the freezing temperatures of winter, marked the billets of young soldiers, who had been sent across the Atlantic, leaving their homes and families far behind, to train to fight on the beaches of France and begin the liberation of Europe from the grasp of the Nazi overlords.

Fifty of the tents stood apart from the others. They were conspicuously bigger, standing more than fourteen feet high, sixty feet wide and one hundred feet long. Supported by three heavy beams, similar to those in a traveling circus, these were used for special purposes; four designated as hospital and medical facilities, forty for dining and commissary areas, and six for meeting places. It was in one of these oversized canvas structures a hundred NCOs stood and faced their camp's commander as he stepped onto a small wooden stage to address the corporals, sergeants, and warrant officers.

"Over the past three weeks I've met many of you as we've worked to put together this rag-tag base. For those of you I haven't had the chance of being introduced to, I am Brigadier General Walters, your post commander. From what I've seen of the layout of our base, no one could have done a better job in the time allotted, and you are to be congratulated for it. You are ten days ahead of schedule. The brass wanted us to be ready by January the twentieth, but you've shown them what good, motivated men can do. I've passed on word to High Command and they've moved everything up, so our full complement will be arriving over the next few days to bring the number of soldiers and marines here in the South Hams to over sixty-two thousand."

The was an audible gasp from the men. This was a lot higher than expected.

The ranking officer smiled. "I know. That's more than we anticipated. They'll be accompanied by a secondary engineering corp with supplies and building materials to increase the number of huts, tents and latrines here, but as you can imagine for the first week or so after their arrival, things will be a little crowded around here, so make sure you let your men know it's only going to be that way for a short period of time. Will you do that, because it is vitally important we maintain morale?"

An affirmative series of grunts and yeses came from the NCOs.

"Good. It's no secret why we are here. Everyone knows, even Hitler, that we are preparing to invade Europe and kick the Nazis out, and God knows it's been long enough coming. But what is a secret, is where and when the invasion will take place. There are over two thousand miles of coastline we could land on, and nobody, apart from Ike and Churchill, has a clue where we will come ashore, and we want to keep it that way until our boots hit the sand, and we return to France."

The Brigadier General had a minor vocal tick few noticed, except the aides closest to him. Whenever he mentioned France, he added the words '*return to.*' This was because on his twenty-first birthday he was in the front-line trenches of France, serving as a corporal in the 91st Division. On the morning of his coming-of-age, September 26th, 1918, the whistle blew and he and his entire division went over the top to begin the final major battle of the World War One, the Meuse-Argonne offensive. For forty-seven days his division fought continuously, until on November 10th they were given the word an armistice would go into effect the next morning at eleven a.m. He was unable to enjoy the celebrations as he was stricken with influenza and sent back to the United States on a hospital ship packed with thousands of others also suffering from the Spanish flu. He had not been able to say farewell to his comrades in arms, and had not returned to mainland Europe since. Now, he felt, this would be his chance to do so, even if it meant facing old enemies once again. He continued addressing his men.

"You will be training for two beach landings with the designated names of Utah and Omaha. They were picked because of the lack of coastline associated with those areas, and if the Germans were to discover our plans included invading Omaha, it would drive them crazy trying to find the appropriate beach in Nebraska."

The men laughed at the cleverness of the names.

"It is funny, but it won't all be laughter. You are about to experience some of the most intense training in the history of the United States Armed Forces. If you thought boot camp was hard, it was a summer vacation compared to what is ahead of you. The exercises lined up will encompass land, sea and air, including many using live fire. It will be so tough, so draining, that at the end of each day, when you finally go to your bunks, you'll be asleep before your head hits the pillow and your eyes close. But it is for a reason. I will not have my men going into battle, facing German guns unprepared; after what you go through here, you'll be ready for anything. You'll be able to breathe fire and spit nails. When I sail with you across the channel to return to France, I want to be able to say, 'I'm not frightened of the Nazis, it's my own men who scare the living shit out of me.' Do I make myself clear?"

The packed tent answered enthusiastically as one. "Yes, sir!"

"And one last thing before you are dismissed."

Silence fell as he paused and the NCOs waited for his next dire pronouncement.

"You worked through Christmas and the New Year and did more than you were asked to do, and did it exceptionally well. Tomorrow, I want you all to relax and pretend the war isn't happening; you deserve a day to recuperate. And to get you ready, there is a special meal prepared and waiting in the mess hall, along with some of the USA's best beer we've had flown in. So, eat and drink and remember the hopes of the free world lie on your shoulders. God bless us all, and God bless America."

If he had wanted to add anything else, no one would have heard his words as cheering and shouts filled the huge tent.

The men were glad of the twenty-four-hour break, because the following few days were non-stop. A seemingly endless stream of new arrivals poured into the camp and were greeted by the soldiers already in place, and by the coldest winter Britain had gone through in decades. Trucks' engines were left running in the fear the radiators would freeze if the diesels were turned off, and the engineers brought in to put together not only the simple Quonset huts but also the complicated and vital radar installations, struggled with the assembly because of the thick gloves they were forced to wear.

Two extra hospital tents were quickly added to supplement the existing four which had been previously thought to be adequate, due to the number of men falling sick from the cold, and both frostbite and bronchial pneumonia developed into a real threat, particularly among the sentries whose thankless job was standing along the two-mile beach enduring not only the freezing rain but also the constant icy salt spray from the storm-driven waves pounding the pebbled beach. It became such a problem that sentry duty was thankfully cut from six to four hours to prevent overloading the hospital tents.

From their eagle's perch on the cliffs above the sprawling military camp, the two members of the Coastal Watch looked down on the constant activity happening along the length of Slapton Sands.

Mary pulled her heavy coat tighter and spoke through the wool scarf wrapped around her face. "The camp's bigger than I thought possible. How many of them do you think are down there now, Grandpa?"

"Don't know, and I'm not interested in guessing. The less we know about what's happening, the better. Stay away from them for your own good."

Before Mary could answer her grandfather's cautionary words a voice from behind interrupted her. "There you go, Reg. Even in this bloody cold, all you can do is fill the poor girl's head with all kinds of frights."

Mary recognized the voice and turned with a grin before she realized the four people approaching couldn't see her smile through the heavy scarf.

Reg was the one who answered. "For your information, Mrs. Northcott, it's not just a bunch of frights. War is not something to take lightly."

"If I was taking it lightly, do you think I'd be up here on this blooming freezing night to take over from you? No bloody way. I'd be back home, tucked up in me warm bed." She nodded to Mary. "Isn't that right, my lovely?"

The pair of GIs accompanying the two women sent to relieve Reg and Mary cut their conversation short. The corporal in charge stepped forward. "Sorry, but we have to make the change now and escort you down the hill."

"Fine with me," said Reg. He grabbed his small bag as he got up from the chair and squeezed out from under the large umbrella's protection.

"I'll have to check the bag, sir." The corporal stretched out his arm.

"They're looking for cameras and notepads. They told Mrs. Higgens and me that now all the soldiers are here, they have to be extra careful."

"That's true," confirmed the other lady. "Opened up my handbag, they did." She shot a disparaging glance at the two soldiers. "I said, do I look like a flaming spy? But they went through everything; even took out me lipstick and purse. Next thing you know, they'll want to search us all over."

Mrs. Northcott grinned as she looked at the two fit young soldiers. "You might be complaining now, Mrs. Higgins, but I bet you wouldn't mind it a bit if those two boys did search you all over."

"Oh, you are a cheeky devil, Mrs. Northcott. You're like a little schoolgirl with naughty thoughts."

"Ladies, please. We have to do this now and return to camp." The corporal was getting both cold and annoyed.

"All right, all right. Mrs. Higgins and I will take our places." With that, the two ladies sat in the vacated chairs. "And don't worry, with us up here, 'itler wouldn't dare invade."

"I'm sure he wouldn't, ma'am." He turned to Reg and Mary. "If you could follow us, we'll escort you down the hill to the checkpoint."

"See you tomorrow night." Mary bade farewell to the two old battleaxes who were ready to do their part in the defense of the British Isles.

As the soldiers led Reg and Mary along the wooded hillside trail, a huge flash of light from sixty miles across the English Channel lit the night. Reg paused for a moment. "Someone's catching it this evening."

Mary agreed. "Do you think it's a bombing raid?"

"Yes. Probably the RAF." He looked at the soldiers. "They're trying to soften up Jerry before you lot go over there. But don't count on it."

"Sir. We've got to keep moving." The corporal knew his orders, and he was not going to engage in any kind of conversation with the members of Coastal Watch.

A series of massive explosions illuminated the dark skies, reflecting off the ominous cloud layer racing above in the offshore winds. "Poor bastards," sighed Reg. "I almost feel sorry for them."

American soldiers trying to stay warm at Slapton Sands, January 1944

CHAPTER FOUR
The Exercises Begin

Ricky Esposito dove face first into the sloping beach and squirmed to find shelter among the small, rounded rocks. He was joined in seconds by Mac Harper, who likewise used the uneven shingle for whatever cover it could provide. Mac looked across to his friend and motioned for him to keep low and follow close behind as he moved forward, worming his way across the unforgiving pebbles.

"Say you feel sorry for me," pleaded Ricky.

"For what?"

"We were told it was beach training. Where's the sand? It's all fucking rocks."

"Guess the Germans didn't think about that when they were planning their defenses. It's a shame they haven't provided lounge chairs for us, and maybe some coconut oil for a tan."

"Screw you, Mac. This place is called Slapton Sands, but there's not a single grain of it here. Should be Slapton Gravel Pit."

"We'll go on a beach vacation after the war. Today we're here to take the flag. Are you ready?"

"I guess so."

"On my mark." Mac slipped the whistle in his mouth, gestured to his squad who were similarly sprawled close by on this long section of the beach, and blew hard twice.

Hearing his signal, twenty men leaped to their feet, and clutching their carbines, raced across the pebbles and up the beach to the blue flag fluttering in the light breeze. In seconds they reached it, and Mac pulled it from the ground, waving it triumphantly. He pointed to his radio operator. "Call base. Tell them Delta section is secured." He checked his watch. "Less than two minutes from waterline to target position. Not bad." Mac was still smiling as Lieutenant Evans strode over.

Mac held out the flag. "This is yours, sir."

"It's definitely not yours, son. You and your squad are all lying dead back there." He waved at the slope where the men had emerged from, minutes before.

"Sir, I beg to disagree. We met no resistance. We sheltered twice on our approach to reconnoiter, saw nothing and continued on."

"You think the Nazi guns will be obvious? They've had three years to dig in, reinforce their positions and presight all the beachheads. That's why it's called Fortress Europe and Hitler's Atlantic Wall. We are simulating some of the defenses you'll be going against. It's the reason we put that tent over there." The lieutenant indicated a small pup tent. Concealed inside the opening flaps were two men manning a machine gun.

The lieutenant continued. "If that was a German machine gun, you'd be facing a 20-millimeter, firing twelve rounds per second with every seventh round, a steel-tipped tracer. It has a seven hundred and forty-foot per second muzzle velocity, and they had you in their sights all the way up the beach. Any questions?"

Mac tried unsuccessfully to mask his frustration. "We had no warning there would be a gun emplacement covering our landing, sir."

"And the Germans are going to post convenient signs, *'warning, machine guns are focused on the beach'*? You didn't get those stripes by being stupid. If you stand up and blindly charge forward, you'll be deader than Custer at Little Big Horn. Use your brain, sergeant. As soon as you're out of the landing craft, you must be ready for anything. You'll have to do whatever it takes to capture your target and stay alive."

"Understood, whatever it takes. Can we try it again, sir?"

The officer looked Mac up and down, and sensed the controlled determination in his tone. This is what he wanted in his soldiers, the desire to win. "Yes, you can try again. But make it quick. With these short days, we only have thirty minutes until dark."

"Will do, sir." Mac spun on his heels and rallied his squad. Ricky hurried after him as they marched back to the tide line.

"*Can we try it again, sir*? What a kiss ass. We're supposed to be demolition and engineering, not infantry."

"Right. And who's going to plant the charges if we can't get off the beach?"

Having addressed Ricky's complaint, Mac fell silent until they reached the water's edge. There, a small raised wall of stones and pebbles arched up, caused by the continuous wave and tide movement. He gathered his squad to brief them on the upcoming action. "We'll take shelter behind this natural barrier. Keep low until Sergeant Esposito and myself head up the beach, then stay close to us. If you are more than two arms lengths away, assume you're dead."

Ricky leaned in so the squad wouldn't hear his question. "Is that smart? If we're all bunched together, we'll be an even easier target. They'll get us for sure."

"Not if they can't see us coming." Mac let his odd answer hang there as he reached into his backpack. "And being demolitions, we have a few things to help us." He pulled out a grenade.

"Jesus, man. You can't use that. This isn't a live-fire exercise today. We're not even shooting blanks, and neither are they. The machine gun nest they set up is only using spotters."

"Right, but you heard the lieutenant. He said to do whatever it takes to capture the target," Mac weighed the pineapple shaped explosive in his hand. "*This* is what it takes."

"Say goodbye to your stripes and hello San Quentin."

Mac ignored Ricky's somber prediction and turned to his huddled squad. "On my command." He pulled the grenade's pin and began his slow count. "One, two, three, four, five, six, seven!" He hurled the grenade to land twenty yards away, between them and the flag.

"Oh, shit!" Ricky clapped his hands over his ears.

There was no explosion, just a loud pop. A billowing red fog appeared, and the late afternoon's onshore breeze carried the thick cloud up the beach.

"That was a smoke grenade!"

Mac nodded and waved his right arm, calling out, "Go."

Under cover of dense crimson smoke, the twenty men raced up the sloping beach. As they passed the halfway mark, Mac yelled to them, "Drop and cover."

As one, the squad buried down into the safety of the pebbles, carbines raised and ready.

Mac spoke softly to his men as they waited for orders. "Stay here until you hear me signal, then head up fast and take the flag." He reached through the heavy smoke, grabbing Ricky's arm. "With me." He pulled him up and across the beach at an angle.

Ricky tried shrugging off his firm grip. "You're turned around in this haze. The flag's that way."

"We're not going for the flag. We're taking out the guns."

"What! How are we doing that?"

Mac ignored Ricky's confused question and kept up his relentless sprint.

Standing next to the enticing blue flag, the lieutenant tried making out what was happening through the thick smoke screen but could see nothing. Impatient, he hurried to the gunners' tent and crawled inside, joining his crew.

He dropped down and lay beside them and the threatening machine gun, relaying his orders. "The smoke will dissipate soon. Keep your aim focused on the flag, but be ready to adjust it quickly and follow them up the beach if they've hunkered down like before. Their little tricks won't work with me."

As he strained his eyes to see any movement through the fog, Mac and Ricky emerged from the enveloping haze and were now six feet behind the gunners' tent.

Ricky realized the beauty of Mac's plan. "Son of a-"

Mac silenced him with a raised finger and stealthily approached the tent. He gestured to the rear tent pole, and bent forward, readying to take care of the opposition. First, he picked up a baseball sized rock and then lifted the tent's canvas back wall. He lobbed the rock inside and yelled, "Boom!"

With that, the two sergeants pulled out the supporting pole and the tent collapsed onto the gunners and the lieutenant.

Mac blew hard on his whistle, and his squad leaped to their feet and rushed through the last wisps of smoke to the flag. There they surrounded it with their rifles raised as if they were protecting the only piece of American soil left on the planet.

In their moment of victory, the lieutenant crawled out from underneath the collapsed tent and stared up at the waiting Sergeant Mac Harper. Before he could speak, Mac snapped to attention, arching to his full six-foot height, and barked out. "Flag captured. Enemy gun emplacement destroyed. Delta section secure for landing, sir."

A hundred yards away, two officers watched the exercise unfold through binoculars. As Mac stood there, ramrod straight, his right hand to his forehead, Brigadier General Walters lowered his binoculars. "Well, I'll be."

The second officer tore his gaze from his own field glasses. "Two questions, sir, if I may."

"Of course, Colonel Brogan. Go ahead."

"Do you want that soldier brought up on charges?"

"Heavens, no. He took the flag, wiped out the machine gun nest, and from here it looks like he did it without incurring any casualties among his squad."

Colonel Brogan nodded his head in agreement and stayed quiet.

"You said you had two questions, colonel."

"I do." He turned to the post commander. "Would you mind if I got that sergeant's name for my records, sir?"

The huge barracks tent was packed with GIs and NCOs recovering from the strenuous day of training. Many were already collapsed in their bunks, while others milled around looking for familiar faces or conscripts from their home town or state to start a conversation with.

Ricky was squeezed in at a square folding table with five other soldiers playing an intense game of poker. A pile of coins and dollar bills lay in the center between them. Ricky tossed another dollar onto the heap.

"I'll take one. Make it a six."

The dealer peeled a card from the top of the deck and slid it to Ricky. As he turned it over, all hope disappeared from his face.

"Shit!" He slammed the cards down. "I'm out, guys." He pushed his chair back, screeching the legs against the hastily laid wooden plank floor, and ambled over to his bunk. Mac was already there, sitting on the edge of the lower bed, sketching on a large drafting pad.

"What are you doing?" questioned Ricky.

"Nothing really. Just working on a couple of ideas I had. Killing time."

"Maybe you could draw me up plans for a casino? One where I win big bucks and never lose."

Mac laughed. "I'm a frustrated designer, not a magician. No such casino like that."

"Tell me about it." Ricky plopped down next to him. "Maybe if we land in Monte Carlo-"

"If we come ashore there, we're screwed. That's the wrong coast."

"It's all France, right?" He tried sneaking a peek at Mac's pad. "Show me. You have to be drawing something."

"A boat." Mac turned the sketch to Ricky. "It's a concept I had."

"Looks like the Queen Mary."

"One of her lifeboats, maybe. She's a twenty-eight-foot off-shore cruiser. Takes her lines from a Chris-Craft, with a forward stateroom and twin diesels."

"Is it yours?"

"Will be one day. After the war's over, when I build her."

"Nice. I'll let you take me out on it sometime. I've only been sailing once, and that was during a vacation with my folks on Fire Island, but the weather was crappy and we all got sick. Hey, can you lend me ten bucks? I just got cleaned out."

"Again?" Though it was a question, Mac's tone revealed he wasn't surprised.

Before Ricky could answer, a sergeant major with a bullhorn cut him off as he stood at the entrance of the barracks tent blasting his words. "Ten minutes to lights out. Operations begin at O-five hundred tomorrow. Sleep tight, sweethearts."

A groan rose from the two hundred men in the tent. Ricky shrugged. "I guess poker's done for the night." He climbed up and crawled into the top bunk, then leaned back over, his head dangling. "Good night, Mac. Keep the snoring down, okay?"

The sun was still pulling itself out of the English Channel as the five hundred non-commissioned officers stood shoulder to shoulder facing their post commander. Many had to squint to make him out as the early morning rays shone directly into their eyes. They knew anytime they were summoned by the man whose word over their training was absolute, the briefing had to be important.

"This will be quick today, men, but don't mistake my brevity for any lack of importance." Brigadier General Walters emphasized his words to make sure his sergeants understood. "We are expecting the LSTs to arrive here at Slapton in a little over an hour, around O-eight hundred. Start Point lighthouse reports having eyes on them already, so despite their slow speed, the Navy is keeping to schedule for once."

He paused and the men laughed.

"Those floating transports are not carrying tanks and armored vehicles today, instead they are bringing the supplies we have been waiting for and the materials to construct the obstacles you can expect to encounter on the invasion beaches when we return to France. The more you become familiar with the complications the Germans have prepared for us, the simpler it will be to deal with on the day itself. I have spent a lot of time planning the upcoming exercises, and they are going to be both rigorous and physically challenging for you all. But before you bitch and moan to each other, which I know you will, understand the reason I have made them so difficult. It's because I believe with every fiber of my being that if you train hard then you fight easy. That's what I am hoping for, because I want to keep my boys safe out there."

Again, he stopped speaking for a moment to let them absorb the information he was giving them.

"Some of the finest soldiers in the world stand before me today. The 1st Engineer Special Brigade, the 2nd Rangers, the 4th Division, and the 82nd and 101st Airborne. To have become a sergeant among those esteemed ranks is an achievement to cherish."

His words were genuine, and he stared at his men with pride.

"Any differences between the brigades and divisions are to be put aside. Together you will have a new designation, Amphibious Force Seven. There has been much talk about where you are going, and I have addressed this with some of you before. You will not know where your landing beaches are until after you have taken them. Only their assigned designations will be used, Omaha and Utah. As we get closer to the day of liberation, we will specifically assign each of you to one of those beachheads, and two secondary groups will be formed, Force U for Utah and Force O for Omaha. But until that is announced, we are all part of the same group, Americans who, when we return to France, will be fighting for freedom and to end fascism's threat forever. Now assemble your men and have them standing by and ready to unload the LSTs when they hit the beach. There's a lot of work to be done today. Dismissed."

Brigadier General Walters stepped from his podium as the NCOs broke from their ranks and returned to the camp to brief their men.

As they walked, Ricky elbowed Mac. "So, what do you think?"

"I like our post commander, he seems to be a good man, but we're not getting anything new. They're keeping where and when we're going to themselves."

"I hope I get assigned Omaha," grinned Ricky. "I used to date a hottie from Nebraska."

"I'm glad it's stopped raining, Grandpa."

"Give it a few minutes, it'll start again," grumbled Reg.

The two Coastal Watch family members sat in their folding chairs, not only staring out to sea, but also keeping an eye on the constant activity on the beach, more than a hundred and twenty feet below them. Hundreds of soldiers were being deployed along the waterline where they took their positions, seemingly waiting.

"What do you think they're doing?" wondered Mary.

"Whatever it is, it's army business, not ours. Keep your eyes off the Yanks and on the channel, watching for Nazis."

"I will. And at least we're off night duty for now. I didn't know how much more of it I could take. I was freezing the whole time."

"I'll agree with you on that, lass. Coldest winter I can remember. I hope Percy has some warm jackets to wear now he's taken over nights or he'll turn into an icicle. The old man's got no meat on his bones."

"Grandpa, what's that?!" Surprise rang through her voice, mixed with a trace of fear.

Reg saw where Mary was pointing, and grabbed his binoculars and scanned Start Point, four miles south-west of them. His mouth dropped open as he squinted through the lenses. "It's ships. At least two of them, and they're big, really big. I can't make out any markings yet through this morning haze. Get ready with your morse code, Mary, in case it is the bloody Huns on their way."

Mary reached into her bag for the field issue signal lantern, while Reg remained transfixed. He kept up his running commentary. "They're transports, not warships. And there are more coming. I can make out at least another three behind the first two. If it is an invasion, then we're really going to get it."

Unable to contain herself, Mary got to her feet, and forgetting her own binoculars, stared at the southernmost point of the South Hams. "There are so many. What are we going to do?"

Reg lowered his binoculars. "Take a deep breath, my girl, and sit yourself back down. They're on our side. I can see a flag flying, it's the American navy that's coming."

"But it looks like they're turning now and heading straight in. If they do that and keep going, they'll crash on the beach."

"That's their plan, alright."

"To crash on the beach?"

"No. They won't crash. They'll come right up on the sand."

"But, Grandpa, they're too big to do that. They'll rip their bottoms out and sink."

"Not the way they're built. Those big ships have a special hollow hull. They load it with water when they're at sea to make them stable, then when they come into shore, they pump the water out and fill the hull with air. That lifts the boat up and they only need a few inches of water below them. They'll land right on the beach, open their bow doors and lower a ramp at the front to unload, just you watch."

"Like a giant landing craft."

"Exactly that. That's why the navy calls them LSTs."

"LSTs?"

"Yes. The little landing craft, they're the ones that carry the troops to the beach. The big ones, these LSTs, carry the heavy stuff, like tanks. That's why they're called Landing Ship, Tank."

"Shouldn't it be TLS, like Tank, Landing Ship?"

"Young lady, you think this old pensioner makes up the names for the Yanks' navy? I only know what they're called. Those big buggers are LSTs, the small ones are LSIs-"

"Landing Ship, Infantry?" guessed Mary.

"Correct, though sometimes they call them LCAs, Landing Craft, Assault, because, I guess, the officers can't make their bloody minds up." Reg scoffed. "And they even have one in between, the LSM, the Landing Ship, Medium, so you can carry a bit of both, men and trucks."

"And you're sure they're friendly?"

Reg instinctively pulled his binoculars back up to his eyes to double-check. As he took in the military might of the oncoming ships heading towards them, he shook his head and whispered under his breath. "They'd better be."

From Coastal Watch – LSTs arriving at Slapton Sands, January 1944

Driving off a beached LST at Slapton Sands

LSTs and LCAs arriving at Slapton Sands, January 1944

CHAPTER FIVE
Meeting

The enormous beach began to feel small. It was jammed with eight massive LSTs pulled up on the shingle and resting fifteen feet above the high-tide line. Four of them had their double bow doors wide open, with the landing ramp deployed onto the sloping beach. Around them, smaller landing craft buzzed in and out, allowing the servicemen, outfitted in full combat gear to board, sail around the bay, then disembark in simulated assaults on German emplacements. Each craft carried a maximum of thirty-six servicemen, so there was a continuous line of soldiers waiting for their turn to practice liberating France.

While the center of the beach had become naval territory, the north-eastern end of Slapton Sands was designated for obstacle training. SI – Signals Intelligence – had reported the German defenses included not only guns and artillery but a series of traps designed to make landing hazardous at best, and in many cases, outright impossible. British commandos had secretly gone ashore at a number of locations and taken photographs of what Hitler's Atlantic wall had lying in wait, and now, using those shots as guides, accurate reproductions were being put together on the South Devon beach to let the American assault teams figure out a way to neutralize them.

Three soldiers, wielding oxy-acetylene torches, sent showers of sparks flying into the air as they worked feverishly to assemble yet another German hedgehog – an anti-tank and anti-landing device looking curiously like a child's set of jacks on steroids. As they put the final touches on the ten-foot-high, interlinked steel crosses, Mac gave them the order to stop. "Good job. Two more to complete and we are done."

A voice from behind contradicted him. "You might be finished with your work for today already, sergeant."

Mac turned to see Lieutenant Evans standing there with another officer, one he hadn't encountered before, but he could see by his insignia, he was facing a colonel.

"How many have been constructed, sergeant?" asked Lieutenant Evans.

"Forty-three of the forty-five on my schedule. I'm getting ready to work on the final two, sir."

"Can your men handle that without you?"

"Yes, sir, I think they can."

"Good. Because you're done here, Sergeant Harper."

"Why is that, sir?"

"This is Colonel Brogan of the 2nd Rangers. He watched you on the beach last week during your practice assault. The one where you took it upon yourself to use the smoke grenade."

Mac involuntarily took half a step back as he focused his eyes on the colonel. "I can explain, sir. I was –"

"No need to explain." To Mac's surprise, the colonel's tone was friendly, not reprimanding. "I saw how you handled the mock gun emplacement, and took note you were able to get all of your squad off the beach, capture the target and take out the machine gunners," he turned to the lieutenant with a smile, "and their officer, without losing any of your own men. It was very impressive."

"Thank you, sir." Mac remained unsure of what was happening.

"I'm told you specialize in demolition and engineering. And by the look of those nasty hedgehogs you've assembled, it seems you know what you're doing."

"I'm only following the plans, sir."

"I think you're being modest, son. My boys are the 2nd Rangers. Two of my combat engineers met with an accident a month ago and the Army has not yet seen fit to replace them. For where we're going, I'll need every one of my men. I want you to join my battalion, and I'd like you to select someone else who has a similar skill set and abilities to yours. And remember, these are the Rangers we're talking about, so when it comes to engineers, they must be able to do both, engineer and fight. And that applies to all the men I command, no matter what their positions. In other words, you serve with me and I'll have you not only building things but blowing shit up as well. Do I make myself clear, sergeant?"

"One hundred percent, sir."

"Are you in?"

"It would be an honor to join your Rangers, sir."

"Good. But from now on it's *our* Rangers, son. We're one team. Got it?"

"Got it, sir."

"Then I will see you at the Rangers' tents at O-seven hundred tomorrow where the quartermaster will issue you a new uniform and billet."

"I'll be there, sir. One question though."

"What is it?"

"In picking the other recruit, along with combat engineering and demolition, are there any other skills I should look for?"

"Yes. A head for heights."

The colonel and the lieutenant snapped a salute to Mac which he smartly returned and held as they walked away.

As he watched them leave, he ran the colonel's last words through his mind, *a head for heights*. What did that mean in the context of a seaborne invasion? Mac was still pondering that question as he noticed where the two officers were heading, the towering cliffs rising from the long shingle beach. His eyes panned up the one hundred and fifty foot sheer rock face and he whispered to himself, "Holy shit!"

The boom from the four-foot-long mortar tube was not overly loud, but it was amplified by the close proximity of the fallen boulders at the base of the cliff, and matched by eleven others also firing on cue, so for a moment the sound was deafening.

Twelve grappling hooks from the climbing mortars hurtled upwards, trailing a curtain of attached ropes dancing through the air. They curved over the top of the cliff before falling to the grassy plain overlooking the beach, where the spiked hooks dug deep into the ground, establishing a firm grip.

One hundred and fifty feet below, the Rangers who had fired the explosive grappling hooks, pulled hard on the ropes, leaning back with all their weight, testing and ensuring they had found a secure hold that would not give way and send a climber dropping to his death. One after another, they gave their supervising officer a deliberate *okay*.

Once the officer in command was certain the safety measures had been checked, he blew his whistle, and twelve Rangers started their hazardous climb up the cliff.

Mac and Ricky stood with Colonel Brogan as they watched the simulated attack begin. The colonel kept his eyes on the climbers as he spoke to the two men with him. "I wanted you to see how we do this before sending you up. The mortars are our preferred method of scaling a cliff as long as the soil surface at the top is firm enough to hold the hooks. If not, we have assault ladders, but with these kinds of heights, they can become unwieldy. My men are also trained in free climbing, but that is always a last resort because in a combat situation with full kit, carbines and explosives, they are carrying a lot of weight."

The second row of twelve Rangers was now starting up and making quick work of the intimidating cliff face.

The colonel noted Mac's admiring look. "My men have practiced this for years. They are the best at what they do. We'll teach you what they know about climbing and fighting, and you can teach them demolition."

"Sir, it's our understanding we will be going into combat with the 2nd Rangers, not just teaching them."

"Son, if all goes as planned, you'll be an integral part of the Rangers and with us in the first wave of landings with the assault force. But I believe in backup. What if you are hurt or killed before we hit the beach? Someone's got to take out the German bunkers and it won't be you if you're busy making apologies to St. Peter for your indiscretions with the under-age girl-next-door back home, and begging him to let you in through the Pearly Gates. You teach us how to use your explosives, we'll teach you how to be a Ranger, and together we'll teach Fritz a lesson he'll never forget."

"Yes, sir!" Mac's enthusiasm rang through his words.

"Look. They're coming back down." The colonel checked his watch. "Three minutes. Forty-eight men up and down the cliffs in three minutes. That works for me."

He watched proudly as the men rappelled down the cliff and jumped the final feet onto the shingles. As they did, instead of waiting to catch their breath, they assembled into a line twelve long and four deep. Their ability and commitment brought a broad smile to their officer's face.

He turned to his newest Ranger recruits. "What do you think?"

"They're good men, sir," answered Mac. "Can we try it now?"

"Now? Today?" The colonel looked him up and down curiously. "Are you sure? I was going to have my boys work with you on it first."

"Sir, they've tested the lines for us and we know they're solid, and Sergeant Esposito and myself both climbed ropes during basic training." Mac stared at the colonel with confidence. "We saw how it should be done; now is the perfect opportunity. Can we try?"

The colonel hesitated before replying. "Okay. I'll have my squad leaders make sure you know how the rope should be fastened around your waist in case you were to tire or fall. After all this, I don't want to lose any more of my explosive experts."

"Thank you, sir."

Mac and Ricky headed across the pebbles to the group of waiting Rangers. Ricky rolled his eyes. "Safety lines in case we fall! Shit, I thought it would be the Germans trying to kill me. I was wrong. It's my best friend who wants to bury me in the ground."

"Don't worry. I'll talk you through it."

"Talk me through it? You can't *talk* someone through climbing a mountain."

"It's not a mountain, and you'll do fine. You were great on the ropes during the obstacle course at training."

"That was, what, twelve feet? Look at the cliff, it's so high it goes up into the clouds. It won't be Krauts waiting at the top, it'll be Jesus and the heavenly choir."

Mac could see Ricky's apprehension and stepped up his efforts to reassure him. "A few rocks shouldn't scare you. Not after the way you led that squad in Sicily to take out the German mortar emplacement. If you hadn't done it, and seized the initiative, none of us would have made it out of the town square."

"That was different. I had my feet on the ground. It was only a couple of Nazis and a few sandbags."

"The CO didn't think it was so simple. You earned your stripes under fire."

Ricky hesitated as he remembered. "Someone had to do it."

"And that someone was you."

Two of the Rangers stepped forward, interrupting their conversation, and after a moment's explanation, helped each of them fasten a Swiss Seat rappel harness around their waists and between their legs, to use as a safety measure for both going up and coming back down. With that in place, the Rangers returned to their ranks to give the two men time to focus.

Mac grabbed one of the ropes and pulled hard. Ricky looked at him, puzzled. "What are you doing? You know they're in place."

"Rule number one in climbing, always make sure. You want to bet your life nothing's changed, that the hook will still hold you?" He pointed at the next rope. "Go ahead. Climb it without checking."

Ricky looked up at the overhanging cliff face and shook his head. He heaved on his rope. It felt firm and didn't move. "It's good. I hope."

"Feed the rope through your harness, lean back, and using your arms to hold you, put your feet on the rock and walk up."

"Walk up? Not climb?"

"Ricky, this thing is almost vertical. If you attempt to muscle yourself to the top you'll burn out your shoulders before you get halfway. With the ropes in place, what I'm saying to do will be much easier on you. Stay at ninety degrees to the face and walk and pull. Like this." Mac took his weight on his arms and started his upward walk.

In seconds, he was ten feet above Ricky and going fast.

"Holy crap. The things you get me into." Ricky began his shaky climb.

Mac yelled back to him. "Doing great, Ricky. Keep your eyes locked on your feet and try not to look down."

"Don't worry, I won't."

From fifty feet away, Colonel Brogan watched as the two men assailed the cliff. Mac was nearly to the peak, while Ricky was not even near the halfway mark. Both seemed confident, but the first one, he struggled to remember his name, he seemed to have something special about him.

It was as he recalled Sergeant Harper's name, that Mac reached the top and pulled himself over onto the flat, grassy pinnacle.

Mac unclipped from the Swiss Seat and dropped to his knees to look back over the cliff's edge and check on his friend's progress. It was then he heard a girl's voice.

"I'd be careful, if I were you. You're too close to the edge."

Mac nearly fell off the cliff at the unexpected sound. He spun around and the most incongruous sight he had ever seen greeted him. Seventy feet away were two civilians seated in folding chairs, an elderly man and a young girl in her early twenties. They were both eating sandwiches, and in between them was a small camping table with two teacups and saucers and a Thermos flask on it. He stayed silent and tried taking in what he was seeing.

Mary spoke again. "I'd move if you want to be safe. When the last lot of soldiers came up over the edge a few minutes ago, some of it started crumbling away, right where you are."

He heard the words, but remained frozen in place.

Mary turned to her grandfather. "Perhaps he can't hear us. Do you think all those loud bangs made him go deaf?"

"Or daft, more like it." Reg raised his voice and yelled. "Move your bum, you silly Yank. The cliff could give way."

Shocked into action, Mac leaped to his feet and took two quick paces from the edge. As he did so, a small stone peeled from the fringing rocks and clattered off the cliff. Hearing that, Mac stepped back to the edge and looked over to make sure it hadn't hit Ricky. Reg and Mary misinterpreted his move.

"Now what's he doing? He's not going to jump, is he?"

Reg again called out loudly. "Don't do it, son. Let it go. Things aren't that bad."

Seeing his friend was okay and still climbing slowly up, Mac turned back to the very English odd couple. "Thanks for the warning. It's sure a long way down."

"A long way down? Oh, he's a bright one, this kid," smirked Reg.

Mary tried to cover for her grandfather's rudeness. "You're welcome. We were only trying to help."

Mac paused in his response as he took in the girl addressing him. The morning sun shone down on her, turning her blond hair a luminescent gold. Her skin was pale, and her lips glowed naturally red. It was hard to tell her build, but like most Brits he'd seen during his posting to England, first in London, then outside to Redding, she seemed slim. All the English people he'd run into appeared slim, some downright skinny; probably, he thought, because of the strict rationing the island nation had been under for the past four years. Either way, she was the most beautiful thing he had seen in a long time.

He knew he had to say something, anything, but all he could manage was, "What are you doing up here?"

Reg looked at Mary, then held up his sandwich. "Eating. We call it having lunch here in Britain."

"But why here? I thought all the locals were…"

"Nearly all," answered Mary. "We live over in Stoke Fleming, and come here every day to do our bit for the war effort. We're with the Coastal Watch." She saw the name didn't mean anything to Mac. "We have papers if you need to see them." She stood up and reached for her bag to get them out and show him.

"It's okay, it's okay, I believe-"

Mac was interrupted by a familiar voice a few feet behind him. "Hey, human fly. I made it. Now what?'

He turned to Ricky. "I guess we go down."

"You don't have to ask me twice, I'm on my way now." Ricky was done with the cliff and climbing. He wanted to get back on solid ground.

As he disappeared, Mac looked again at the couple, his eyes fixed on Mary. "I gotta go."

He picked up the trailing rope extending from the grappling hook and attached it to his harness. He stepped back to the cliff and waved to the two Coastal Watch members. "Cheerio," he said, failing in his attempt at an English accent. Unconsciously showing off, he leaped from the edge and swung into the cliff face, barely cushioning the impact with his feet.

It was Reg and Mary's turn to fall silent after his departure. Reg was the first to speak. "Peculiar lot, these Yanks."

"I thought he was quite handsome." Mary regretted her choice of words as soon as she'd said them when she saw her grandfather's scowl. "In a peculiar kind of way, of course."

Ricky was still ten feet from the base of the cliff when Mac passed him and dropped onto the shingle beach. He detached the harness and hurried over to Colonel Brogan, who greeted him with a salute.

"That was excellent, sergeant. Where did you learn to climb a cliff like that?"

"It wasn't on cliffs, sir, but something more difficult."

"More difficult than that nastiness?" He pointed to the almost sheer, rugged face.

"Yes, sir. Something narrow, wet, and moving. I grew up on boats, sir. When I was eight years old, my father had me up and down the rigging of a two-master in all kinds of weather. I'd fix sails, untangle ropes, oil the pulleys, check the masthead light. Became a sport for me, really."

"It must have been an exceptional way to learn, Harper. I hate to say this, but you're faster than most of my men, and they are the best in the service."

"Sir, it was my first time tackling a cliff face and using a harness. May I try one more time now I have the feel for it?"

The colonel checked the sun. "Certainly. Training is done here for the day and we've got quite a few hours of daylight left. But don't get hurt. I think we're going to need you."

"Thank you, sir."

"How about your friend?"

Mac looked at Ricky and stumbled through his words. "I think maybe I should work with him first on a few things." He pulled himself together. "And I'm going for speed, if that's okay?"

"Good with me. When you're climbing a cliff under fire, trying to get to a German gun emplacement, speed is what might stand between you and the big sleep. You work on it, then teach Sergeant Esposito."

"Will do, sir. I'll have him come with me now, recheck the ropes, then be my spotter and wait at the bottom of the cliffs."

"Agreed."

The two sergeants returned to the foot of the sheer face. Colonel Brogan studied Mac as he walked. "That's Ranger material," he murmured to himself.

At the base of the cliff, Mac erupted into a fury of speed, once again attaching his Swiss Seat to the climbing rope. For all his hurry, he made sure to double check the knots and the carabiner.

Ricky watched in amazement. "You are certifiable, you know that?'

"Yup, I know. I'll see you in the nuthouse." With that, Mac was away and racing up the rocky face.

In less than forty seconds he summited the cliff and hauled himself, up and over, onto the grass. He unclipped equally fast and sprinted to Reg and Mary. Breathing hard from his exertion, he struggled to speak. "Hello again. How often are you up here?"

"None of your business. We don't talk to soldiers about schedules and what we do. Loose lips sink ships."

Mary shot a disparaging glance at her grandfather. "We're here six hours, every day."

"What if the weather's bad, like if it's raining?"

Reg snorted and lifted a rolled-up umbrella. "You're in England now, not the bloody Sahara Desert. We don't leave home without one of these."

"Got it. I'm Mac Harper, by the way."

"Did you say Max, like Maxwell?" asked Mary.

"No, it's Mac."

"Mac?" Mary's grandfather scoffed at the thought. "Like a bleeding raincoat? Is that even a name?"

Mac closed his eyes for a second. He'd only been asked this about a million times before, and knew he couldn't stay up here too long without arousing suspicion. "Yes, Mac, M-A-C." He spelled it out. "Before my grandparents moved to the States, our family first emigrated to Canada about two hundred years ago and it's become a family tradition that every generation a boy is named after a river where they first settled, The Mackenzie. They just shortened the name and used the first part."

"Bloody good job they didn't move to Mississippi, or we'd be calling you Miss." Reg laughed at his own joke.

Mac glanced over his shoulder to the cliff, knowing time was running out, and then back to Mary. As their eyes met, she understood. "I'm Mary. Mary Sheppard. That's my grandfather, Reginald Sheppard."

"Nice to meet you both." He took a deep breath. "I've gotta go."

"Don't let us keep you," said Reg.

"But you'll be here tomorrow?"

"Weren't you listening when my granddaughter said we're here every day? I would have thought even an American would know that meant tomorrow and the next day and the next, until you lot finally get around to winning the bloody war."

"Good." He smiled at Mary. "I'll try and find an excuse to come back. Until then, see ya!"

He turned for the cliff. As he moved, Mary called after him, in a vain attempt at an American accent, "See ya, Mac."

Mac rappelled to the base of the cliff where Ricky was waiting. He studied Mac as he shed the harness. "And?"

"And what?"

"You got up to the top in no time flat, disappeared for six minutes, then come sailing back down. What were you doing up there? Making friends with the locals?"

"It was nothing important."

"Really? I'm your buddy. Tell me."

"Can't do it. You know the slogan; loose lips sink ships." With that, Mac grabbed his harness and started his trek across the slippery shingles back to the base camp.

A morning haze filled the air as the two hundred and twenty-five men of the 2nd Rangers assembled on the field behind the sprawling military encampment.

Colonel Brogan addressed his men with an easy familiarity. "So far, the training here at Slapton is going well, and I've just received intel that when we do get the word to go, whenever that might be, we will be assigned to Easy, Dog, and Fox companies. Those boys are among the best here, so with the 2nd to lead them in, I feel sorry for whoever we will be facing."

He paused, letting his men absorb the information. "As you have probably guessed from our recent training, our target will be taking out the guns mounted high above whatever landing beach the brass have selected. I know you will have no trouble storming the cliffs, but the guns themselves pose a different problem. The Germans have had years to strengthen their positions, and the British Commandos who did the recon, say the emplacements are heavily fortified with steel and concrete. A straightforward assault would be tantamount to suicide, and I will not let any of you be put in that position."

The four lines of Rangers suppressed a smile. They knew how much their commanding officer cared for them.

"Instead of running at their guns, our plan is to blow them to kingdom come so there'll be no one left to shoot at us. Now, the Navy claims they can do that by shelling them before we reach the beaches, but between you and me, I've seen them miss their targets as often as they hit them, so I'm thinking it's going to be up to us to take out the armored bunkers. That's why for the next few days we are leaving our climbing exercises and concentrating on demolition. Sergeants Harper and Esposito, step forward."

Ricky and Mac left the line of Rangers and joined the colonel.

"These two men are experts in demolition and engineering. I asked them to join the glorious 2nd to teach us about high explosives, setting fuses, and using Bangalore Torpedoes. The training will be done here in Newland's Field. Report to your squad leader for scheduling and assignment. Dismissed."

Colonel Brogan turned to the duo as the men fell out. "Will four days be enough?"

Mac checked with Ricky before answering. "It should be. They won't be experts but they'll be able to handle the charges safely and effectively."

"Good. Go to it." The colonel turned and left.

Ricky waited until he was out of earshot before speaking. "At least we get a break from Everest for a few days."

Mac shook his head slightly as he replied. "Yeah, I guess."

Newland's Field, a wide strip of grassland bordering Slapton Ley, the marshy lagoon lying inland of Slapton Sands' rocky beach, was empty of the sheep which had grazed there for more than two centuries. A long airstrip had been bulldozed down the center of the pasture, and though the ground was too soft to allow the landing and take-off of heavier planes like transports or bombers, it was fine for spotter aircraft, and even, at a pinch, a fighter like the Mustang P-51. Two sets of anti-aircraft guns guarded the north and south sides of the field, and the far western edge was used for parking and storage of the military vehicles including tanks and APCs.

Mac and Ricky stood with two platoons, each consisting of four squads of ten Rangers. Mac had decided that even though the training would take longer by breaking up the 2nd into platoons, it would be a safer and more effective way of learning for the men. He began his briefing. "You'll see there are two abandoned vehicles about a hundred yards apart, a tractor and a truck. Sergeant Esposito will take his platoon to the tractor. My men follow me to the truck. The supplies we need are already in position."

With a nod to Ricky, Mac led his four squads over to the rusted transport vehicle. Lying close to it on the damp grass were a series of five-foot tubes. Mac stopped his platoon by the pile. "What you are looking at is an M1A1 Bangalore Torpedo. It's basically a pipe bomb on an extended stick you push ahead of you. That way you can stay safe while the enemy are greeted by the nasty end which is packed with TNT. It can be used for clearing brush or exploding exposed mines, but what you are training for, is to use it against a fortified emplacement too dangerous for a direct frontal approach."

The men nodded in appreciation of the logic of this.

"The business end of the Bangalore is sealed," Mac pointed at the rounded closure on one of the tubes. "The other nine tubes you simply clip on, one after another to lengthen it up to fifty feet. That way, you stay safe from the blast, and God willing, from any enemy fire. We don't have a convenient gun emplacement to blow up today," he smiled. "But we do have this old truck as a stand in. Hopefully, the first blast won't blow it to bits, because I want to do this a least four times to give you the hang of it. If there's not enough left of the truck, there are several logs and a diseased oak tree we can attack."

The platoon laughed.

"Which squad wants to go first?"

Forty arms shot skyward, so Mac chose the men closest.

"Start by finding a secure spot or dugout within fifty feet of your intended target. Shelter there, then push the explosive end over the top. Screw on the second tube, then the third, until it's long enough to reach your target. Go!"

The Rangers followed his directions without question, and in less than two minutes had six lengths attached, so it stretched thirty-five feet from their shallow foxhole to underneath the rusted old farm vehicle. With it complete, they looked to their supervising sergeant for approval and final instructions.

"Good work. You are going to be close to the explosion, so make sure you are eating dirt when you set it off. Ideally, you could run a set of wires to your end of the Bangalore then retire even further to a really safe distance before you set it off, but in the field, pinned down under constant fire, you might not have that luxury. We're going to assume you don't, so whoever is doing fire control, alert your other team members, cover your ears and hug the ground. Got it?"

"Got it, sarge."

The lead Ranger motioned for the other nine to get as flat as they could behind the natural rise in the field acting as a shielding trench, while he counted out loud. "Three – two – one."

He twisted the detonator. There was a massive boom and the heavy truck lifted off the ground in a ball of flame, spinning in the air, its rear axle separating from the frame and crashing down a dozen feet from the burning vehicle.

Slowly, the demolition team raised their heads to survey the results of their work. As they did, Mac stepped forward and joined them. "Great job. I'd say the gun emplacement has been neutralized." He looked back at the three other squads who were waiting and now eager for their turn. "Who's next?"

The light was fading and the creeping arrival of evening turned the rolling green hills behind Newland's Field into an azure blue, as Colonel Brogan addressed the assembled force of the 2nd Rangers. "The reports I've received over the past three days tell me you have been quick and able in your mastery and use of explosives. I'm not surprised. I expected nothing less from the 2nd. We will revisit demolition in a few weeks if the invasion doesn't occur before then, but as of tomorrow we return to landings, climbing, and assault exercises. Get some sleep tonight, you'll need it. Dismissed."

As the two hundred and twenty-five men broke apart and started their slow walk to the tents at the base camp, Ricky shook his head. "Climbing the cliffs again."

"Yup."

Ricky looked at him, puzzled, not understanding the happiness in his friend's voice at being told he once again had to tackle that formidable rock face.

The early February weather was cold and miserable. An endless drizzle oozed from the heavy skies, and the temperature hovered a few degrees above freezing. The grey seas were no better, as a four-foot swell rolled constantly in from the English Channel to crash relentlessly upon the sloping beach.

Six LCA – Landing Craft, Assault – bobbed out in the cold waters, a half-mile from shore, their twin Ford V8 engines turned off to conserve the sixty-four gallons of fuel they carried.

The thirty-six Rangers onboard sat squashed together, and shivered in unison as wave after wave rolled the small boat, soaking their uniforms and chilling their flesh.

"I'm going to be sick again." Ricky's pallor shamed the grey skies.

"Get to the side. Don't throw up in the boat. It already stinks to high heaven from everyone who has." Mac helped Ricky up and he barely made it to the gunwale of the little craft before he dry heaved from his already empty stomach.

None of the other Rangers gave him a disparaging look as he returned to the wooden bench and plopped back down; most of them had done exactly the same thing.

Mac checked his watch. "Ten-fifteen."

"We've only been out here three hours? Shit, it feels like a month. I can't ever remember being so cold, wet, and miserable."

Mac said nothing. No words of his could change the situation, calm the seas, or make the situation better.

"You're like a fucking statue. Doesn't this affect you, floating out here, going up and down?"

"It's not the rocking, it's the cold I'm trying to handle."

"You're handling it better than me, Mac. I wish I could be like you right now, but I'm an east coast, big city, kid."

"It is something you get used to. At first, when I was a little boy, I'd cry when Dad took me on his boat in the winter. But as I got older, I learned to ignore the cold, and love being out on the ocean, no matter what the weather."

"How long before I get to love it?'

Mac looked as his friend's pallor. "Give it a while."

"A couple more hours?"

"A couple more years, maybe," Mac laughed.

"Oh, great. By then the war will be over. When Hitler surrenders, he'll say it was because of all the Rangers throwing up on him." He managed to move his head a little without bringing up more bile, and looked at the sectional assault ladders lying stacked along the center of the craft.

"At least, when we get ashore, the climbing should be easier. We get to use ladders. Not damned ropes like last time."

A whistle blew, cutting off Ricky's whining, and the twin diesels roared into life.

"Finally. Here we go." For the first time in hours there was excitement in Ricky's voice.

The boat lurched forward and picked up speed as it, and the five other LCAs, raced in to the beach.

Mac turned his head, looking back and down to the engine compartment. His brow furrowed deeply.

"Smile, buddy. We're moving." Ricky gave him a thumbs up.

"The engines are out of sync." Mac shot a glance at the coxswain captaining the craft to see if he had noticed the problem.

Ricky couldn't understand his friend's concern. "What is it?"

"Can't you hear that? The engines are off-pitch."

"Sounds okay to me."

"It's not. The engines aren't working together; it's like they're fighting against each other."

"How the hell are you hearing that?"

"I worked on a twin diesel tug that had the same mechanics as this, with my dad in San Pedro for four years. When the engines start making that sound, you have to fix them, quick."

"Jeez, I hope they don't crap out before we reach dry land. I need off this floating barge."

Before Mac could answer, the landing sergeant stood up at the front of the speeding boat, putting his back to the ramp and called out to his men. "We're going in. We'll be on the beach in two minutes. Keep your heads down, your carbines dry, and prepare for immediate evac when I call landing stations."

Following orders, the squads checked their weapons, adjusted their helmet straps and cinched the buckles holding their gear, making sure it wouldn't be lost in the water as they raced off the assault vessel. The forward squad reached down and placed one hand each on the collapsible ladders as they had been taught in training, ready to run with them down the ramp and across the beach to the cliff. Today would be their first chance to see if all the instruction drilled into them actually worked in a real situation.

The coxswain raised his hand in a fist. The landing sergeant saw the prearranged signal and yelled, "Ten seconds. Ready, Rangers." It wasn't a question.

A grinding noise overtook the roar of the diesels and the craft shuddered as its flat bottom made contact and ground up onto the shingled slope of Slapton Sands. Several of the Rangers were thrown from the wet wooden seats as the landing craft stopped abruptly, its short voyage completed.

A heavy rattle filled the air as the metal front acting as the little vessel's bow fell forward to become a sloping ramp, the soldiers' sole access from the boat to the beach.

"Go, go, go!" The ramp had barely settled in place before the order was given.

On command, the first two squads, carrying the assault ladders, raced down the ramp, through the breaking waves washing around them, and up the beach toward the cliffs.

"We're next." Mac gripped his carbine.

"Second squad, go!"

Mac, Ricky and their team were already on their feet and racing to the craft's yawning opening, knowing when the day of the real invasion came, speed could mean the difference between life and death.

A four-foot roller broke over the boys as they ran down the metal ramp. Ricky slowed for a second. "Shit, that's cold."

"Don't stop. We can't stay here at the tideline. This will be the kill zone." Mac used the butt of his carbine to push Ricky forward,

"Okay, I'm going."

The thirty-six Rangers powered across the slippery rocks toward their towering target.

At the foot of the cliffs, the first two squads, designated as the base crews, worked feverishly to assemble the ladders until finally two one hundred and fifty-foot ladders were complete and swung into position against the menacing crag. Because of the cliff's height and the ladders' limited length, the assault would be almost ninety degrees, a vertical climb.

The base crews used their grips and bodies to brace the flimsy ladders.

Seeing them in position, the landing sergeant again barked his commands. "Teams ready. Two at a time only on each ladder. On my mark. Go!"

Mac singled out one of his squad. "I'll take point. You follow." He grabbed the sides and started up, the flimsy ladder shuddering before he was even a few feet from the ground. Unperturbed, he kept going. When he reached the halfway point of the cliff, the second designated climber started up after him. Now the ladder shook violently, and the ground crew fought to keep it stable.

Taking a glimpse over his shoulder at the other assault ladder, he could see he was well ahead of the second squad leader. Mac didn't slow, he pushed harder until he reached the cliff's edge, and threw himself from the ladder onto the solid ground and assumed a firing position, to cover the next climber.

The following soldier appeared and took a similar prone position. Mac called to him. "Stay with the ladders. Give them cover and help them over the top. I'll reconnoiter the surroundings." He got to his feet and ran forward in a crouch toward two distant figures sitting in deckchairs.

As he rapidly approached them, he saw Mary wasn't there, only her grandfather, who sat with an older woman. Mac stopped in front of them, his carbine still in a firing position.

"Careful with that bloody thing. If it goes off, it'll blow Mrs. Higgens' head from her shoulders."

"Where's Mary, Mr. Sheppard?"

"And a hello to you, too. First, they move us all the way back here so you boys can play soldiers, then you come running up with your gun pointed at us, and not even a blooming good morning."

"Excuse him, son. He's in a bad mood. He got out of bed on the wrong side this morning."

"Like you would know, Mrs. Higgens."

"You only wish." Mrs. Higgens smiled at the handsome young American soldier. "They moved Mary to nightwatch for a while. Her eyes are better than mine."

"And now look what I'm stuck with," huffed Reg.

"Thanks." Crestfallen, Mac turned and raced back to the cliff to help the rest of the squad summit their goal.

The barracks bustled as the men compared stories about the first of their '*real*' exercises carried out across the length of the beach earlier in the day. In addition to taking the cliff, three regiments had come ashore in an infantry assault, and six tanks had been successfully landed, along with multiple Jeeps and a dozen trucks. There had only been minor hitches and those had been quickly overcome, so even the top brass had been satisfied, and made it a short day for the men, dismissing them to their quarters for food and relaxation.

Ricky held five cards to his face, spread out before him like an oriental fan, deciding which ones to get rid of. His dwindling pile of coins reflected his lack of success so far. With a shake of his head, he threw in his hand, swept up the last of his stake, pushed the chair from the table and stomped back to his bunk.

Sitting there, waiting, Mac was hunched forward, sullen and deep in thought. Ricky knew his friend and it was impossible to overlook his mood. "What is it, man?"

Mac hesitated before he answered, lowering his voice so only Ricky could hear him. "I want you to cover for me."

"Doing what?"

"I'm going off base tonight."

It was Ricky's turn to be taken aback. "Off base? Do you have a pass?" He knew the answer before he'd even finished his question and saw Mac shake his head. "Can you spell AWOL? They could take your stripes if you do that. And worse. Put you in the hole and hold you for court martial. What the fuck is worth that?"

"The less you know, the better. I don't want to take you down. too."

"I know you're not running and you sure ain't a spy. Maybe just nuts. And I do owe you big time. I wouldn't be here today if you hadn't put yourself on the line for me in Sorrento. Then I would have never had fun with all those Italian girls..." Ricky paused as a light went off in his brain. "That's what it is. It's a girl. There's nothing else that would make you sneak out of camp and risk going to the stockade for. Who is she? I hope she's cute."

Mac kept silent.

"She'd better be." Ricky slapped him on the shoulder. "Tell me what you need me to do."

American GIs on Slapton Sands - the cliffs in the distance

Rangers in LCAs approaching the cliffs at Slapton Sands

Rangers training to scale the cliffs and eliminate the German gun emplacements

CHAPTER SIX
Chocolate

The lights burning from the Quonset huts and tents were behind Mac as he slipped through the darkness, sticking to the shadows and hedgerows as he made his way up the winding cliff road, avoiding the two sets of sentries, who laughed together at an unheard joke, and had no reason to be alert. After all, if there was an attack, it wouldn't be from inland, the Germans would come across the channel.

Mac reached the flat plain of the cliff top and saw, with the aid of the rising quarter moon, the backs of the two civilians of Coastal Watch, huddled in their chairs, trying to ward off the night's chill. He noticed they were once again closer to the cliff's edge, having been allowed to return there after the completion of the day's exercises.

He stepped up behind them, and with a smile in his voice, said, "Good evening, ladies."

The women jumped in shock at the unexpected sound, knocking a Thermos flask from the little table and sending it flying into the air. The elder of the two leaped to her feet and spun around, not sure whether to run or to confront this unexpected intruder. "Who the bloody hell are you?"

Mary answered for him, surprise lining her words. "That's Mac, Mrs. Northcott. He's one of the American soldiers."

"I can see he's a Yank with me own flaming eyes. I didn't think he was a Nazi with that GI Joe uniform on. But what are you doing up here? Checking on us?"

"Sort of. And I'm sorry if I startled you."

"Well, what did you think was going to 'appen, sneaking up on us, quiet as a blooming church mouse. You scared the bejesus out of me. Next time, if you come up here, give us fair warning. Make some noise. Maybe rattle the bushes, or shine a light, or whistle or cough. Not tiptoe behind us and go boo!"

"I'm sure Mac didn't mean to frighten us."

Mrs. Northcott looked at Mary curiously. "That's twice you've said his name. How do you know each other?"

"We met when I was up here with Granddad."

"Oh, you have my sympathy then. He can be a miserable old sod. But you two seem to have hit it off."

"Mary was nice to me," replied Mac.

"I bet she was." Mrs. Northcott delivered her zinger with a wink, sensing the attraction between the two of them. "Tell you what I'm going to do. I believe I should check on the far side of the hill and make sure the Germans aren't launching a surprise attack there."

"You don't have to go."

She grinned at Mary. "Oh yes I do, my love. I was young once; don't you forget it." Mrs. Northcott turned and began her slow amble out of sight.

Mary waited to speak until she was gone. "I didn't know if I'd see you again."

"Same with me. I was shocked today when you weren't here."

"Grandpa told me you asked after me. Actually, he said you came over the cliff like a madman, waving your gun around as if it was a kite in the wind."

"I don't think I was that bad. I just wanted to say hi."

"Well then, hi."

The two fell into an uneasy silence for a moment before Mary continued. "Do you want to sit down?" She pointed to Mrs. Northcott's empty chair.

"She won't mind?"

"Umm.. she might bite your head off if she catches you in it." Mary giggled. "Only joking, it'll be fine."

Mac dropped into the English deckchair and took a second to get acquainted with the awkward leaning back position the chair's strange angle forced him to adopt.

Mary laughed. "You don't look comfortable."

"That's because I'm used to real chairs. You know, ones with four legs, a seat and a back."

"These are everywhere in England in the summer. Go on your holidays to the seaside and they have stacks of them you can rent."

"People pay to be tortured by these things?" It was Mac's turn to laugh.

"Oh yes, there's even a deckchair man who walks up and down the beach to check you've paid your thruppence for the chair."

"Thruppence?"

"Three pennies."

"That's way overcharging for this."

They laughed together at their two different upbringings and backgrounds.

After a moment, Mary took a serious tone. "Is it all right for you to be up here, Mac? From what I know, which isn't much, most soldiers aren't allowed to leave their camps at night. Only the sentries."

"You're correct. But I had a reason to leave."

"What?"

Mac paused before admitting, "You."

"Me? That is quite a compliment. I did hope to see you again. I got excited when Grandpa told me you'd asked where I was, but I didn't know how it would happen, with me being put on nights and all."

"Did your grandfather say anything else?"

"Not much really. Only what I said earlier about you running around looking crazy."

"He doesn't like me, does he?"

"It's not you, it's the fact you're a soldier. He doesn't like any soldiers."

"But we came here to help. Why wouldn't he like us?"

"Because of the war." Mary struggled to sit up in the chair as she became very serious. "Not just this war, but the First World War. He fought in it for two years and suffered badly. So bad, he won't ever talk about it. You can ask him questions about what happened but he shakes his head and stays quiet. Then he was in London in the summer of 'forty, when the Battle of Britain was going on. Him, and mum and dad were there when the Blitz started. Our house was hit, and my parents were both killed by the bombs. I only made it through because they put me under the stairs when the sirens went off. When grandpa found out, rather than letting the authorities stick me in a home, he came and got me, and brought me down here to live with him in his cottage, far away from the bombing. My father was his only child and I'm his only grandchild."

"I'm so sorry."

"I am too. I miss mum and dad every day. But it is much safer here than in London or Bristol or the big cities. The only times the German planes fly over is when they come to bomb the dockyards, but that's getting less and less all the time. I can't even remember when the last raid was. It's been quiet here for quite a while, that is until you lot came." Mary waved her arm in the direction of the sprawling American encampment below. "Where are you from in America?"

"California."

"Cal-i-forn-i-a." Mary said it slowly, savoring each syllable. "I saw loads of films about California and the Wild West when I used to go to the pictures before the war started. Lots of cowboys and gold mines." She was excited now. "Have you ever been to Hollywood? Have you met Clark Gable or Vivien Leigh or maybe John Wayne?"

"I've been to Hollywood a couple of times, but the only stars I've seen are the ones on the Walk of Fame. I've never met any real movie stars."

Mary shrugged. "Me neither, but movie stars don't come to Devon. Where are you from in California?"

"From a place on the water, like this area is. It's called San Pedro."

"San Pedro." Mary enjoyed how it sounded. "American city names are so glamourous – Hollywood, San Pedro, Chicago, New York. In England and Europe our names are boring – London, Paris, Rome...." She changed subjects. "What did you do in San Pedro?"

"I worked on boats. My dad had a job as a longshoreman, unloading ships in the harbor. Then he saved up and bought a boat and started his own company. He would go out to the cargo ships that were anchored offshore, waiting for dock space, and bring their goods in for them. Dad was like a ferry service who saved those ships a lot of time and money. Then he got a tugboat so he could pilot and guide in the really big ships who couldn't safely maneuver to their berths. Me and my brother worked on his boats, and we both kind of fell in love with the sea. After all this is over, I want to build boats."

"You'd build the boats yourself?"

"Yeah. Design them, build them, and sail them." He looked out at the moonlight shimmering across the long bay. "This wouldn't be a bad place to do something like that."

"If you love boats so much, why aren't you in the navy?"

"That's a bit of a sore point in my family. My brother is in the navy. He's on the USS Indianapolis somewhere in the

Pacific. Our folks didn't want us both in the same branch of the service, and because Donovan enlisted first, he got to choose the navy. I joined the 1st Engineers because of all the mechanical work I've done on engines, and I'm pretty good with my hands."

Mac looked again at the bay then down at his base. "I think I have to get back before I'm missed. Would it be okay if I came up here again to see you another night?"

"That would be delightful, Sergeant Harper."

Mac tried unsuccessfully to suppress a smile as Mary remembered his last name. "Great. I'll be back tomorrow night if I can make it past the sentry."

"Mac, could I ask you something?" The nervousness rang through in her words.

"Sure. Anything?"

"Could you get me some chocolate? Would that be possible? I read in the newspapers American soldiers have chocolate, and because of rationing, I haven't had any in nearly five years since the war started. But if you can't-"

"I can and I will. I'll make a point of getting you some."

"Thank you. I can hardly wait."

"Me neither. Until next time, Mary."

"Until next time, Mac."

The absent-without-leave sergeant clumsily got out of the low canvas deckchair and headed to the treeline marking the border between the clifftop and the coast road. As he walked, he risked a glance back at the lovely English girl who had unknowingly made him risk his rank and freedom. His gaze caught hers as she stared after him. Embarrassed, they both instantly averted their eyes, but not before a bolt of electricity passed between them, and Mac disappeared into the dark.

A second day of amphibious landings was behind the men of the 2nd Rangers, and as they disembarked the landing craft, tired and soaked through, all but one of the men headed back to their assigned quarters for showers, food, and rest. That lone soldier strode purposefully across the camp to the quartermaster's tent.

He stepped through the twin canvas flaps, the second hanging in place to keep the plentiful supplies dry and warm, and stopped at the counter where the heavy-set quartermaster stared him down, trying to guess the soldier's request. If he'd been a betting man, he would have put his money on cigarettes.

"You're here late. What's it going to be, sarge, Lucky Strikes?"

"No, sir. Chocolate."

"Chocolate?" He had plenty of chocolate but he was rarely asked for such. Pleas for cigarettes and bribes for bourbon were the usual. "How many bars do you need?"

Mac held up four fingers.

It was thirty minutes after midnight when Mac again slipped past the sentry stations posted along the cliff road. Knowing the last sentry change was at ten, he figured after two and a half hours of staring out at the empty British countryside, the sentries would have settled into their unenviable shifts, and both boredom and carelessness might have set in. Hoping that was the case, he stealthily worked his way to the clifftop.

Mac had learned his lesson the previous night, and wanting to make a good impression, and trying not to scare the life out of Mrs. Northcott again, he paused where the trees ended and reached up to shake the low-hanging branches and make a rustling noise. After a minute he stopped, and unsure of whether they'd been alerted of his presence by the sound, he whistled softly twice, and coughed. He then walked forward into the growing moonlight and saw both of the Coastal Watch staring in his direction.

Mac smiled. "I hope I didn't alarm you tonight."

"You didn't," scoffed Mrs. Northcott. "You made plenty of noise. In fact, the Germans sent a message asking if you could keep it down. They can't get a wink of sleep over there with all the hullaballoo you're making."

"Good. Tired Germans are what we want when we cross the channel." He laughed and reached into his pocket. "I brought you both something." Mac pulled out two large Hersey bars. "One for you," he handed Mary one. "And one for you." He passed the other to Mrs. Northcott.

The older lady took it, not understanding what she was getting. As she stared at the bar, her eyes bulged. "Is this chocolate?"

"Yes. An American chocolate bar. I hope you-"

Mac was unable to finish his words because Mrs. Northcott leaped from her deckchair and planted a big, sloppy wet kiss directly on his lips.

"Bless you, son, bless you," she blurted out as she pulled away. "I've been dreaming about having chocolate again ever since Hitler drove the French out of Paris." She shot a look to Mary. "Come on, lass, don't be shy. Show some appreciation and thank our soldier boy."

Mary got up from the chair slowly, unsure at first. But as she approached Mac, she regained her confidence, stood on her toes and kissed him, closing her eyes as their lips met.

The kiss was broken by their mutual laughter as Mrs. Northcott continued her monologue. "I'm going to take this bar over to the trees and eat the whole blooming thing before anyone else can ask for a single piece. Chocolate…" She trotted off to the tree line, leaving Mac and Mary dangerously close.

Mac looked down at this gorgeous girl, the moonlight dappling her face, causing her skin to glow, and so wanted to grab her and kiss her again. Similar thoughts bounded through Mary's mind as she took in this strong, caring young soldier standing only inches from her, but worried it could be the wrong thing to do. She broke the impasse by popping a piece of chocolate into her mouth and stepping back a pace. As the dark flavor washed through her, she closed her eyes, relishing the taste. "I'd forgotten how good chocolate is. It's been so long."

"I'm glad you like it."

"I don't *like* it, Mac. I love it. Thank you."

"Was it a good trade?"

Mary wrinkled her brow, making her, in Mac's eyes, even more adorable. "What was the trade?"

"A kiss for a candy bar? Was that fair?"

"I'll say it was fair. I'd do that trade anytime."

It was Mac's turn to grin. "In that case..." He slipped his hand inside his heavy khaki jacket and pulled out another Hersey bar. "Daa – dah!" he trumpeted, simulating a fanfare.

Mary almost dropped the first bar in shock at the appearance of another. To go from no chocolate for nearly five years to two bars in one night was inconceivable. "Sir, you are a veritable sweet shop."

"Sweet shop? What's that?"

"It's where we'd buy our sweets before the war."

"You mean, like desserts?"

"No, silly. Sweets are chocolates, and things like Turkish Delight, and liquorice allsorts. Don't you have sweet shops in America?"

"Yeah, we do. But we call them candy stores."

"Candy stores. All right, I'll remember that."

"And there's something else you shouldn't forget."

"What?"

"Our deal. The trade for the chocolate."

"How could I forget?" Mary inched forward, closer to Mac. This time he held her gently, his arms partially around her waist as they kissed for a fraction longer.

When they finally broke apart, Mac didn't hesitate and in seconds had the fourth candy bar in his hand.

"Oh, my goodness. You're a magician."

"I brought it for your grandfather. Sort of a peace offering."

"I'll make sure he gets it." Mary took the bar and slipped it into her small bag.

"And our deal?"

"Right." She giggled, remembering the fine art of flirting. "As it's for Grandpa, I'll have him kiss you." She started to sit back into the deckchair but reconsidered, and instead dropped softly onto the damp grass. She sat there looking up at Mac and patted the spot next to her. "You should sit down as well. I'm sure you're tired. I see the soldiers running around all day."

"It's called training." Mac sat by her. "But it is good to sit. I do have something else for you."

"Something sweet?"

"Yes, something sweet." He took out a pack of gum. "You can have this after you finish the chocolate."

"You think I'm going to finish all the chocolate tonight? Not me. Maybe Mrs. Northcott might, wherever she went, but I'm saving mine. It's too good to hurry."

"I can get more. If you want something different, try this." He slipped a stick from the silver foil and held it out to Mary.

She looked at it with surprise. "It's pink. I didn't think they made pink chewing gum."

"It's bubble gum. It's different."

"Why do they call it bubble gum?"

"You Brits are behind the times, aren't you? You put it in your mouth and blow bubbles."

"Why would you do that?"

"There's no *why*. It's just fun. I'll show you."

Mac popped a piece in his mouth and started chewing. Mary watched curiously then slipped the partially opened gum from the wrapper and put it in her mouth, almost inhaling it.

"Hey, slow down. Don't swallow it, chew it."

"You Yanks are crazy."

"Crazy like a fox."

They lay back on the grass, chewing, and stared up at the starlit sky. They were so close together they nearly touched, and both could feel the magic of the moment, but neither was sure what should happen next.

Mac was the one who broke the silence. "Okay. When you've got it soft, you kind of stretch it with your mouth and tongue, then stick your tongue in the middle of it and blow. Watch."

He contorted his face as he readied the gum, then slowly blew a small but perfect bubble. Mary clapped her hands in delight as he drew the bubble back into his mouth and chewed it again. "Got it? Now it's your turn."

"I'll try." She puckered her face as she readied the gum and positioned her tongue. Then she blew hard, way too hard. The gum flew out of her mouth, landing on the grass two feet from her.

"Don't worry about it," consoled Mac. "I've got plenty more."

Mary sat up and reached for the gum. "And waste this perfectly good piece? That's not happening, mister. Don't you know there's a war on?" She dusted the gum off and with an exaggerated gesture, popped it back into her mouth. Mac grinned; this was his type of girl.

"Show me again. I'm not someone who gives up easily. If you can do it, so can I."

"Okay, but you've got to promise to keep it in your mouth this time."

Mary nodded in agreement, too busy chewing to speak. She locked her eyes on Mac trying to pick up on his every move as once again he blew a perfect bubble.

"Got it?" he asked as he bit down on the bubble.

"I got it. Watch me."

There was a second of silence as she finished chewing, then started to blow, more slowly and controlled this time. A small bubble began to form, and Mac nodded in appreciation.

Encouraged, Mary kept blowing, and soon the bubble was big and continuing to get larger. As she looked down and saw it forming, she blew even more, wondering how big she could get it.

Mac knew what was about to occur and quickly raised his hand in warning, but too late. With a loud pop, the bubble ruptured and splattered across Mary's face.

Mary sat there, speechless, covered in bubble gum. Before Mac could say anything, she laughed. A deep, unaffected belly laugh. No shame, no embarrassment, only a sense of fun and discovery. And as she laughed, Mary realized, for the first time in years, she was genuinely happy.

"It's my fault, I should have warned you. Let me get it off you."

Mac reached out and gently peeled the gum from her face. His fingers brushed her skin and Mary closed her eyes, delighting in the feel of his soft touch.

"At least it didn't get in your hair. If it had, it would have been a real mess."

She stuck her hand out. "One more piece, please. I told you I don't give up easily."

"Okay, here you go." Mac passed her another stick.

She unwrapped it and dropped back down on the grass. Mac followed suit. The two lay there, chewing silently, saying nothing, enjoying each other's company.

Mary turned her head to Mac. "What is it you like about boats?"

"That's a good question. So many things. First, when I'm on a boat it takes me back to my childhood; those were good times. I remember it as always being sunny, always fun. My brother and I were so close, and while we were out with dad, he gave us all the freedom two boys could want, swimming, fishing, diving. As for the boat, it depends what kind I'm on. If it's a power boat, then maybe it's the way the engine sounds, or how she trims at speed. On a yacht, I love the sound of the sails unfurling and the snap they make when they fill with wind, and it's hard to beat the slap of the waves against the hull. Like I said, so many things." He turned his gaze to Mary. "They say boats are like people; every one is a little different. And that's why I want to design special boats. Get to know someone who wants a boat and then build it so it fits what they're looking for perfectly."

"What kind of boat would be right for me? I've often thought it would be lovely to have one of my own."

"You have?"

"You sound surprised. Don't be. You're in a seafaring community here. You can't live along the coast by the water and not dream about sailing."

Those words made Mac sit back up. "I could design one for you. I even know what I'd call her, and that's usually tough, naming a boat."

"You said *her*?"

"Yes, boats are always female, because they are sleek, compact, and beautiful, like you."

"Sergeant, you do know how to flatter a lady. So, what would *her* name be?"

"You said you've dreamed about having your own boat."

"Yes."

"Then it would be *Mary's Dream*. That's her name for sure. Now we have the tough part sorted out, all I have to do is design and build her."

"So, what's next to do before you start your designing?"

"I have to get to know my client."

"I'm your client now?"

"Yes, ma'am, I consider myself hired. I've accepted your commission."

"It all sounds very formal. What do you need to know I haven't already told you?"

"Well, you talked about your parents and how your grandpa brought you here, but what about other people in your life. Any, err…" it was something he dreaded bringing up, but knew he had to ask, "boyfriends?"

"Why would that be important?"

Mac hesitated as he thought for a reason he might have asked that personal question. "Just getting to know you, and anyone else who might sail on Mary's Dream with you."

Mary tore her eyes from Mac as she remembered. "I did have a boyfriend once. It was back when I was in London. We were together for nearly two years. Then he got called up in the early days of the war and joined the Royal Artillery. After that we only saw each other when he was on leave. But I wrote to him almost every day."

Mac was taken aback. No way would he ever move in on a girlfriend of another service member. "Do you still write him?"

"No." Mary swallowed her words as her eyes misted over. "Not since his regiment joined Field Marshal Montgomery and the Eighth Army, and was sent to El Alamein to fight in 'forty-two. His parents wrote me after that. They said they were told it was all over very quickly and he didn't suffer." Tears poured down her face. "This war. This bloody war."

"I'm so sorry." He reached out and took her hand, holding it in a gesture of comfort. "Would you do something for me?"

Mary fought through her tears. "What?"

"When I'm sent to France, will you write me?"

Mary wiped her eyes with her free hand and forced a smile. "Can Americans read English?"

Mac chuckled. "Only the easy words."

As they laughed, a shooting star appeared overhead, streaking across the clear sky.

"Quickly," urged Mary, "make a wish."

She closed her eyes tightly as she thought about what she wanted to come true. As she did, Mac studied her face, taking in her beauty, and suddenly realized she was making it hard for him to breathe. Her eyes flickered open and she saw Mac staring at her. "You were meant to have made a wish."

"I did."

"What did you wish for?"

"Mary, you know I can't tell you. If I do, it won't come true. It'll be my secret."

"Spoilsport. Let's see if my wish comes true." She chewed quickly and then blew. In moments, a perfect bubble formed. She let it stay there for a few seconds, then drew it back into her mouth as Mac had. "It did come true. The wish worked." She dropped back down onto the grass. "Let's wait and see if we can spot another shooting star."

Mac stood slowly, his body language showing his sadness. "I wish I could but I have to get back before they notice I'm gone."

"Can you come here again tomorrow?"

"I'll try. It all depends on the assignments and training. But I will see you again, I promise. If not tomorrow, then real soon."

"You'd better make it real soon, Mac. I'll stay here and look for another star to wish upon. I won't tell you what my wish will be, but you might be able to guess. Now go, and don't get caught."

CHAPTER SEVEN
Live Fire

A flare burned across the clear sky; its long crimson smoke trail etched against the icy blue firmament. On its signal, the heavy guns opened up.

Two cruisers and three destroyers of Britain's Royal Navy, stationed four miles out into the channel, began their precise bombardment of the deserted beach. All the soldiers, machinery and vehicles had been moved to the encampment, on the far side of Slapton Ley, safely out of target range from the heavy explosives speeding inbound.

The shells passed over the eight Landing Ship, Tanks that hours earlier had unloaded seven thousand men into the landing craft waiting to transport them. The red flare and thundering naval guns alerted the tired men crammed onboard the small vessels to get ready; it would soon be time to cover the three hundred yards to reach the beach, and the first of the long-anticipated live-fire exercises would be under way.

Seconds after the booms reached them, the men pressed their hands to their ears as the screaming shells drowned out every other sound, even the ever-present thudding of the twin diesels, and the high-pitched, terrifying screech of the one hundred and twenty-millimeter rounds soaring overhead threatened to render them deaf.

The first salvo fell fifty yards short of the shoreline, crashing into the shallows and sending huge sprays of water into the air. Ricky spun on the wet bench to Mac in panic. "They missed the beach! Jesus, the Limeys need to watch where they're shooting, they could hit us next."

Before Mac could respond, the landing sergeant called out. "That's the signal. Prepare to go ashore. We're separating from the rest. They'll be going in to secure the beach; our job, Rangers, is to scale the cliffs and take out the guns which have the shoreline pre-sighted. If we don't pull it off, they'll rule the entire landing force is dead meat, and the day will be lost, because of us."

"No pressure then," Ricky whispered to Mac, rolling his eyes.

As the men grabbed their rifles and adjusted their helmets, the big diesels rumbled to life, and the landing craft stretching for a mile across the bay kicked up a thick white wake behind them as the block-shaped boats began their coordinated rapid assault on Slapton Sands. The six craft carrying the Rangers peeled from the main group, turning toward the bluffs overlooking the landing site.

A second salvo flew above and impacted again in the water, this time twenty-five yards from the shingled shore.

"They keep missing, and all the landing squads are going straight for where they're firing. This is nuts."

Mac heard the fear in his friend's voice. "It's okay, Ricky. The navy is right on target."

"Then why are they firing into the water? If they shelled the beach, they'd blow up the Germans. The only thing they're hitting now are fish and seaweed."

"They're paving the way for the assault squads. First, they take out the obstacles in the water and at the tideline, then they keep moving the shelling up, a few yards at a time, clearing a path. It's called a creeping barrage. Our troops come in behind it as the navy opens it up for them."

"They'd better shoot straight, or the Nazis won't have to kill us, the British navy will have done the job for them."

The third salvo thundered over the main force, and this time impacted the beach, sending rocks and pebbles flying into the air and creating craters perfect for giving the attacking troops much needed cover. Ricky saw this and fell quiet, realizing the brilliant logic behind the strategy.

"One minute to go." The landing sergeant stood tall to see over the raised sides of his boat to check their positioning. He nodded in satisfaction. They were holding their own with the five other LCAs as the small vessels roared toward the shore.

A shudder shook the boat, and one of the pounding engines emitted a high-pitched whine.

"Did we hit something?" asked Ricky.

"No. We're losing the port diesel." Mac turned and saw the landing sergeant moving back through the seated Rangers to speak with the helmsman. "Maybe I can help." He got to his feet and hurried to the stern.

"What's the problem? Why are we slowing down?" The landing sergeant demanded of the helm. "We need to keep up with the rest of the 2nd."

"One of the engines is acting up. Without it we'll be stuck out here," answered the stressed coxswain.

"Not if you cut it before it seizes. Shut it down, then turn the wheel hard to port and hold it there."

The landing sergeant heard Mac's voice and looked back at the interloper. "Why aren't you in your place, soldier?"

"I heard the pitch of the port engine change. It's out of sync and losing revs. The problem's been developing for days. The twin diesels are meant to work together. Lose one, and it screws up the steering."

Hearing the confidence in Mac's words, the sergeant paused. "What should we do?"

"Like I said, sarge, without sync we have to alter the way we steer to get in. Normally the wheel isn't used, the engines do the steering by increasing or decreasing their power. With only one side running, it'll spin us in circles. If we go against the spin by using the wheel and slow to half revs, we can still make it in to the beach. It's either that or float out here until they send a tug to bring us in."

There was no hesitation from the landing sergeant. "Do as he says, helm. Cut the failing engine and lean on the wheel hard." He stared at Mac. "You'd better be right."

"It's the only way. It'll take us longer but we can get in and still be a part of the landing."

"Okay. As long as it gets us to the shore. And see me after the exercise is complete, soldier."

The other five landing craft carrying the 2nd Rangers had already beached and discharged the squads. Mac saw the teams racing toward the cliff face and staying low as machine gun fire rained down on them from above. The bullets impacted either side of the sprinting soldiers, only yards from them, carefully aimed to make sure no one was hit, but still giving a real sense of fear and danger to prepare the GIs for what waited for them on the French beaches where the Germans would be shooting to kill, not scare.

"Shit. They're nearly at their assault positions already."

Ricky raised his hands slightly. "Fine with me. The gunfire is nuts."

As they moved in closer to their disembarkation point, Ricky and Mac watched the Rangers huddle close to the base of the cliff which gave them natural cover as the steep angle made it impossible for the gunners on the clifftop to fire straight down. Instead, the machine gun on top now turned its attention to the final landing craft slowly approaching the beach. Water sprayed across the open vessel as bullets smacked into the sea either side of the boat.

"If this was for real, we'd all be dead coming in at this speed."

Mac said nothing in reply to Ricky's words; he knew his friend was right.

The two kept low but managed to peer over the flat ramp acting as the bow, and saw twenty of the Rangers step back five paces from the rocky face. In almost perfect synchronization they snapped the climbing mortars into place and triggered the explosive launch. Twenty grappling hooks and trailing ropes arched through the air with all but one soaring over the clifftop to find a place for their barbed ends to grab into the ground.

"It's going to be over before we start climbing."

Even as Mac vocalized his disappointment, the LCA scraped across the shingles and the landing sergeant called out, "Ramp down."

The serrated metal front fell forward and crashed onto the rocky shore. The sergeant barked again. "Two pairs at a time. Go! Keep moving and stay low."

In seconds the craft was empty as the men ran hell for leather up the beach to the cliffs, spurred on by bullets flying all around them.

As they reached the base, the Ranger lieutenant acting as beachmaster and overseeing the assault yelled to the final team arriving. "About time. We've got men over the top already. As soon as the ropes are clear, go. I want you up there. And for Christ's sake, be quicker climbing than you were coming in."

Mac leaned back and looked up. The last of the Rangers were pulling themselves over the edge and out of sight. All nineteen of the ropes hung there, free of climbers. "Let's go, Ricky. It'll be two on a rope. You go first, I'll follow."

Ricky grabbed the heavy rope, attached his harness and started up. A machine gun situated on the beach started firing live rounds at the cliff face, the steel-jacketed bullets ricocheting off the rocks and sending shattered fragments spinning down on them. Ricky was barely thirty feet up, less than a third of the way, when he stopped climbing and hung there, wedging himself against the sheer face.

Mac caught up with him in seconds, Ricky's feet blocking him from going any higher. He yelled to his friend, "Are you okay? Did you get hit?"

"I'm fine. I'm just…just…"

"You can't stay here; the gunners would pick you off in seconds. You have to climb."

Mac was right, stuck on a cliff face under fire was not a place to be.

"Okay, okay, I'm going." Ricky pulled on the rope and restarted upward. Mac stayed close, only a few feet below, giving him the incentive to keep moving.

Finally, they reached the top, and as Mac hauled himself over, he knew they were the last pair to make the summit, and the simulated German gun emplacement had already been captured and a Stars and Stripes was being raised to signal their success to the main landing force stretched across Slapton Sands, a quarter of a mile from the cliffs.

The officer, observing the exercise, positioned at the top of the cliff, addressed the triumphant assault team of Rangers. "Congratulations, men. You achieved your objective with minimum casualties, and had this been the actual invasion, by destroying the guns you would have saved countless lives on the beach. Head back down in the order you made it to the top. Tell the lieutenant it was a job well done and no one could have done it better."

A cheer rose from the relieved Rangers and they returned to the climbing ropes to begin their rappel down.

Mac scanned the flat grass plain and spotted Reg and Mrs. Higgens in the distance. They had been moved back over a hundred yards, almost to the trees, for their safety. He waited until the men were on the ropes and the officer was not watching him, and he waved to the two elderly members of the Coastal Watch.

Mrs. Higgens spotted his wave and elbowed Reg to get his attention before she waved back. Reg remained seated, arms folded, behaving as though the two of them were alone on the clifftop and disregarding the recent mini war that had been fought in front of them.

Mac had no time to react to this affront. The officer snapped his order. "You two. On the ropes, now."

Heeding his command, the two boys started their quick climb down, but now without the deliberate and dangerous distraction of the gunfire. With the mission accomplished, their part of the live-fire exercise was over.

They stepped away from the ropes and headed across the sloping shingles to the landing craft where the beachmaster was dividing up the men from Mac's crippled vessel to go back on the other five boats. As they walked, Mac turned to Ricky. "What happened on the climb?"

"I froze for a minute, that's all."

"But if-"

Mac was cut off as the landing sergeant called to him. "Sergeant Harper. To me."

"I'll see you back at base." With that, Mac hurried to the sergeant in charge.

The beachmaster nodded at his prompt arrival and wasted no time getting to the point. "The helmsman can't find the problem. He admits the diesels on these LCAs aren't his strong point. You said you worked on them, right?"

"Right. Grew up on them. We had exactly the same engines in my dad's boats."

"Is there anything we can do while we're waiting for one of the other five to come back and give us a tow?"

"That depends. Do you want to return to the main beach under your own power?"

"How's that possible? The helm said the port diesel was crapped out."

"It's not the engine that's damaged; at least I don't think so. I'm pretty sure we shut it down in time to prevent that. It's the sync mechanism which is the problem. If that's not functioning, the engines aren't aligned and fight each other instead of working together and that means you're screwed."

"Can you do something to fix it?

"I can try to realign the sync, yes."

"What do you need to do that?"

"To do it properly, it would take calipers, spacers, maybe a gasket or two and a few hours. But if we go into the onboard tool box and find a wrench, some heavy tape, a flashlight and about twenty minutes, then I should be able to do a field repair which will hold together long enough to get us back."

"Do it, Sergeant Harper. Make the Rangers look good."

"I'm on it." Mac made his way up the still deployed ramp, pushing back his sleeves as he walked.

An hour later, the landing craft, with a crew of three – the landing sergeant, the crestfallen helmsman, and Mac at the controls, slowly approached the main beach of Slapton Sands to take its place next to the other five boats assigned to the Rangers' assault exercise.

Mac gently worked the two levers controlling the twin diesels. Though there was a ship's wheel, most of the steering was done through adjusting the engines' speed; increasing the port diesel would turn the boat to starboard and vice versa. For a craft with such a blunt profile creating so much resistance against the water, this was by far the easiest and most efficient way of operating the vessel.

The shore was approaching, and Mac throttled back both engines allowing the craft to drift in and make contact with the rounded pebbles so softly the boat barely rocked.

The landing sergeant couldn't conceal his admiration for Mac's skill. "You are a natural, Sergeant Harper. I'm going to write that in my report."

"Thank you, I appreciate it. But honestly, after all the old barges and tugs I grew up on, handling anything in this bay," he waved at the mass of ships assembled off of Slapton Sands, "would be a piece of cake. It's my dad who should get the credit; he taught me everything."

"Then thanks to Harper senior. He saved the Rangers embarrassment today. Instead, this first live-fire exercise has been a huge success. I'm sure the big brass will be happy with how it turned out."

Landing Craft – LCAs – racing to shore at Slapton Sands

GIs disembarking during exercises at Slapton Sands

CHAPTER EIGHT
City In Flames

"Geronimo!"
The wild scream alerted Mac of the incoming body as Ricky leaped onto his bunk. "Three days R & R. Who would have thought the brass cared enough for us grunts to give us leave while they get the next live-fire shitstorm ready?" His wide grin lit his face. "What are you going to do for three days?"

Mac smiled back at him. "I'll find something to keep me busy."

"Something or someone? Want to bet I can't guess who and what it is?"

"And let you take my money? Think I'm a sucker? No, thank you."

The rain sliced down in a deluge, sucking the light away and darkening the evening sky to a midnight blue. Two figures huddled together sharing a raincoat and an umbrella, trying to keep dry as they laughed and treasured each other's company.

"It's three whole days. What should I do?"

"There are so many things. You could go to Torquay, that town is always fun, there's lots of pubs there and even a ballroom right next to the harbor. And because you love boats so much, you'd like Brixham; they have a really big fishing fleet and a great aquarium. But…" Mary paused as she decided.

"But what?" asked Mac.

"If it was me, and it was my first time in the West Country, I'd go to Plymouth. It's a lovely city by the water. You've got it all there, hundreds of shops, some wonderful parks, and even cinemas with the latest films, a lot of them from Hollywood. They might make you homesick."

"I told you, I've been to Hollywood; I didn't live there."

"Oh, you are such a nitpicker. Yes, you should go to Plymouth."

Mac drew in his breath. It was time for the moment of truth. "Would you go with me?"

"You want me to come? Really?"

"Yes, really. No one has any idea exactly when the invasion is going to happen, it could be any day, so I don't know if we'll get any more leave before we're sent over there. I'd love you to come with me. Maybe tomorrow?"

"I can't tomorrow." Mary saw, even in the darkness, disappointment cross Mac's face. "I want to go with you, but I have to plan it because of Grandpa, and come up with some excuse so he doesn't know I've gone."

"Would he be that against it?"

"Oh yes. The very mention of you gets his knickers in a twist. He'd kill me. When I gave him the chocolate bar, he refused it and handed it straight back. Said he'd never take anything from you and I should have nothing to do with a *'soldier boy'*."

"I don't want to get you in trouble-"

"I don't want to get in trouble, that's why we have to work it out."

"Could you leave in the daytime when he's on watch? That way, he'd never know you're gone."

"Maybe. It might work. I'll talk to Mrs. Northcott when she gets back here. We can make up some story about me sleeping at her place during the day, after tomorrow's night shift. She's a good sport. She'll back me up. That would be Friday, and that's the night I can take off from Coastal Watch, so it would be perfect. Could we go then?"

"Yes, Friday would be great. How about if we meet down on the cliff road right after your change over, at eight-fifteen?"

"Let's make it eight-thirty. Then I can chat with Grandpa for a few minutes, make it seem like everything is normal, and he can settle into his shift."

"Eight-thirty, Friday morning, You're on. Can't wait to see Plymouth with you." Mac paused. "What happened to your grandfather's chocolate bar?"

Mary laughed. "What do you think happened? I ate it, of course."

"Really?" Mac assumed a serious tone. "So, what about our agreement?"

"Our agreement. Let me think." She rubbed her chin, then unexpectedly grabbed Mac and pulled him in close, kissing him long and hard on the lips. After a few seconds, she pushed him away. "See, mister, I always honor my word. There's your trade."

Mac reached out for another kiss, but Mary backed away, waving her finger at him. "No more tonight. You should go now, and I'll see you Friday. As the great Bard of Stratford said, 'absence makes the heart grow fonder'."

Mac laughed. "Okay, you have me with that one." He stood up and slipped out from under the umbrella into the pouring rain. "I never got the chance to study Shakespeare at school, so I'm not good with his quotes. The only one I know is, Toby or not Toby, what is his question?"

Mary almost fell from her chair as she cracked up. "Toby? It's not a name; there's no one in his classic play, *Hamlet, Prince of Denmark,* called Toby. It's 'to be or not to be, that is the question.' It's about living or dying. Shakespeare wrote that line about a troubled prince pondering his existence. Maybe we should skip Plymouth and get you into a good English school instead."

Mac shook his head. "I'm done with school. I'll stick to exploring a new town with you."

"And we'll do that together, Friday. Until then, begone young sir, parting is such sweet sorrow." With a deliberately exaggerated move, Mary whipped her head around and stared out to sea through the rain.

"Friday," called out Mac, as he vanished from view into the downpour.

Friday, February 19th, 1944

The sun struggled to break through the light cloud cover as Mary hurried down the cliff road, not wanting to be late for her arranged meeting with Mac. As she turned a corner, the hedgerow revealed her date, pressed into the bushes, waiting for her.

"Mac!" she called out excitedly.

He raised his finger to his lips to silence her. She reached him, puzzled. He took her hand and led her further down the winding lane, keeping his voice low as he spoke. "Sorry, I wasn't trying to be rude. I didn't want the sentries hearing us."

Mary was confused. "But you said you had three days leave?"

"I do, and I have my off-base papers with me." He patted his chest pocket. "But I don't have a pass for this. Wait here." He left her for a second, standing alone on the little path as he disappeared into the greenery. Equally quickly, he reappeared pushing a single-seater motorcycle with an attached sidecar. "I borrowed it from the motorpool. Hopefully, it won't be missed before I can get it back."

Mary couldn't contain her excitement and jumped into the air, clapping her hands.

"So, I did good? You like motorbikes?"

"I don't know. I've never been on one. But I've seen them in the movies and they look such fun."

"This will be better than the movies, I promise. Climb into the sidecar, I'll drive."

"Is there room in there for my handbag? It's not very big."

"There should be. Push it to the front where your legs go."

"I will." She hesitated before continuing to speak. "I wanted to bring a different dress to change into for our trip today, but I couldn't smuggle it out with Grandpa noticing."

"Don't worry, you look great. As for me, I've only got this to wear."

Mary turned her gaze to the striking young soldier's clothes. "Your uniform and cap looks very good on you."

"It's my dress uniform. I'd normally only put it on if we're mustered for a parade or an officer's address. It's the best I have."

"Then it's very smart."

"Smart?"

"I thought you spoke English? Smart – you know, fashionable, presentable, handsome."

"I like that. I'll take any of those." A smile lit up his face. "Want to climb on in so we can get going?"

"Got it." The thrilled young girl clambered awkwardly into the narrow sidecar and tried to find a comfortable position.

"Ready?" asked Mac.

"I'm ready!" confirmed Mary.

Mac pushed down on the kickstart and the two hundred and fifty cc engine thundered into life. "We have to get going, in case the sentries come to check out the noise." He slipped the engine into gear and the two of them headed rapidly up the hill away from the base.

Within a few minutes, they had reached the final checkpoint to leave the American occupation area of the South Hams. Mac presented his off-base papers to the heavily-armed sentries who barely glanced at them, showing little concern. For the past day, they had seen many troops from the base coming through with their seventy-two-hour passes. This sergeant was just the latest to pull up to their post. The supervising sentry took in Mac's gorgeous passenger and winked enviously at the soldier, his mind conjuring up images of what the two of them would be getting up to later.

He raised the barrier, and Mac drove the motorcycle through at a respectable speed, hoping it wouldn't be questioned, and held back on accelerating until the guards, sandbags, barbed wire and gun emplacements were a way behind them.

"Do you know where we're going?" questioned Mary.

"Plymouth," answered Mac.

"Ha ha, smart aleck. Do you know how to get there?"

"Yes. I picked up a map. The main road is four miles ahead. We turn left, stay on it for forty minutes and it'll take us right into the town."

"I guess you have it all figured out." Mac beamed at Mary's approval as she continued. "But there's a few places on the way we should stop and see; they're really pretty, and not too far off the road. And when we do get there, I take over. I'll be the best tour guide in Plymouth."

"I bet you'll be the best tour guide in England."

"Why just England? Maybe the whole world." Mary threw her arms in the air, savoring the wind whipping through her fingers. "This is so much fun."

"I hope it doesn't rain," said Mac, as he glanced up at the patchy cloud cover.

"Don't worry about that." Mary was full of good cheer. "We should be alright, there's enough blue sky to make a rabbit's underpants."

Mac was so taken aback by her words that he pulled the bike over for a moment. "What does that even mean?"

"It's a saying the locals have. If you can see enough blue sky through the clouds to make a rabbit's underpants then it probably won't rain."

Her answer cracked Mac up. "How are you going to make a rabbit's underwear out of blue sky? And how much is enough? You Brits are so funny."

"I'm glad we make you laugh, and I hope that's meant as a compliment, mister. I'm sure you have some sayings we would find strange. Now would you please get going and drive; I'd like to be in Plymouth sometime today. Keep your eyes on the road and watch out for-"

"-rabbits running around in underpants!" Mac interjected with a laugh. "Hold on, here we go." He twisted the throttle, and the motorbike picked up speed as they continued on their way.

The drive flew by as they left the narrow country lane, barely big enough for one vehicle to make its way along without the encroaching hedgerows on either side scratching the paint, and reached the main thoroughfare, a blacktop two-lane road masquerading as Britain's version of a highway. Mac accelerated, but made sure he kept the speed within reason as he was not only on the wrong side of the road for him, but it was the first time he had ever driven a motorbike with a sidecar attached, and he didn't want to risk losing – or upsetting – his precious passenger.

Twice, Mary had them take a detour then stop to enjoy the incredible views of the lush countryside they were driving through; once to look out across Bantham's long beach covered with golden sand, and tiny Burgh Island laying off of it, and then to pull up alongside a babbling brook leading into the estuary forming the River Tamar.

"It's really beautiful here," stated Mac.

"I'm glad you like it. Is it very different to California?"

"Sure is. We have the beaches and the coastline, and we even have mountains as well, but everything's a lot drier in California. We get used to the grass being brown and the same with the trees. Here, everything is green, and there's so many different shades of it." He pointed. "That bush is so green it's almost blue. I know that sounds nuts, but that's how it looks to me."

"It's the rain. We get so much of it. That's why it's all green."

"How about in the summer? Does it turn brown then?"

"No, it doesn't have time to change colour. Our summer is a lot shorter than yours in California."

"When is your summer?"

"July 30th and 31st, then we're done," laughed Mary. "I told you it was short."

"Right. Like I believe you. Come on. Back in the sidecar; we've got a big city waiting for us."

With Mary safely ensconced in place, Mac kickstarted the bike and left the brook behind them as they continued on the final few miles to their destination.

The countryside began to give way to homes and small shops, and in the distance the sound of church bells rang out over the growl of the engine.

Mac slowed as they approached the magnificent three hundred and fifty-year-old house of God, its gothic arches and towering spire designed to inspire the worshipers within.

"This building is amazing. Is it a cathedral?" Mac called to Mary.

"No, it's Charles Church. It's Church of England. We call it God's gateway to Plymouth. It's like he's watching you approach and warning you not to misbehave."

"I promise I won't. So, I guess Plymouth doesn't have a cathedral?"

"Of course it does, silly, it's about two miles from here. Every city has one. In England, that's what makes it a city. Without a cathedral, you're just a town."

"And what's the difference between a town and a village?"

"A town is smaller than a city but bigger than a village. And every town has a mayor, only a few villages, like Slapton and Torcross, have a mayor."

"You have so many different rules for things over here. If a village doesn't have a mayor, what does it have?"

"I don't know." Mary thought. "Maybe a postman," she smiled, "and definitely a pub. And a village is a little bigger than a hamlet."

"I thought Hamlet was the Prince of Denmark? Isn't that what you said?"

Mary rolled her eyes. "Yanks. I guess everything they say about you is true."

Mac grinned. "I hope it's only good things they're saying." He looked up at the soaring spire. "Why are the bells ringing now?"

"They're calling the parishioners to an early service. If you keep going slow, you'll probably be able to hear it starting as we ride past. There's no other way into Plymouth from here."

Mary was right. The main road into the city wound around Charles Church which predated cars and motor vehicles by more than three centuries. When traffic demanded the road be widened, the only choice was to curve it round the imposing church.

Mac kept the revs down as they passed by, and caught the sound of an organ drifting through the air.

"Told you," said Mary. "The service is getting underway."

As they left the church behind them, Mac saw the buildings and shops getting bigger and closer together, and recognized a familiar American store, Woolworths.

"Anywhere special we should park?"

"I could keep riding all day. I love it."

"Yeah, but you brought me here to see the town, so I think we should pull over soon."

"You're right." Mary reluctantly admitted. "Anywhere here would be good. There's lots of shops, and over there," she pointed, "is the seafront."

"Done." Mac swung the bike to a stop alongside the curb fringing a small park, a green area in the middle of the city, and stepped from his seat. He reached out to help Mary emerge from the semi-recumbent position the sidecar forced her to assume. "I hope you weren't too uncomfortable."

"I'm fine. I'm happy to be here." She almost said *with you*, but caught herself.

"Good, because I'm ready for the grand tour."

"If you insist. Follow me. You like boats, so we'll explore the harbor first, then come back into the town and go shopping. I brought some money I've been saving; maybe I can find a new dress."

Mary led the way down a narrow street which quickly opened up to a gently sloping hill framing a small part of Plymouth's immense natural harbor.

Mac was taken aback by its size. "Holy crap, I wasn't expecting anything like this, it's massive. I thought Long Beach had a big harbor but you could put that one in here three or four times and still have room for more."

"I don't know about Long Beach, but people have sailed from here forever. Where we're standing now is called Westward Hoe. They named it that because it looks west and that was the direction a lot of the ships went as they left Plymouth. Sir Francis Drake and his fleet assembled here to fight the Spanish Armada, and your people, I think they were called the Pilgrim Fathers, left from down there," she pointed to a small jetty with a series of well-worn stone steps leading to the water, "to go over to America."

"And that's why they called the place they landed, Plymouth Rock, right?"

"Right. And the best view of the harbor is from over there." She nodded to a nearby tall, narrow, red and white structure. "That's the Edison Lighthouse."

"Can we go up?"

"It's usually open. Do you want to see?"

She grasped his hand and they ran together across the damp grass to the small wooden door at the base of the old lighthouse and grinned as it swung open.

"Ladies first."

"Thank you, kind sir, but not in here. It's dark and damp, and there's a lot of steps going up the spiral staircase. You go first in case there are any spiders or creepy crawlies inside."

"Okay, I'll take the lead."

The excited couple scaled the two hundred stairs, reaching the circular platform surrounding the warning light, and gratefully caught their breath from the climb as they took in the harbor.

"You know I said your people sailed from here?"

"Yes."

"Well, it seems like a lot of them have come back now. Look at all the American flags on the boats out there."

Mac scanned the enormous harbor and saw dozens of warships, both American and British. "That's a huge amount of naval firepower." He was genuinely impressed, and started counting. "I see two carriers, three battleships, a cruiser, and at least fifteen destroyers, maybe more."

"I see a lot of guns."

"This place must have been quite a target for the Germans in the early days of the war, but they're ready for them now," he gestured upward. "There are over thirty anti-aircraft balloons flying. I wouldn't want to be the pilot trying to get in between them."

"They don't come often anymore, nothing like when the Blitz was going on. The last raid was months and months ago, and they said on the radio it was very small and there wasn't much damage." She shrugged off the tragic memories of the bombings she had endured in London in the summer of 1940 and changed the topic. "No more talk of Germans and planes and bombs. Let's go back down to the Hoe and enjoy the view from there."

"Fine with me. I'll race you." Mac took off at a run for the metal spiral staircase.

"Wait for me, soldier!" yelled Mary as she chased after him.

They sat close together on a park bench, sharing each other's warmth against the February chill, as they gazed across the spectacular natural harbor.

"Tell me another story about California, Mac."

"Sure. What would you like me to talk about?"

"Anything. America is so fascinating." Mary's eyes glistened as she spoke. "What other places have you been to outside of San Pedro and Hollywood? Have you traveled a lot?"

"I wouldn't say a lot, but my mom and dad took me and Donovan on some road trips-"

"Road trips?" Mary didn't know the expression.

"Yeah. When you load up the car and go away for a few days."

"That's right, I forgot. Everybody in America has a car. Not many do in England, and you used yours for a holiday. How wonderful."

"They were good times. We went south to San Diego and stayed there for a week. It's a great town with beautiful beaches and some incredible Mexican food."

"Mexican? How does that taste?"

"Spicy." Mac chuckled. "All the meals come with salsa and guacamole."

"Guacamole? That's a funny word. What is it?"

"It's something really good. They make it from avocados."

"I've never heard of avocados."

"They're green and grow on trees."

"Like apples?"

Mac laughed. "Not exactly. I tell you what; you come and visit me in the States, and I'll make sure you try some."

"I'd love to. Maybe we could go on a road trip?"

"Maybe we could. If we do, we'll head up north, because I think the best vacation I ever had with my family was first to Santa Barbara, then up through Big Sur…" Mac saw Mary's face crinkle as she didn't understand *Big Sur*. "Don't worry, it's not a huge guy, it's a place. It's on the coast; lots of high cliffs there that tumble down into the sea, and forests of giant trees called Redwoods, some of them growing hundreds of feet high. It's really very special. We ended up in San Francisco, which I loved."

As Mac talked, Mary listened to the lilt of his voice, and how his accent made certain words seem almost magical as they danced from his lips. To her, the way he spoke played like music in her ears and was so different to the people she heard around her in Devon. Here, they spoke with a long rolling *r*, which made the locals sound like pirates when they talked of *ourrr* mum and *ourrr* dad. Mary knew she could listen to Mac forever and never grow tired of his voice.

Her mind began wandering as she imagined being with Mac at his home in California, and Mac noticed the change in her.

"Am I boring you? You look a little…distant?"

"No, no, quite the opposite. I was lost in my thoughts, that's all. I'm sorry."

"No need to apologize. I think I've talked enough for both of us," Mac grinned. "How about I shut up and we do what you wanted to do, go shopping?"

Mary clapped her hands excitedly. "Yes, let's do that. Let's go shopping."

She jumped from the park bench and grabbed Mac's hand, pulling him to his feet. "Come on, lazybones, we haven't got all day!"

Mac was surprised at how busy the stores were, and there were moments he almost forgot there was a war on. But the reminders were everywhere; uniformed British and American sailors roamed the aisles hunting for gifts to take home to their distant families, and outside of the shops every window had a crisscross of thick tape across them to prevent the glass from shattering and crashing into the street should there be a bomb blast nearby.

They went in and out of several large shops, spending most of the time in the women's clothing sections. After going in and out of several stores, Mary caught herself for monopolizing the day, and apologized to Mac and asked if there was anything he wanted to find or buy. Mac shook his head and told Mary shopping was her thing; he was more than happy to be her companion and give his opinion on the clothes she tried on, and whether the hats and gloves she modeled for him suited her.

The third time she emerged from a dressing room, Mary became upset because Mac said everything looked good on her, but when she realized he truly meant it, her heart skipped a beat as she savored the warm feelings he generated inside of her.

She was parading between the racks of coats, swinging a patterned handbag she couldn't afford, doing her best impression of a society woman out on the town when the first siren sounded. She stopped, freezing in place.

"Maybe it's a drill."

The siren blared again, dashing Mac's hopeful words. A second siren joined in, adding its wail, and throughout the store concerned shoppers and employees looked for the exits and shelters.

Now, it seemed a half-dozen sirens were sounding together. As their noise ripped through the air, even inside the building, Mary stood motionless, a statue locked in place, only her eyes showing the terror she felt.

Mac gripped her hand. "Come on. If this is real, we can't stay here."

Mary still didn't move, so Mac pulled her toward him. "Mary, we've got to go. I'll carry you if I have to."

Those words snapped her from her panicked freeze, and Mary dropped the expensive bag she had been eying and ran with Mac, sprinting for the exit.

As they rushed onto the street, scores of people, running for their lives, banged into them as they raced to find a shelter or get home to their loved ones. In the distance, even above the screaming sirens, the pounding of heavy guns rang out.

Mac stared through the fading light and saw that four miles away, over the harbor and docks, the sky was alight with exploding shells and flak, all targeting a dense mass of planes – German bombers.

"Shit. It is a bombing raid. A big one. There are at least a hundred planes up there trying to make a run at the fleet. We were told the Luftwaffe was nearly done. This must be a last-ditch effort to sink our ships before we come over there for them."

"Can we go? Please?" The dread of the situation broke the spell, and the desperation in Mary's voice shocked Mac. "Please. Anywhere but here."

"Okay. Let's go to the bike and get out of here."

He kept his hand locked around hers to avoid losing her in the surging crowds, and ran through the streets to where they had parked.

Behind them a tremendous roar shook the air, and Mac swung around to see a Junkers 88 bomber had taken a shell directly into its bomb bay, blowing it apart in a gigantic explosion.

The air defense searchlights came on, piercing the twilight with their burning beams and highlighting the German bombers. The planes were already restricted in their flight path by the anti-aircraft balloons flying high above the fleet, the metal cables tethering them down, designed to sever an aircraft's wing like a hot knife through butter, limiting their approach and herding them toward the waiting guns below.

Pinpointed by the two hundred thousand candlepower lights, the German raiders became easy targets for not only Plymouth harbor's entrenched anti-aircraft guns, but now also the combined force of the British and American fleet's armament, manned by veteran crews who pounded the ill-fated bombers with deadly accurate fire.

Three more Junkers burst into flames, leaving blazing trails of oil and shattered fuselage stretching across the sky behind them, as they spun down in their death throes.

The racing couple reached the bike, and as Mac helped her clamber into the sidecar, he watched a dying bomber crash into another German plane attempting to weave its way through the web of balloons and constant fire. For a moment, it looked as if the two planes were embracing as their wings broke off and wrapped around each other, before they both disappeared in an enormous fireball.

"They'll never try this again. Jerry's getting murdered." Mac's words had a degree of sympathy in them. A sign of respect for fellow brave warriors, even if they were the enemy.

The respect was fleeting, because as he spoke, he saw the lead planes turn away from the dockyard and the protecting balloons and change direction, but not back over the channel to occupied France and comparative safety; instead, they set a course directly toward the heart of the city center, a purely civilian target, the place where they were standing.

"They know it's suicide! The Germans have given up on the fleet. They're going to drop their bombs on Plymouth."

The whites of Mary's eyes appeared as she understood the awful implications of what Mac was saying. "Please. We have to find a shelter." She tried to lift herself out of the sidecar.

"Stay right where you are!" Mac's abrupt tone shocked Mary and she sunk back into her seat. "There's no time. Our only chance is getting out of here. Hang on."

Mac kickstarted the bike and dropped it into gear, roaring off in a desperate attempt to leave the doomed city.

As they sped up the street, the air reverberated from the city's own anti-aircraft guns opening up. On both sides of them shells shot into the sky ready to explode in a deadly hail of flak hoping to rip apart their incoming targets. But the city only had a few guns; it was not a military target and had not been designated for protection, after all, it was five years into the war and constant British and American air raids had crippled most of Germany's factories responsible for their armament production. Why would the Germans waste valuable bombs on civilians when they were needed against military targets? The majority of the defensive guns were positioned at the dockyards where a successful air raid would have the most impact on the war effort.

But now, unable to complete their mission and destroy the invasion fleet, the squadron's commander refused to return to his home base in shame with a full bomb bay and be brought up on charges by the Reichsmarschall for dereliction of duty, so a new target had quickly been decided upon, and that was the city of Plymouth and all the innocent families who made their homes there.

The searchlights surrounding the docks readjusted their focus and swung in toward the city center in a vain attempt to help the limited defense there. The powerful beams picked out dancing fireflies descending from the planes. Mac knew only too well what he was seeing, these were clusters of bombs falling and glistening silver in the glow of the intense lights.

Behind them, the street exploded in a series of massive blasts as the first of the bombs impacted where they had been. If they'd hesitated a few seconds longer…Mac couldn't consider it.

As fast as he could drive the bike, the Junkers 88s were faster and bombs fell around and ahead of them. Mary buried her face in her hands, hiding her eyes, terrified of what she might see and reliving the horrors she'd experienced first-hand, years before, when she survived the Blitz in London. Mac's focus was on getting them out of there as he swerved and accelerated around the burning rubble, and could feel the intense heat as one building after another was pounded by the incendiary charges and erupted in flames. The historic coastal town Mary had been so excited to show him had become a city of fire.

A lamppost, torn from its mounting bolts, crashed down, blocking the roadway in front of them. Mac veered the bike off the street and around the fallen bricks blown across the sidewalk, avoiding a collision, then bumped back onto the road and pushed the bike faster. Mary dug her fingers into the edges of the sidecar to cling on and stop from being thrown out.

Mac saw how his seemly crazy driving was tossing Mary violently around in the semi-prone position the sidecar's cramped design made her assume, and yelled, "I'm sorry."

Mary heard him but didn't lift her head and kept her eyes closed, only calling out in reply, "Just go!"

Mac needed no encouragement; he already had the throttle wide open and was silently praying they wouldn't blow a tire as they zigzagged through the smoking debris and scorching embers.

He saw the magnificent church a hundred yards ahead and knew exactly where they were now. Excitedly, he shouted to Mary. "The church is coming up. We're almost out of the city. We're going to make it."

The falling bombs gave Mac no warning. The heat from the incendiary blast smashed into his face like a blowtorch, and the following shockwave shook them so hard he let go of the handlebars before regaining control and slamming the brakes on. He twisted the front wheel to the right to help protect Mary from the explosion and flying shrapnel, and the bike came to a skidding stop.

In front of them, Charles Church, large enough to hold fifteen hundred worshippers for a service, was on fire. There was a terrifying roar as the roof collapsed in on the nave and pews below. The intense heat from the firebombs caused the stained-glass windows, crafted to illuminate the devout inside, to explode outward in a cascade of jagged shards smashing onto the roadway and spraying across the graveyard holding twenty generations of families.

"Oh my God. There were people in there for evening prayers." The flames lit Mary's face and Mac saw the tears streaming uncontrollably down her cheeks.

Before he could answer or console her, the most grotesque sight he had ever seen silenced him. Three figures stumbled from the inferno that had been the beloved church. He knew they had to be people because of the way they moved, one step at a time, but that was all he could see of them. There was no way to tell if they were men or women; it was impossible to make out clothes or faces as they were hidden by the sheets of flames rising from walking corpses. They were human torches desperate to escape the holy building which had become a nightmarish gateway to hell.

Mac was already off the bike as he yelled to Mary. "I have to help. Stay here."

"No. I'm coming with you."

The two of them ran toward the firestorm and the blazing victims, only yards away.

Mac pulled off his heavy military jacket as he sprinted to the first burning person. He flung it around them in a frantic attempt to smother the blaze, shouting as he moved. "I'm going to lay you on the ground. I'll roll you to put out the flames."

There was no reply. Whether the person could still speak was unknown, but Mac was not waiting for an answer. Ignoring his own pain from the flames and heat coming from the dying victim, he reached out with his hands to stabilize them and lower them to the ground. As soon as they were down, he rolled them back and forth, pulling his jacket tight around their body. In seconds he had the fire smothered and the person lay there, shaking uncontrollably from the agony of their burns.

Mac called to Mary. "Stay with this one. Make sure the flames are out. And let me have your jacket."

Mary peeled off her coat and tossed it to Mac as she dropped to her knees beside the person he had helped. Mac leaped to his feet to locate the other two burning people he'd seen. One had dropped to the grass already, but not to attempt to quell the flames. It was merciful death that caused them to fall. The other stumbled in circles, trying to scream, but the noise coming from their mouth was unlike any sound Mac had heard a human make before.

He approached the victim from behind and spread out Mary's coat, wrapping it across the person's back. As he did, a flare up from the burning clothes engulfed his fingers, causing him to involuntarily recoil. But he only paused for a second. If he didn't do something he would never forgive himself. He stuck his hands into the blaze, fighting through the intense pain, and this time was able to pull the jacket tight. Starved of oxygen, the fire went out and Mac lay the suffering person down.

The sound of ringing bells filled the air and Mac whispered a silent thank you. A fire engine and two ambulances raced to the church, the first to arrive at the terrible scene.

Two of the rescue vehicles came to a stop; the second ambulance hurtling past on an unknown mission, its bell still ringing.

Mac watched it go, wondering how many more would be needed, both to put out the raging inferno and to transport any injured survivors to waiting hospitals.

His thoughts came to an abrupt end as the speeding ambulance disappeared in a huge explosion, as one of the last bombs of the devastating raid found its target and turned the white vehicle with the big red cross painted on its sides and roof, into a ball of molten steel.

The lone fire crew unspooled their hoses and started their valiant but hopeless attempt to save the historic church, rather than wait for more support engines to arrive.

The three-person team from the ambulance ran across the burning debris field that had been the church's lawn and reached Mac and Mary. "What's happening here?" demanded the first of the medics.

"Only three have gotten out of the church on this side. We've lost one, but these two are still alive. I don't know their condition, I'm not a doctor, but they're bad, really bad." He pointed at the prone bodies.

The ambulance driver scanned the two moaning victims and agreed with Mac's limited assessment. "Bad is putting it lightly. They won't have a chance if we don't get them to hospital now." He noticed Mac's hands. "And you, son. Your hands are in a shocking state. You should come with us too."

Mac looked down at the burns wrapping around his fingers and palms, and said nothing. Mary saw his charred flesh and peeling skin for the first time and gasped out loud. "Mac, your poor hands."

"Get in the back of the ambulance. We'll make room for the other two. But we have to hurry; they don't have much time."

Mac shook his head. "No. I'll survive. You're going to need all the doctors and beds you've got to take care of the bombing victims. I'd slow you down."

The driver nodded, then turned to Mary. "Look, Miss. Your boyfriend needs treatment whether he likes it or not. Burns are nasty things and can get infected very easily, and he's got them all over both his hands. If he's not careful, he could lose all his fingers."

Mary stiffened at the thought.

"If I leave you some antiseptic and bandages, can you take care of him until he gets to a doctor?"

"I'll try."

"We have good doctors back at the base," offered Mac.

"I know you do. You Yanks have everything." He turned again to Mary. "It's important to clean his hands first with fresh water; get all the dirt and grime out, otherwise a nasty infection could start. After you've done that, rub in the antiseptic lotion, and don't be sparing, use it all. Then bandage his hands, but not too tight. That should tide him over until his doctors can take care of him."

"I understand."

"I'll get it for you." He saw the two other members of the ambulance crew rolling the victims on gurneys into the ambulance. "But I have to hurry, I'm needed over there." He sprinted to the ambulance and returned with a small bag stuffed with bandages and lotion. "It's our burn kit, it's pretty good. And here's two pills. Swallow them, they'll ease some of your pain." He held them out.

"I can't take them." Mac raised his useless hands.

"Miss?" the driver offered her the tablets.

Mary took them and lifted the pills to Mac's mouth, slipping them between his lips. He swallowed both gratefully without water.

"Best of luck, and thank you, sergeant, I think you saved two lives tonight." With that, the medic returned to the rear of the ambulance to help load the victims onboard.

Mary opened the bag containing the burn kit. "Kneel down, so I can work on your hands."

Mac shook his head. "Not here. They'll be more trucks coming to fight the fire and look for survivors, and we'll only be in the way. We need to head out and find somewhere quiet, away from here and the bombing, and you can do it there." A thought hit him. "The only problem is finding fresh water to wash these damn burns first. Maybe we'll have to skip that."

"No, we won't. Remember the brook we stopped at on the way here? It has all the fresh water in the world. That's where we'll go first, then we've got to get you back to your base so the doctors can see you."

Mac looked at the bike and waved with his burnt hands before the pain of the movement made him flinch and drop them to his side. "I won't be able to drive it. I'm sorry, I can't even close my fingers to grip the accelerator."

"Show me how to do it."

"You're sure?"

"Yes." Mary turned and led the way back to the motorbike with Mac following.

"What do I do?"

"You can ride a pedal bike, right?"

"Of course. That's how I got to school as a little girl."

"This is almost the same. You've got the brakes on either side of the handlebars; squeeze them to stop."

"I can do that."

"And the grip on the right is the accelerator. Twist it toward you to go faster, then back to slow down the speed."

"Okay."

"And the silver knob thing by your right foot, use it to change gears."

"How?"

"By pressing it with your foot."

"But how will I know when to do it?"

"I'll tell you. Hopefully, once we get going, we can stay in the same gear. And don't worry about balance; the sidecar does it for you, like having an extended training wheel."

"All right. Get on in then."

"Not yet. We have to start the bike. It'll take both of us to do it. The keys are in there." He looked helplessly at his pants' pocket. "I can't use my hands to get them."

Mary understood and reached in, quickly finding them.

"I guess you have to do everything, I'm useless now."

"That's all right, Mac. You'll be better soon."

"I hope so." He pulled himself from the well of self-pity and continued with his instructions. "Put the key in the ignition, then turn it."

Mary did as she was asked but looked quizzically at Mac. "It didn't start."

"It won't yet. The key unlocks the bike. We have to kickstart the engine."

"How does that work?"

"It's hard the first time so we'll do it together. I'll take care of the kickstart. You twist the throttle. We do it at the same time and that'll get the engine going."

"Okay." Mary gripped the throttle as Mac raised his left foot and rested it on the kickstart.

"I'll count to three, then twist it toward you. Ready?"

Mary nodded.

"One, two, three." He pressed down hard on the pedal as Mary twisted and the engine roared to life.

Mary kept the throttle open wide and the engine screamed. Mac flinched as he forced a smile through his pain. "Back it off, speedy. Let her idle while I get in and you climb on."

Mary released the throttle and the engine quieted to a low rumble as she helped Mac into the sidecar and they got ready to begin their twenty-five-mile journey.

Mac looked up and checked out Mary's position on the bike. "Okay, you're good. What you've got to do now is, when I tell you, press the gear pedal once. That'll put it into first and you're going to slowly open up the throttle."

"Open up?"

"Sorry. Twist it. But slowly. We don't want to do it all the way or we'll jump forward and stall the engine. Nice and easy."

"Nice and easy. Got it."

"Then let's try."

Mary pushed down on the gear pedal and twisted the gear. The bike began moving and she immediately backed off on the speed, causing them both to jerk in their seats.

"Sorry. What did I do wrong?"

"You can't be frightened of the movement. It's what we need, to go forward. You're still in gear. Try it again and concentrate on steering the bike. There's lots of things in the roadway, and we don't want to run into anything burning, if we do, we could blow a tire." He nodded with his head to the roaring fire raging inside the church. Behind them the sound of bells could be heard. "That's more ambulances and firetrucks coming. We should go now and get out of their way. Ready?"

"I'm ready."

Mary twisted the throttle and the motorbike lunged forward. She backed off the speed only a little this time and was rewarded as the bike continued on.

"That's it! You're doing it!" encouraged Mac.

"I'm trying."

Slowly, haltingly, Mary drove the bike through the wreckage and left the flames of Charles Church behind them.

Mac looked back and saw two more fire engines pulling to a stop, accompanied by a half dozen ambulances hoping to find at least a few more people who had survived the merciless attack.

As the hoses opened up on what was left of the shattered ruins of one of Devon's largest parish churches, Mac had no idea that even after the flames were extinguished, it would not be rebuilt and the windows and roof never replaced, but kept instead as a wrecked shell, standing in the honor and memory of the hundreds of civilians who were killed in the fire-bombing of Plymouth.

Charles Church memorial, Plymouth, Devon - 2024

CHAPTER NINE
The Brook

The country lane was dark, lit only by the crescent moon hanging high in the sky. Its soft light glinted from the steel handlebars of the motorbike and sidecar pulled up close to the hedgerow.

Thirty feet past the bushes, a small, battery-powered flashlight gave the two people gathered there a little of the illumination they needed.

They kneeled on an old blanket alongside a quickly flowing stream which brought life to the night with its chattering waters and a slight phosphorescence that added a glow to the clearing. Mary took control of the moment.

"We can't get your shirt off. If we pulled the sleeves over your hands, it would hurt too much and might scrape off even more skin. I'm going to try pushing the sleeves back before we wash your hands."

"Makes sense. But should we use this water? The ambulance guy said it had to be fresh. You think this is clean enough?"

"Clean? It doesn't get any better than this." Mary reached down and scooped up a handful of water, drinking it without hesitation. "This stream starts with the rainwater falling on Dartmoor, about thirty miles from here and it keeps going all the way to the River Tamar. It splashes over granite rocks to filter it even more. People drink from it all the time, they always have. It'll be just right for cleaning your burns."

"Okay, nurse. I'll take your word for it." He held out his arms.

As gentle as Mary was, Mac flinched multiple times as the burns and open sores played havoc with his scorched nerve endings. He knew the pain would have been much worse without the two tablets the ambulance driver had given him. He tried toughing it out, but Mary could see how badly it was affecting him.

"I'm sorry. I'm trying not to hurt you."

"Keep going. It's got to be done."

Mary nodded in agreement and tugged on the sleeve of her blouse.

"What are you doing?" asked Mac.

"I have to use something to wet your hands with. My jacket got burned up and I left it back at the church with yours, and I can't stick your hands in the water, you'd probably faint from the shock and fall in the stream, then we'd be in a right pickle." She pulled hard and tore off a strip of the cotton fabric. "This should do. I don't want to waste the bandages for this; we'll need every single one of them to wrap your burns."

She dipped the cloth into the brook, soaking it thoroughly. As she lifted it back out, she let the drips fall into the stream before facing Mac. "You sure you're ready for this? It's really cold and your burns are new and open."

"As ready as I'll ever be."

"Here we go." She lightly pressed the wet cotton against Mac's right hand. As gentle as Mary was, the sudden dampness and temperature change shocked his fried nerve endings, and he reacted to the searing pain shooting through him by wrenching backward, and unsuccessfully tried suppressing his involuntary scream which instead came out as a low growl.

"Are you okay?" The alarm was obvious in Mary's words.

"I'm sorry. I won't do that again." Embarrassed, Mac couldn't meet her eyes.

"Do whatever you have to do to get through this, Mac. I can't imagine how bad it hurts."

"I'll make it. I'm so grateful having you here to help me." He held out both hands in a peace offering, and gritted his teeth.

Mary reached forward again with the wet rag and slowly pressed it against one of his hands, gently holding it there. This time, Mac masked his agony and kept his arms outstretched. Encouraged by this, Mary carefully dabbed his hand until the entire back of it was wet, and now, hopefully clean.

"You're doing so good. Can you turn your hand over, please? I need to wipe any dirt and ash from your palm."

Mac complied, and Mary once again dipped the cloth into the steam to ensure it was soaked through.

"Here we go."

This time, knowing what was coming, Mac was able to withstand the pain, and Mary's cautious pressure on his blistered skin limited to a minimum the shards of electricity shooting up his arms.

"Now we've got your hands clean, we have to dry them before I can put the lotion on." Mary looked around for something to use as a towel but could find nothing. The worn blanket they knelt on was too old and dirty. "This blanket's no good," she explained. "It was fine for the sidecar but who knows if it's ever been washed and how many filthy pairs of army boots have been on it."

Mac had no disagreement with her statement; even in the dim moonlight he could see the grimy oil stains discoloring the rough cloth.

Mary drew in her breath. "I'll have to use my skirt." She adjusted her position to get as close to Mac as possible and lifted the colorful fabric, revealing her legs. She tried not be self-conscious as she gently wiped the back of Mac's hands dry. He turned them as she rubbed so she could dab his palms. As she stroked his fingers, making sure there was no water left between them, he looked into her eyes. The pain seemed to flee his body, and all he could feel was a deep attraction for this beautiful English girl who wanted nothing but to help him.

Mary felt the moment as well, and a smile creased her face before she caught herself. "We've got to get this done. I think they're dry enough now. It's time for the lotion. The ambulance man said it would help prevent an infection. Hold still if you can."

She undid the tube and squeezed a line of thick white medication from it.

Mac laughed through his pain. "That looks like what I put on my toothbrush at night."

"I bet it doesn't taste the same." Mary grinned before issuing her warning. "I'm going to rub it in now."

As softly as she could, she massaged the heavy lotion into his hands, taking special care with the scorched burns.

For Mac, the cool antiseptic felt good and formed a welcome block between the open sores and the night air.

"Bandages next. Lift your hands, please. I'm going to start wrapping the wrists then work up to your hands and finish with the fingers and thumb."

She expertly looped the first of the bandages around his wrist and continued on, going around his thumb and then covering each of his fingers individually before securing them together for protection with one final loop.

"Now your other hand."

"You're very good at this. Have you done it before?"

A cloud crossed Mary's face as she replied. "A few times. When the Blitz started, my dad taught me first aid so I could help out. And when it got bad, and the Germans kept coming back, it was useful to know it so I could help people. But it's been a couple of years since I've had to do it."

"You certainly haven't forgotten how to."

"Thank you. But stop talking now; you're distracting me, and it's important I get this right."

Mac remained silent as Mary finished the intricate bandaging, then turned from him to wash her hands clean in the stream. "All right, I think we're done. It's the best I can do."

"You did great." Mac sighed and dropped his head, falling silent.

Mistaking this for anger, Mary sought to encourage the injured soldier. "You'll be all right. The doctors at your base will fix you up a treat."

"That's not what I'm thinking about. I know it could have been worse, much worse. I mean, Christ, look at those poor people back at the church. Bandages couldn't help them."

Mary nodded in agreement, and it was her turn to remain silent.

"But we made it through, and here I am with you. This could have been the perfect end to a perfect day; the stars," he gestured to the clear night sky, "the babbling brook, the countryside…" His voice trailed off.

"Yes, the war has a way of bollixing things up."

They remained quiet until Mac's laughter broke the awkward silence.

"What's so funny?"

"I was just thinking; I should have brought another chocolate bar I could trade with you."

Mary's expression changed as she realized Mac's silence was not caused by him feeling sorry for himself, but his feelings for her. She whispered, "You don't need a chocolate bar."

Before Mac could answer, she leaned forward and kissed him on the lips. But this was not a peck. Their lips met and she pushed against him, her eyes closing as her thoughts and hopes of the past few days were coming true.

After a moment of surprise, Mac responded in kind, and he reached out for her.

"No, no, no!" Mary pulled away.

Mac stiffened. "I'm sorry. I misunderstood. I thought maybe you-"

"I do. You were right. I just don't want you to hurt more. Can you do what I say?'

Mac nodded.

"Good. Put your hands down."

He obediently dropped his hands.

"Lie back on the grass. Relax, like you did when I was bandaging your hands. Let me do this."

"Okay." Mac lay back and waited. He didn't have to wait long. Mary laid down next to Mac and stroked his face, running her fingers through his hair.

"I've wanted to do this since the first time I saw you. You're so handsome. You could be a movie star."

"No one would want to see me in the movies."

"I would. But it would have to be a thrilling, romantic film. Something like *Gone With The Wind*. That's my favorite."

"Frankly, my dear, I don't give a damn."

Mary laughed at his Clark Gable impression. "You've seen it too!"

"I think everybody has. Would you be my Scarlett O'Hara?"

"Why yes, kind sir. But only if you'll be my Rhett Butler."

"I will. But it's funny. They're another couple that had to escape a burning city."

"They didn't have a motorbike to ride."

"They had a horse and buggy. I bet you'd be able to drive one of those. I can see you holding the reins, going giddy-up."

"If I had to." She tensed. "But not now. Not here. There are other things to do." Mary stopped rubbing Mac's hair and tilted his head toward her and kissed him again.

As their lips locked, she started undoing the buttons on his shirt. Mac understood what was happening and his kiss became more passionate in response. He extended his arms to embrace this incredible girl.

"Stop that, mister. You'll hurt your hands. If I can drive a motorbike and a buggy, let me do this."

"Are you sure?"

"So sure. And it shouldn't be tough for you. You're a soldier; aren't you used to taking orders?"

"Yes, but from officers, and they aren't usually trying to kiss me." Mac grinned.

"I'm happy to hear that. Now lie back."

Mary climbed onto him, pulling off her blouse. Mac's shirt was open, and she had left it on him to avoid disturbing the bandages and irritating his wounds. She pressed her body hard against his, suppressing a gasp of pleasure at the warmth radiating from the feel of his firm chest.

Mac felt her tense and mistook it for apprehension. "Do you want to stop?"

"No. Not unless you want to."

Mac's eyes gave her the answer she wanted, and she cut off any further words with a kiss that began slowly, then reflected the passion the two young lovers had suppressed for weeks.

Mac fought the urge to hold her, knowing any movement with his hands would trigger a rebuke and possibly shatter the mood, so he lay there, letting this gorgeous creature take the lead.

Her hands slipped down from his chest to his flat stomach, running across his muscular abs before finding his belt. She lifted her body to give herself room to move and undid the buckle. It was Mac's turn to gasp. He knew what was happening, but the reality of it coming to pass was still tenuous. After the unexpected events of the day, he had a gut feeling this was too good to reach fruition and something would intervene to stop them, but for all his concern, there was no unwelcome intrusion. Instead, she undid his pants and tugged to get them off him. Mac responded by raising his butt, and the military khakis slid down to his knees.

Mary pulled off her own panties and moved her body up on Mac, ready to consummate their desires. She paused, staring into his brown eyes. "I know after tonight, you won't think the same of me, and if you don't want to see me again, I'll understand. I won't like it, but I'll know why. It's just I –"

"Shh," urged Mac. "I'll want to see you again and again, and forever, after this war is over. Tonight is only our next step."

"I do hope so." Mary reached back and slipped him inside of her as she pressed down, his warmth filling her body. Pleasure pushed her head forward and she sucked in a deep breath, drowning out the babbling brook, as the soulmates made love under the stars.

The moon had risen high in the sky as the two lovers lay cuddled together under the shelter of the rough blanket. Neither wanted to speak for fear of shattering the beauty of the moment. Finally, Mary had to break their silence. "Was it all right for you?"

"All right? That would be quite an understatement." He leaned over and kissed her. "It was," he looked for the appropriate words, failing in his quest. "It was everything."

"Everything?"

"Yes, everything. Being here with you like this is all I ever wanted, all I ever needed." He turned his head from her as he considered what he would say next. "There's only one thing that would make it better."

"What would that be? Not having burned hands?"

Mac smiled. "Okay, two things would make it better. My hands, and taking you to meet my family. When all this is done would you come to the States with me so I could introduce you to my mom and dad and my brother?"

"Do they talk funny like you?"

"You'll be the one who talks funny over there."

They both laughed out loud and Mary good-naturedly shoved Mac causing him to roll over and squeeze down on one of his bandaged hands. He jerked from the shaft of pain shooting up his arm and through his body.

"I'm so sorry. I forgot for a moment."

"So did I, and they're my hands." He shook his head at the humor of their situation, then remembered. "Much as I love being here with you, I need to get some medical attention for these damn burns back at base, and you should go home to your grandfather."

"Oh, no! I'll be so late. Mac, I'm in such trouble."

"Is there anything I can do to help?"

"Yes, maybe. When I get you back to your base, can you find someone to take me to my house in Stoke Fleming? It's only a few miles outside of the American camp."

"Sure, I'll have one of the guys from the motorpool drive you." He picked up on the concern running through her voice. "Can I ask, are you mad at me? Is it okay to see each other again?"

Hearing the innocence in his words, a little of the tension fled from Mary and she gently leaned forward and kissed him. "You'd better want to see me again, soldier. Especially when your burns are healed; I can't wait to find out if you really are good with your hands." She giggled, then became serious. "Now we should get dressed and go back to the bike. If you can start it for me, I'll have you to your doctors in no time."

CHAPTER TEN
The Old Soldier

Reg Sheppard sat back in the worn leather armchair; his old body warmed by the roaring log fire; the flickering flames the only source of light for the small living room. But Reg didn't need it brighter, the darkness helped him concentrate. He focused on the radio, listening to the grim news being delivered by the BBC Home Service.

The voice crackling from the wireless's speaker continued. "The first reports coming in from the unexpected air raid on Plymouth late this afternoon show the German's initial target were the military ships and personnel gathered in the harbor and Westward Hoe area of the dockyard."

Reg drew on his pipe as he took in the announcer's words.

"It was the Luftwaffe's first major raid on the West Country in more than eighteen months, and after failing to get through both the land and naval defenses posted there, and incurring heavy losses, which is reported to be over thirty bombers, the remaining squadrons, estimated in excess of seventy planes, crossed the River Tamar and began to indiscriminately bomb the unprotected city center of Plymouth."

Reg grunted at the words, and shook his head in disgust at this murderous action.

"Both high explosive and incendiary bombs are reported to have been used, devastating entire areas of the city which remain in flames at this hour. RAF Perranporth in Cornwall, dispatched two squadrons of Spitfires, which intercepted the Germans over the channel. The Spitfires brought down a further twenty-three planes, resulting in a total confirmed German loss of fifty-seven. This accounts for more than half of the bombers used in this ill-thought-out attack."

A noise from behind caught Reg's attention and he turned to see the big wooden front door creaking open and Mary inching her way inside. He quickly raised his hand to indicate to her to be quiet until he had heard the rest of the news report.

"We have no firm estimates as to the number of civilian casualties in Plymouth, but the BBC has been told that all available hospital beds in the city are already full with burn victims and those injured by the explosions and collapsing buildings. Many of the victims are being transported to Truro, Torquay, and Exeter for treatment at medical facilities there. The Home Office has delivered to our studios a memo informing us they hope to have a preliminary list of confirmed fatalities and those reported missing by late this evening, and will have the list posted by tomorrow lunch-time at all post-offices throughout Devon and Cornwall.

His Majesty, King George, is preparing a speech, and at this time sends his thoughts and well wishes to the people of Plymouth in their hour of need, and prays that God will be with them."

The announcer paused out of respect for His Royal Highness before continuing. "In Burma today, Allied troops…"

Reg reached from his chair and clicked the radio off, plunging the room into silence. He said nothing as he stared at Mary, standing by the door. Finally, he spoke.

"You look bloody awful and your clothes are filthy. Where the hell have you been?"

"I was there. Plymouth."

Reg jerked upright. "Are you hurt, love?"

"No. I'm fine."

"Are you sure?"

"I'm sure."

"Then you are a lucky bugger. They said on the wireless how bad it was." He waited before his next question. "Were you with him?"

"Yes."

"Damn it!" Reg exploded in fury, pushing himself out of the chair and stomping toward the hearth, his fists clenched so tightly the white of the knuckles seemed to glow in the firelight. "I told you not to see him." He spun around to Mary. "You disobeyed me."

"Because I don't understand. Why do you hate him? What has he done to you?"

"It's not what he's done to me, it's what he could do to you. He's wrong for you, wrong!"

"No, Grandpa, he's not. He's wonderful. He helps others. He talks about his family, his interests – and *my* interests. And when I speak, he listens to me like no one else I've ever known. You'd like him if you got to know him."

"I don't want to know him, now or ever."

Mary shook her head, puzzled. "But why not? He's a soldier like you were, and he's going off to fight for us, like you did."

"That's why."

"Because he's like you?"

"Yes, goddamn it, that's right, if you have to know. I've had enough of soldiers and soldiering."

"How am I meant to know that? You've never talked to me about what you did when you were a soldier."

"Maybe I should have. Maybe then you would understand." He gestured to the couch as he tried controlling his outburst. "Perhaps now is the time to do that. We should both sit down if you want me to tell you about it."

Mary moved to the patterned sofa and took her seat as Reg crossed the little room to a wooden cabinet and took out a decanter half full of whisky and poured himself a glass. "I'm going to need a dram or two of this if I have to dig up my memories."

He returned to his armchair and slipped back into its waiting embrace. He took two sips of the smooth, Scottish beverage before beginning his story.

"I was a few years older than this boy of yours when I went over to France in 1916. We were told it would be a great adventure going off for King and country to fight the Kaiser's men. They gave us uniforms and rifles and taught us how to march, and crowds turned out to see us as we paraded through the streets down to the harbor to board the ships waiting to take us across the water to teach the Huns a lesson. We all felt honored to be the chosen ones."

He took another swig.

"I was in a Pals Battalion."

Mary looked at him, not understanding the reference.

"They called them that during the recruiting drives. They promised you could serve with your family members and friends from the same town. That way you knew everyone in your company. It made for camaraderie. And at first it was great. We were all there; my brother, my old schoolmates, my drinking friends from the pub, my whole cricket team. It really was a battalion of pals. We marched together across the French countryside for days, singing songs as we went, enjoying the sun on our faces and the wonderful June weather, camping out at night and laughing that the Germans wouldn't dare show themselves and fight, or else we'd give them a good what for; we had a grand old time. Our march ended in a beautiful stretch of land, all green fields and woods, with a gorgeous river running nearby called The Somme. It was a little piece of paradise; we didn't know it then and neither did any of the French farmers living around the area, but heaven was waiting to become hell on earth."

He shook as the memory enveloped him.

"We found out the Germans were dug in on the far side of our field, so our commanders told us to dig trenches on our side and wait for orders. We did just that, and so did all the Allied troops along a twenty-five-mile front. With us safe in our trenches and Jerry in theirs, it became a stalemate. No one was going anywhere and no one was getting shot."

Reg closed his eyes as he knew what was coming.

"The generals didn't like that. In their way of thinking, what's a war without shooting? So, on the 24th of June they ordered the Royal Artillery to start shelling. Our big guns opened up along the entire frontline and didn't stop, day or night, for seven whole days. The history books say we fired over one and a half million shells at the Germans. It was loud for us, with the shells whizzing overhead, and then all those constant bangs and booms, but for the Huns in their trenches, it must have been like every demon from Hades was raining down on them. Finally, on July 1st, it stopped. It became so quiet we thought we'd gone deaf. Then, suddenly, at seven-thirty in the morning, there were two enormous blasts from behind the German lines. Our sappers had dug long tunnels reaching under their trenches and filled them full of dynamite. When they got the signal, they set them off. The explosions were so big they could be heard back in London, hundreds of miles away. That was the moment the generals had been waiting for."

Reg got to his feet and paced the small room.

"Our commander, Sir Henry Rawlinson, was so sure all the Germans had been killed that he ordered us to leave the trenches and go over the top in parade formation and march slowly forward to give a good representation of the British army. I remember his exact words, *'There's no hurry, boys, those dead Huns aren't going anywhere. I want shoulder to shoulder, forward march. No running or pushing. You'll all get to the German lines at the same time and they'll be plenty of souvenirs for everybody to take back home and show your families.'* He even called up a squad of Bengal Lancers to lead our parade, those poor bastards and their horses..." He shook his head as he recalled that day. "But we didn't know any better so we did as we were told. We had a Scottish brigade on our left and they began playing their bagpipes as they came out of their trench, so we responded by sending two drummer boys and three pipers ahead of our men to give us some good old English music. Those little kids couldn't have been more than eleven years old. So, with the pipes, drums, horses and lancers leading us, we slowly marched on those empty lines."

He drained his glass and paused as he refilled it, knowing he would need another.

"But the lines weren't empty and the Germans weren't dead. They had dug in deep and suffered through the worst we could throw at them. When they heard the music and saw us parading toward them in long, straight lines, all done up in dress uniforms and waving flags like crazy men, they came out of their shelters, set up their machine guns and opened fire."

The old soldier choked on the word *fire*, and tears flowed down his face.

"To this day, I still can't remember who took the first bullet. Whether it was my brother on my left, or my best friend, Tommy, who was marching to my right, but in seconds they were both gone. But before either had hit the ground, I realized I was the only one in my entire platoon who hadn't been shot. How the gunners missed me, I don't know, but everybody else, Tommy, Ian, Nigel, Colin, they were all killed in a second. And the noise was horrendous. The air was alive with whistling as bullets zipped past, some so close they lifted up your hair, and that sound mixed with the screams of dying men calling for their mothers, and the shriek of the horses, rolling in the mud with their legs shot off. It was bedlam, so horrible that nearly thirty years later it still wakes me up in a cold sweat at night. I heard one officer yelling, '*Don't break rank, keep going.*' But then he fell silent as the bullets took him too."

Reg stopped pacing as his memory took over his movement.

"I just stood there, lost. I froze in place, not knowing what to do. Then the second wave reached me, but they went straight past, and they weren't marching; this time they were running straight at the German lines. But they weren't fast enough, and the guns kept firing and in the blink of an eye, they were all gone as well. The same happened with the third and fourth wave; it was as if men were offering themselves up to the bullets. The few that reached the edge of the German lines were hung up on the barbed wire."

He locked his eyes on Mary.

"The so-smart generals didn't take into consideration that you can't blow apart barbed wire. Hit it dead on with an artillery shell and it bounces and flexes with the explosion, but stays pretty much intact. Our boys had to stop and try to pick their way through it and became sitting ducks for the machine gunners who slaughtered every single one of them, leaving their bodies, twisted and contorted, hanging on that bloody web of sharpened wire. Finally, when they had no more soldiers left to send, the recall whistles sounded, and I made my way back toward them, stepping over a bloody carpet of bodies, leaving everyone I had ever known dead on that field; my whole village, every man and boy I'd grown up with, gone in the first seconds of that stupid nightmare. During the first morning, before noon came, over nineteen thousand of our men were killed there and another thirty-five thousand wounded."

Reg blew out a long breath as he pulled himself together, "We fought that battle from July 1st, 1916 until November, when the brains trust at high command decided The Somme could be bypassed. We marched away from it leaving behind over one million dead, their lives sacrificed for a field eventually deemed unimportant."

He got out of his chair and moved over to the couch, sitting close to Mary.

"There's a particular reason I couldn't tell you this, Mary. As I said, Tommy was my best friend. His wife hanged herself when she got news of his death, leaving their only son, Ben, an orphan. He was barely fifteen and still in school, and had no way to survive by himself during those tough times, and being as my wife and I had no kids of our own, we took him in and raised him as our son. It was the best thing I ever did. We were so happy when Ben found a lovely young lady and married her at the age of twenty. Within a year they gave birth to a child, an even more beautiful baby girl, and we were over the moon when Ben told us he was going to name her after my wife, Mary. The christening and the party afterwards was really something; we all laughed and danced and toasted to the future. A few years later, my wife got sick, and I promised on her deathbed I'd never let anything happen to any of them, but then Ben had to move his family to London for work, and this bloody war started and he and your mother were killed in the Blitz."

It was Mary's turn to gasp as she realized the implications of the old soldier's confession.

Reg fought through tears as he continued. "That's why I hate war and everyone who fights in it. It takes everything good and kills it. It's brought our family nothing but sorrow."

Mary reached out and wrapped him in her arms. "I love you, Grandpa."

"Mary, I'm not really your-"

"Hush now. You are. You always have been and always will be."

She pulled him closer, feeling the frailty in his bones, and cradled him, hoping to protect him from his troubled past and never wanting to let go. Locked in the embrace, the old man and the young girl cried together in the firelight.

CHAPTER ELEVEN
Support

"Show me your hands." Colonel Brogan's words carried authority, not anger.

Mac, who stood across from the commanding officer's desk in his billet which had formerly been a beloved home for a family from Slapton Sands, complied and extended his arms, displaying the extensive bandages the US Army's medics had applied only a few hours before.

"Jesus, I've had men with mortar wounds that required less dressings. I can't see anything under them. How bad are your burns? And be honest sergeant; I can get the report sent to me in minutes."

"The doctor said they were third degree, sir." Mac was reluctant revealing how extensive his injuries were. "A couple of weeks and they should be fine."

"A couple of weeks? I might not have a red cross on my door but I'm no fool. I was burned when I was a kid doing a stupid stunt with fireworks, and it took me a month just to get my fingers working enough so I could pick up a cherry bomb again."

"I don't think mine are that bad, sir."

The colonel stared down the anxious soldier standing before him. "Okay, Sergeant Harper, pass me my water." He nodded to the glass resting on his desk.

Mac moved forward and reached out to grasp it, but realized how impossible the simple task was and lowered his thickly wrapped hands. "I can't, sir."

"Exactly. That's why I'm taking you off active duty and assault exercises until you are fully recovered."

"But sir, that could be after-"

"-the invasion. It could well be. No one knows when it's going to happen, but it will, and I won't have a soldier who is not one hundred percent on my Ranger team, because that's what it is sergeant, a team. We all rely on each other. And if we're in combat and someone is not able to do their assigned job, it could cost another member of my team their life. I have not only your safety but theirs to worry about."

"It doesn't seem fair, sir. I had an off-base pass. It was part of a three-day furlough-"

"Harper, you are not understanding me. I am not punishing you." Colonel Brogan sat back in his chair. "Do you know how I found out about this and why I called you in?"

"From the doctors?"

"No. I have fourteen thousand men under my supervision here in the South Hams. With all the heavy machinery, weapons and live-fire exercises, we have at least a dozen injuries on base every day. Most are minor, it's true, but the doctors don't come to me with every medical report otherwise I'd have no time to get anything else done."

"Then how, sir?"

"This morning, at daybreak, our sentries on the southern side of the camp were approached by a member of the Devon Constabulary. He knew he had no access to the base, but he was on a courtesy mission. He dropped off a burned jacket, US military issue. He also carried a letter from a medic at one of Plymouth's hospitals." The officer reached behind him and pulled out the blackened jacket, holding it up. "Recognize this?"

"Sir, yes. It's mine."

"I know that. There was a letter to your parents in the inside pocket. Lucky it didn't burn."

"I didn't mean to leave it behind."

"Would you just listen a minute and stop being so damn defensive? This isn't about losing a ruined jacket. Go see the Quartermaster, he'll give you a dozen more; this is about what you did last night. It was all in the note from the limey doctor. He said the jacket was wrapped around a burned British civilian by someone putting out flames. Apparently, the poor guy was a bonfire on two legs."

Mac started to speak but Brogan's glance quieted him.

"If I can continue, the doctor also wrote that a second injured civilian, a female, was saved by the same American soldier who risked his life in the fire-bombing. His exact words are…" He lifted the letter from his desk and read, "If it hadn't been for the prompt and fearless actions of the soldier, then both people would have died at the scene. Instead, they will live, after what will be a long recovery." He put the paper down and focused on Mac. "You know what that means, sergeant?"

"No, sir."

"You are a goddamn hero, son. If those two Brits had been our boys, I'd be pinning a medal on you right now."

"But sir, if I can speak plainly?"

"Go ahead."

"You seemed so angry at me."

"I am angry. But not at you. I'm angry you won't be with me and the other Rangers in the first wave ashore when we hit the French beaches, I need men like you alongside of us."

"Sir, is there anything I can do to change your mind?"

"Go to the Chaplain and pray for a miracle. Unless your burns go away overnight, you are off assault and assigned to divisional support."

"Divisional support?"

"I'm glad the bombing didn't affect your hearing. That's what I said. Without support, none of this can happen. You'll be as important as the guys on the front line doing the shooting. Someone has to get it done. And as of today, that someone is you."

Colonel Brogan saw Mac tense to continue to argue his case, but was having none of it and rose from behind his desk. "You are assigned divisional support. That's an order, soldier."

Mac snapped to attention and attempted a salute that was thwarted by the heavy bandages. "Yes, sir."

"The sergeant at arms outside will take you to the support section and they'll designate your assignments there. Get going, Sergeant Harper."

"Sir." Mac turned and headed out of the office where he was met by the waiting sergeant who had been made aware of his task. "Follow me, I'll get you situated. And cheer up. The colonel probably just saved your life. You'll be coming in long after the beaches have been secured."

Mac stayed silent. That was exactly why he was burning inside now, more than he had been when fighting the previous night's flames.

The mess tent buzzed as the evening drew in. Soldiers collapsed on their mattresses, full from dinner and exhausted after yet another day of intensive training. Mac sat with Ricky on his bunk.

Ricky broke out laughing. "You, of all people. I wondered where you were today when we hit the beach. Off combat and sentenced to divisional support? Oh, Lordy! I guess I'll be sending you postcards from the front. I'll let you know how grateful the French mademoiselles are when we liberate them."

"Give me a break." Mac was in no mood for humor. "I'll be with you all the way through training."

"Right." Ricky grinned widely. "You'll be at our beck and call, the one we tell to, 'run and get us a ladder. We need to climb the cliffs now. And don't forget to make us a baloney sandwich in case we're hungry when we come back down.'"

"Try that and there'll be a big problem."

Ricky stared at the multiple layers of gauze and bandages wrapped around Mac's hands. "And what would you do with those Mickey Mouse fists? A punch from those would probably feel good."

"Wanna find out?"

"No thanks, Steamboat Willie."

"It won't be this way for too long; the doc says they'll come off in about three weeks, and after that I'll be reassigned."

"But not to combat?"

Mac shook his head sadly. "No, I'll have missed too much training. Word is I'll be supervising tank and armor support on the Ranger's landing ship, LST 289."

"An LST? A Large Slow Target? I guess you found a way to make the navy after all."

Mac rolled his eyes. "It's hardly the navy. Certainly not a warship. They barely have any armament, just a couple of anti-aircraft guns. Those LSTs are the trucks of the sea, with three decks for men, trucks, and tanks."

"You can always pretend it's the real navy." He beamed at Mac. "All the good girls love a sailor. Hell, you'll be in bell-bottoms before the war is over."

The low moon spread a silver light across the clifftop, casting long shadows from the fringing trees marking the start of the flat grassy area stretching over a hundred yards to the rocky edge and sheer drop to the beach below.

Two figures sat in their folding chairs, scanning the empty waters of the English Channel, their backs to the treeline, and didn't react to the lone figure emerging from the bushes. Mac approached and coughed slightly to let them know he was there and not startle them.

"No need to alert us of your presence, son, we heard you coming a mile away."

Mac froze in place as he recognized both the voice and the face of the person addressing him. Moonlight lit him as he swiveled in his chair to look back at the lovesick American soldier.

"I guess the flames not only scorched your hands but burned your tongue off as well. Can't you speak, boy?" quipped Mary's grandfather.

Mac opened his mouth, but the surprise of seeing Reg still held him silent.

Mary quickly intervened. "It's all right, Mac. I told him about you; about us."

Her words broke the spell, and the dumbstruck sergeant stepped forward. "But I thought..." He looked at Reg and his voice faded again.

"Here's the thing. My eyes aren't good in the dark, and Lord knows my frail old body could do without the evening's bitter cold, but I've been up here the past three nights waiting to find out more about this *'great person'* my lass keeps going on about."

"I was getting worried about you. I thought they might have sent you home to America to recover from your burns."

Mac breathed in deeply, hearing Mary's words, and composed himself. "They're not that bad." He raised his bandaged hands. "I had to get some movement back into them first, before I could..." Again, he stopped talking, searching for the right words.

"Sneak out?" Reg finished the sentence for him. "You're lucky most of the Yankee sentries posted at the roads and approaches to the South Hams are there to stop people getting in, not to be looking for their own boys going out for a nighttime jaunt. I'm pretty certain there's only a couple around the village and the camp. At least, that's all we can see from up here."

"You're right, sir." He grinned. "But I still didn't want to get caught sneaking out. Too many awkward questions."

"Like, *'what are you doing, soldier? Off for a romp with a local girl?'*"

"Grandpa!"

"Come on, Mary, why else is he here, to bring us a pot of tea? If so, where's the flask with my hot cup of char?" It was Reg's turn to smile. "You're here now, son. Why don't you head over to the trees and romance the young lady?"

Again, Mary called out the same refrain. "Grandpa!"

"Neither of us are stupid, my love. What's he going to talk to you about, military strategy? Be off, the both of you." He raised a finger and pointed it at Mac. "But behave yourself, son, understand?"

"Understood, sir."

Still shocked at the turn of events, Mac waited as Mary rose from her chair and joined him, and the two of them walked together to the shelter of the trees.

It was Mac who spoke first after waiting until he was sure they were far enough away that Reg couldn't overhear them, but even then, he lowered his voice to stay on the safe side. "I thought he hated me. What happened?"

"We talked."

"It must have been quite the conversation. What did you talk about?"

"About love, about family."

"And now he's good with you seeing me?"

"I wouldn't exactly say that. It was more like," Mary deepened her voice as she attempted to echo her crusty grandfather's tone, "Is that wet behind the ears Yank the best you can do?"

"What did you say?"

"I told him, with the war on and all the single men going off to fight, it was pretty slim pickings for a girl around here, so I had to make do."

Mary saw Mac's expression change as he took her words seriously.

"I'm joking." She shoved him gently to emphasize her point. "His big thing is, he doesn't want me hurt."

"I'd never hurt you."

Mary laughed again. "You couldn't. Not with those big mitts all wrapped up in cotton."

"Even when they come off, you won't have to worry, I promise."

"I know that."

"I can't stay too long tonight. I start helping supervise beach exercises tomorrow."

"So, you're staying with the Rangers? I know how worried you were."

"Yes, I am." He sighed and she could feel his regret. "But no longer part of the assault squads. I have to stand around and watch while they do the work."

"It could be worse, you know that, much worse. This way, I still have you."

She locked eyes with him, an unspoken invitation, so Mac leaned forward and kissed her softly, but not for too long because after all, Grandpa might be able to see.

A whistle blast ripped the air, triggering the Rangers at the foot of the cliff to begin their assault. Before the echo reverberating from the rocks had died out, the waiting squads exploded into action and were tackling the cliff face. Their speed was astonishing, reflecting both the constant training they had already endured, and the knowledge they carried that when the actual day of the invasion arrived, it could be how fast they summited the cliff that would keep them alive.

Mac stood twenty yards from the climbers with three other Rangers, two wearing a white wrapping bearing a red cross on their right arms, indicating they were prepared to act should anyone fall or be injured.

Colonel Brogan approached the group, and after a quick visual assessment of his men's progress, turned his eyes to Mac. "Report."

"The first squad reached the top in under ninety seconds, sir. And that was carrying full gear."

"Excellent. Do you think they can push that?"

Mac nodded to his superior officer. "They get faster every time, sir. Come the day, I would estimate their time will be closer to a minute."

"Pray God, it'll be fast enough." Colonel Brogan's concern for his men was obvious. "Let's give them a little more incentive. We'll begin the live-fire exercise this afternoon at fifteen hundred hours. Have them stand offshore two hundred yards in LCAs, then come into the beach under fire and tackle the cliffs and gun emplacements. They should be able to get two runs in before we start losing the light."

"I'll requisition an infantry squad to take positions on the grass at the top and fire down on the men."

"Make sure those flatfoots are good shots. The rounds should be close, but there's no room for accidents. Yesterday, the 101st lost two men because the shooters got too damned excited. Terrible. There's no fucking excuse for it."

"Sir, I'll fully brief them myself."

"And I want a lot of smoke and magnesium grenades going off continuously on the beach. Who knows what Jerry has in store for us, so let's make it as bad as we can, that way, when the real thing comes, our boys will be ready."

"Yes, sir."

"Now call them back and give them a break to rest and eat. They'll need all their faculties to get through what we have in store for them later."

Mac, still struggling with his bandaged fingers, clumsily put his whistle to his mouth and blew hard twice, sounding the recall. For the exhausted men, the signal didn't come a moment too soon, and in seconds, the rugged rock face was covered with Rangers rappelling down, knowing food and rest awaited.

The two-hour break went by too fast for the Rangers, and with the taste of the sandwiches they'd had for lunch still fresh in their mouths, the squads loaded back into their landing crafts and motored out to stand off two hundred yards from the beach, ready for the signal indicating the live-fire exercises had begun.

Mac stood with Colonel Brogan; the sergeant's eyes fixed on the sweeping hand of the stopwatch he held.

"Right at fifteen hundred hours. That way we can calculate the assault time accurately," ordered the colonel.

Mac nodded, but said nothing, not wanting to be distracted and miss the watch's cue. The second hand hit sixty, and Mac lit a signal flare that scorched into the sky.

The result was immediate. The twin diesels of the six landing craft roared to life and the heavily loaded boats lurched forward. At the same time a series of mortars fired from the cliff tops, their shells landing fifty yards in front of the now speeding vessels, the resulting explosions showering the sheltering Rangers inside the open craft with ice-cold sea water.

Machine guns opened up, the skilled gunners firing even closer to the LCAs than the less accurate mortars, and the whining bullets screamed above the huddled men.

In less than a minute, the six craft hit the sloping shore and the bow ramps dropped to allow the troops inside to disembark. The Rangers didn't hesitate and raced shoulder to shoulder down the ramps onto the wet pebbles.

"Now," commanded the colonel, and Mac sounded his whistle.

This time, a dozen men planted either side of the landing area threw grenades into the grouped Rangers sprinting up the beach. Though their shape looked exactly like the standard issue MK II grenade, their color was different.

Instead of the drab olive-green grenades servicemen carried into combat, these were painted light blue to show they did not contain the TNT or Trojan explosive inside, but had been specially adapted for training and held either a smoke bomb or a magnesium flash-bang discharge designed to disorient any soldiers nearby in much the same way as a real grenade's blast would. As they detonated, the illusion of an actual battle was complete.

Undeterred, the 2nd Rangers powered through the chaos and blinding smoke, and made it to the foot of the cliffs, hugging the rock tightly to avoid being fired on from above.

A lieutenant called out a command to his sheltering men. "On my mark, have three squads lay down covering fire on the top of the cliffs. As they are doing that, ladder squads get your ladders assembled and in position. Do it fast, but do it right, you'll have less than a minute. Speed is everything. The longer we're on the beach, the more men we lose." He swept his eyes across the group. "Ready?" He didn't wait for an answer and barked, "Now!"

There was zero hesitation as eighteen Rangers opened up on the hilltop with their carbines. One of the men, Ricky, struggled with his gun, as his M1 rifle jammed immediately. He tried ejecting the stuck shell and replacing the eight-shot clip, but the semi-automatic continued to foul, the clip release latch not responding. He banged the butt plate into the rocks in frustration, hoping to free the rounds, as the men beside him kept up their covering fire, effectively quelling any opposition from above.

Taking advantage of this lull, the ladder teams slid together the long sections and raised the six assault ladders into place, one member of each team standing at the base to stabilize the towering ladder.

The lieutenant saw it was done and called out, "First climbing squads, GO!"

In groups of four, the Rangers raced to the ladders and swarmed upward, going hell for leather. Their speed was faster than at any previous point in training, the realism of the moment kicking in, giving them added motivation.

Smoke grenades erupted around the base of the ladders as the lieutenant yelled, "Second climbing squads. Take the cliff, NOW!"

That was Ricky's cue, and he slung his useless rifle across his back and started up the ladder. Small rocks and debris from the first squad above showered down on him, dirt and grime lodging in his eyes. He paused, trying to wipe them clean so he could see, but his team mates below were only inches away and pounded on his boots, screaming, "Move it, Esposito, move it. We're going to die here."

A flash bang grenade, dropped by the defenders at the top of the cliff, exploded twelve feet above Ricky, the blast rocking him, and its magnesium charge and acrid smoke temporarily obliterating what was left of his vision.

"Give me a minute," he called back to the men below.

"A minute! We don't have a fucking second!" roared the corporal, blocked by the helpless soldier.

"Get off the ladder, asshole," came another call.

Unable to see anything, Ricky knew he had to clear the way, and took a hand from the ladder and blindly felt for the cliff. The face was rough and filled with cracks and ledges. He took the chance and slipped his fingers into a small opening and swung from the ladder onto the rocky face, clinging there for dear life as the three other members of his team raced past him, heading to the top, trying to make up for lost time, leaving their disgraced squad mate not moving as he hung motionless against the cliff.

Slowly his vision returned, and he reached back for the ladder but realized he wouldn't be able to get onto it as there was no opening and no pause from the other squads who were heading up fast. He looked down; he was barely twenty feet above the beach, that would be his best and probably only option. Shamed and defeated, he climbed down the rock face to the shingles below, while the rest of the 2nd Rangers completed their successful assault on both the cliff top and the simulated German gun emplacements waiting for them.

Colonel Brogan lowered his field glasses and glared at Mac. "Goddammit."

"But they took the guns, sir, and in record time."

"Of course they did, my Rangers are the best. But no thanks to that man. One bad apple like him could put too many of my men in the ground. Have him report directly to me tonight."

"Will do, sir!"

It was getting close to lights out in the sprawling tent housing the 2nd Rangers. Already, the men, knowing time was drawing in, were wrapping up their card games and returning to their bunks, as four giant fans blowing through propane-fed flames, acting as the tent's forced air heaters, were cranked to the max to fight off the night's oncoming cold and yet another freeze warning.

Mac flipped his drafting pad closed, frustrated the bandages had once again prevented him from completing his work on the sketches which filled much of his idle time between dinner and sleep.

A pair of arms wrapped around his neck from behind and a wet kiss was planted firmly on his cheek. The voice revealed his would-be lover. "Pucker up, buddy. I owe you."

With a laugh, Mac pushed Ricky away. "What did I do to deserve all this uncalled-for affection?"

"Saving my ass, that's what!" Ricky plopped down onto the bunk next to his friend. "I don't know what you said to the old man, but it worked. I thought after today's disaster he would take away my stripes for sure and put me on toilet duty for the duration."

"I told him to skip the latrine and stick your head straight in the crapper." Mac's smile gave lie to his words.

Ricky grinned, then became serious. "Whatever you did say, thanks. The colonel was right to take me off beach assault. I can't handle climbing, particularly under pressure. Ropes are one thing, being shot at while going up some cliff is entirely different. I could have got people killed."

"Starting with yourself."

"Yeah, you're right; starting with me."

"So, what did he come down with?"

"Like I said, I'm off the beach assault team; at least the initial waves. But he didn't kick me out of the Rangers. He pulled my records and said there were some good things in there, and what I needed was to be under supervision. I think his words were, *'with a watchful eye, you could be useful.'*"

"And whose watchful eye will you be under?"

"That's the kicker – yours! He read what we did together in Sicily, and it was you who had recommended me, and with so few people to spare in the unit, it's going to be you who is my supervisor and I report to."

"Me? That's nuts."

"I wanted to tell him that, but I didn't because latrine duty was the only other option. It's divisional support and vehicle distribution for me. You're looking at your new right-hand man. I'll be on LST 289 with you."

LST 289 beached on Slapton Sands, March, 1944

CHAPTER TWELVE
LST 289

The enormous bow of LST 289 rose fifty feet from the ocean's surface as the huge craft pushed through the waves. Unlike a regular ship with a bow coming to a point made to cut through the water, this gigantic vessel, stretching back three hundred and twenty-eight feet, was designed solely as a transport for troops and the heavy machinery they needed in battle, both tanks and trucks, and this dictated the bow had to be able to swing open like a set of doors, drop an immense ramp from within, and allow the military vehicles inside to drive off quickly under their own power through the yawning opening. Because of this, the bow was not as sharp as on a normal ocean-going vessel, and this increased resistance drastically limited the boat's speed while under way.

The LST was born when the war broke out and engineers were given a unique transportation problem to solve, how to get armored vehicles to an enemy shore and land them directly on a beach, with no harbor around. Within months, they came up with a revolutionary breakthrough, an enormous ship which could carry a dozen Sherman tanks, sixteen trucks, and a thousand men. Construction began on the LSTs in June 1942, and featured multiple innovations, including a ballast system with internal siphons so the ship could take in huge amounts of seawater, allowing it to become heavier and have a much deeper draft while making open ocean crossings, and oversized pumps which could empty those ballast chambers quickly and give a fully loaded LST a draft of a little over two feet so it didn't need a dock or a pier to unload, and could run right up on a beach and discharge its deadly cargo onto the sand.

The boat's main challenge was caused by its shape, which was by force of the design, a block. Because of this, it didn't slide through the water; it had to push and bludgeon its way, which meant, even with its oversized twin diesels firing at their full capacity of two hundred and twenty-five pounds per square inch, the LSTs had a maximum speed of ten knots. This did not go unnoticed by their crews or the troops assigned to them, and they gave the Landing Ship, Tank, the unwelcome nickname of LST – Large, Slow Target.

Mac stood in LST 289's wheelhouse at the stern of the vessel, looking out across the upper troop transport deck, filled with several hundred soldiers who sat and lay around, with nothing to do until the boat landed and they were dispatched onto the shore.

A voice from behind grabbed his attention. "How are your hands, Sergeant Harper?"

Surprised, Mac turned quickly to address the ship's captain, Lieutenant Commander Rogers. "Much better, sir. I'm glad to finally have the bandages off." He held up his hands to his commanding officer, showing them to be intact, but heavily discolored from the still healing burns,

"Do you have all your motion back?"

"Happy to say, yes, sir. There was no damage to any of the joints or muscles in my hands." He flexed his fingers to reinforce his words. "They look bad, but everything works."

"That's good news. Do you want to try taking the helm, sergeant?"

"Me, sir?" The question took Mac by surprise. "I'm here to coordinate the dispersal of the men of the 2nd, and the storage of their support vehicles and equipment."

"I'm aware of that, sergeant. I've been watching you since you've been onboard these past few weeks, and I've gone through your history and know Navy was your first choice, and it was our boat's engineer who you helped out on the landing craft when the sync mechanism failed. He told me you were instrumental in getting everyone back to Slapton, and that's high praise coming from him. I also heard you borrowed the operational manuals to learn how this ship runs, and you've spent more time on the bridge this month than me. Based on all that, I think you might be ready. So, tell me, do you want to try handling that landing craft's big sister?"

"Yes, sir!!"

Lieutenant Commander Rogers broke out in a smile at Mac's enthusiasm, and nodded to the helmsman. "Stand down for a few minutes, Sergeant Harper is taking the helm."

"Sir." The helmsman stepped away from the console, moving to the rear of the cabin, but keeping his eyes glued on the panel, ready to resume control at a moment's notice.

Mac moved forward, placing his hands gently on the two levers working the steering of the lumbering boat much more effectively than a wheel. "Orders, sir?" he asked.

"Correct the course and take her ashore at Slapton. Use a visual reading so we beach just east of the village. I want her on the sand, where we will unload the trucks. Current speed is…" he checked the gauge, "six knots. Maintain that until we are two miles out. At that point, empty the ballast and float her higher. Then, continue with standard landing procedures." He looked at Mac with a knowing grin. "Exactly like we've been doing these last few weeks. I'm pretty sure you're a quick learner, son."

"Thank you, sir. Standard landing procedures it is." He increased throttle on the port engine, while decreasing slightly on the starboard. This maintained forward speed while beginning a long, slow turn of LST 289 toward their destination, the sloping beach of Slapton Sands.

On deck, the soldiers heard the change in the engines and felt the boat swinging toward the coastline. Ricky, who had been assigned the role of beachmaster, was supervising a squad working on ammunition storage, and looked up at the glass enclosed bridge at the rear of the vessel. He saw Mac through the heavy window, piloting the ship. A huge smile crossed his face, "Well I'll be. You'll make Admiral yet."

Ricky wasn't the only one assessing Mac's performance. Lieutenant Commander Rogers stood right behind Mac monitoring his every move, subtly checking the gauges displayed across the console on the bridge. The compass heading was true, the visual lined up, and the speed remained locked in at six knots. He'd been right to trust this boy.

Understanding the others watching him must have concerns, Mac spoke aloud to convey his actions to the captain and his helmsman. "Approaching two miles offshore. Initiating ballast pumps. Going to shallow draft to prepare for landing." Mac clicked the four stainless steel switches to turn on the port and starboard ballast pumps.

There was a shudder as the pumps started, and an intense bubbling commenced on both sides of the ship as the ballast water was rapidly pumped out and air took its place. Very quickly the waterline appeared as the boat rose higher in the sea.

Mac looked at the gauges displayed in front of him and continued to explain his actions. "Pumps at full efficiency. Boat should reach minimum draft in less than two minutes." He pushed both of the throttle levers forward. "Increasing speed as we approach the landing beach. Two reasons for this. First, it makes it harder for the enemy to target the ship, and secondly, it increases the ability of the pumps to fully empty the ballast chambers."

Lieutenant Commander Rogers watched the speed increase to eight knots and shot a worried glance back at the helmsman who raised his hands in a *I don't know* gesture. The boy was quoting the book, after all.

Mac turned to his superior officer. "Permission to alert the men of the upcoming landing, sir?"

"Sure. Go ahead." Though he replied positively, uncertainty rang through the captain's voice.

Mac grabbed the wired microphone and clicked it on, opening up the public address system across the ship. "We should be ashore in four minutes. Man all vehicles for immediate evac and brace for beach contact."

The sprawling deck below became a hive of activity as men rushed to their positions.

As they approached the landing spot, Mac wrapped his hands around the levers. Rogers saw Mac's veins tighten through his purple scars, as he tensed to make a move. Unsure what he was planning, the captain poised to take over the helm. He shot a glance out of the wide glass window; from high up in the bridge, it looked as though they were about to run up on the beach already, and yet they were still speeding forward. Should he-

Mac's voice ended his doubts. "All stop." He pushed the two levers upright and continued explaining his actions aloud as he completed his moves. "Now full reverse, port and starboard diesels. Three seconds then," he waited, "cut engines."

He thrust both levers back into their locked positions, shutting down the two big diesels.

His maneuver worked perfectly. The huge ship, its ballast tanks empty, floating high in the water, drifted the last few yards, beaching softly on the pebbles of Slapton Sands.

Mac again took the P.A. microphone, announcing, "Beaching complete. Opening bow." He flipped a large switch on the console operating the massive forward watertight doors. "Deck now has control of ramp. When lowered, follow the beachmaster's instructions and begin moving out the vehicles."

Eighty feet away, Ricky listened to the page and reacted accordingly. "You heard the man. Get in your trucks and tanks. Evac by the numbers. Move it!"

The men sprinted to their vehicles, happy to get off the boat and feel dry land beneath their feet again.

A corporal fired up the engines of his troop transport, but hesitated before putting it in gear. He leaned from the open driver's side window and called to Ricky. "You coming with us, sir?"

"Move it out, soldier. I'll be in the back."

The camouflage-painted truck began its slow roll forward, waiting its turn in the line of Jimmys to disembark, as Ricky ran behind it and pulled himself inside. He was gone for a moment before reappearing holding a large, hand-painted sign he unfurled to hang over the tailgate, reading *PARIS OR BUST!*

As the vehicles headed down the ramp and onto the beach, Ricky's words were proudly visible, fluttering in the light breeze.

From his eagle's perch, Mac cracked a smile as he saw the sign, knowing who was responsible for it.

"Glad you're smiling, son." Lieutenant Commander Rogers interrupted Mac's thoughts. "You had me going there for a while."

"Really, sir?" Mac was genuinely surprised. "You said to use standard landing procedures, and I was only following the book."

Rogers responded in mild amazement. "The book is one thing. Do you know how long it takes most people to learn to operate a behemoth like an LST? You have quite a gift with boats."

"I have my father to thank for that, sir. While the other kids got bicycles and BB guns for their birthdays, my dad would take me out to learn to sail his tugs and pilot vessels in Long Beach."

"How old were you then?"

"Couldn't really tell you, Captain. Some of my earliest memories were on his boats, and whenever he earned enough to get a new one, he had me go through it with him; the engines, the steering, the mechanics, until I knew it inside out. He built everything with hard work. He always said to me, without the bend of your back and the sweat of your brow, you have nothing. But I loved every second of it."

"It shows." Rogers laid his hand gently on Mac's shoulder. "It was through my family I became a navy man. I was the third generation to graduate from USNA in Annapolis. I hope after all this nonsense is over, I can meet your father and let him know the kind of son he raised. I'd look forward to it; I've always wanted to spend some time in California."

"He'd like that, sir, and so would I. Maybe you could captain one of our boats for the day and check out some of the big merchant vessels in Long Beach."

"Now that's an offer I'll take you up on. We'll definitely try to make it happen," smiled the ranking officer. "But for now, you're dismissed, Sergeant Harper. Go to the barracks and relax. This was a job well done. I'll have a pass waiting for you."

"A pass, sir?"

"Yes, a pass. You deserve a little time off, then you can come back refreshed and ready to go. And we have our major exercises coming up, and they're scheduled to last three days or more. I'll need you alert for those. Now get going before I change my mind."

Mac clicked his heels together as he snapped to attention and saluted. "Yes, sir!"

The barracks tent bustled with activity as the soldiers inside relaxed and joked and took advantage of the fact the day's activities had ended while the early springtime sun was still an hour from setting.

Mac sat bent over his drafting pad, checking and rechecking the multiple pages of detailed designs he poured over. Ricky interrupted his scrutiny as he flopped on the bunk next to him.

"I thought you'd finished it?"

"I have. But there are always the tiny details you can miss. I want it to be perfect."

"Like my sign?"

Mac laughed. "I saw that. Very creative."

"Wasn't my first choice. I wanted to write, *WE'RE COMING TO GET YOU, ADOLPH*, but it wouldn't fit on the sheet."

"I like *Paris or Bust* better, anyway." Mac closed the drafting pad. "I hope this goes over well tonight."

"Tonight? Why? What's happening in the mess tent?"

"Not the mess tent, Ricky. This!" Mac pulled a signed letter out of his pocket.

Ricky scanned it quickly. "Holy shit. Aren't you a lucky bastard, an off-base pass, and it's not a holiday or anything. Let me guess where you're going, Mary?"

"Yup, Mary. A little home cooking this evening."

CHAPTER THIRTEEN
Three gifts

The small kitchen inside the stone cottage buzzed as Mary moved quickly around the tiny room, checking first the stove, then the pans on the two electric burners acting as the range. She had very little counter space and no island to use for preparing, cutting, and placing items on, so instead she improvised with a pair of sturdy boxes stacked one on top of the other.

Anxiety crossed her face as she dipped a spoon into a warm pot then lifted it back out to sample the sauce. As the flavor hit her taste buds she broke out with a satisfied sigh and poured the contents of the saucepan into a waiting gravy boat.

A voice drifted through the partially open door. "It smells wonderful. Can I help with anything?"

Mary's smile widened as she answered. "No, it's all under control, Mac. Give me another five minutes and you'll be eating."

"You sure you're okay?"

"I'm fine. It's taking a little longer than I thought because I've never cooked for a man before."

"Then what the hell am I, bloody Peter Pan?" came a gruff second voice.

Mary laughed. "You know what I mean, Grandpa."

The table in the living room was loaded with empty plates, marking the end of a feast. The three occupants of the cottage sat around the roaring log fire, too full to move.

"This could be the third Thursday in November, I'm so stuffed." Mac rubbed his stomach for effect.

"What happens the third Thursday in November?" wondered Mary.

"That's when we have Thanksgiving. It's a tradition where all the family members get together and celebrate the end of a successful growing season with a feast. But instead of the chicken we had tonight, it's usually turkey with all the fixings."

"It sounds a bit like our harvest festival. We do that in October and cook up all the fresh food from the farms."

"October, November - who knows what month it is these days? For all I know we could be eating Christmas pudding now, it's so cold. It feels like blooming December to me, not the last week of April. We had snow a few days ago, snow! And you'd know that Mac, camping out in your boy scouts' tents. We should be enjoying springtime, but nobody told that to Mother Nature, or to my old bones. And where are the daffodils? Not a one to be found yet, too cold for them as well." Reg leaned forward and grabbed another freshly cut log, tossing it on the fire. "Let's keep it as warm as toast in here for when I get back." He inched his way out of his favorite armchair.

"Where are you going, sir?" asked Mac.

"I don't want to 'ave to tell you again, son, it's Reg, not sir. I might be Sir Reg one day if King George sees fit, but there's no *sir* here tonight. Leave the military talk back at your base, alright?"

"Understood, Reg. But where are you going?"

Reg was standing now, and talked as he put on his heavy coat. "Someone's got to take the dog out. Billy isn't going to walk himself."

He belted the coat tightly around him, pulled a woolen cap over his head and ears, slid on a pair of gloves, then reached for the dangling leash hanging from the hat rack. This caused the sleeping labrador to suddenly jump to its feet, convulsing in spasms of joy.

Reg grinned and raised his bushy eyebrows, "Look at the cheery bugger. You'd think he'd just won the bleeding football pools." He clipped the leash on the happy doggy's collar and reached for the door handle. He paused, looking at Mac and Mary. "And don't you be worrying. I won't come straight back in, I'll knock first and give you fair warning."

Before the two of them could reply, Reg and his beloved Billy disappeared through the door into the frosty night.

Mac looked wide-eyed at Mary. "I certainly wasn't expecting that."

Mary leaned forward and kissed him. "Were you expecting that?"

"Hoping, yes. Expecting, no."

"I'm so happy you could be here tonight to see our little house."

"It's cute. Everything I thought an English cottage would be."

Mary kissed him again, and with a smile, Mac backed away. "Save those kisses a minute. I have something for you." He reached back, and on a wooden chair by the door, he picked up his drafting pad and presented it to Mary. "I wanted to give you this."

"What is it? A sketchpad?"

"Look and see."

Mary carefully flipped open the large folder, revealing pages of intricate line drawings and diagrams. "Are these pictures of a boat?"

"Not just pictures, and not just any boat. They are plans and schematics for building a special one. If you go to the back page, you'll see what she'll look like completed. She's unique, not another exactly like her in the world."

She turned to the final page, and there was a full color rendering of a gorgeous yacht under sail with the sun setting behind her. The name on the stern proudly reading, *Mary's Dream*.

Tears flooded Mary's eyes. "She's beautiful. Can I frame this?"

"Better than that, you can sail in her." Mac put his hands gently on Mary's shoulders to emphasize his words. "After the war is over, I'm going to build her for you. I know they have a shipyard at Dartmouth and it's only ten miles from here. That is, if you want me to stay."

Mary couldn't speak. Her body shook from tears of joy.

"If that's not right for you, Mary, you could come to America with me. I've been writing my folks about us, and they can't wait to meet you."

"You'd take me to America?"

"I told you I would. And I'd take you anywhere in the world you wanted to go. These have been the best four months of my life."

"Even with what happened to your hands?"

"Yes, even with my hands."

He stared down at the slowly healing red and purple scars across his fingers and palms, and with a grin, bent his hands into claws. "Oh no! It's taking me over." He deepened his voice and continued speaking, but with a growl to his words. "I'm becoming a monster."

Mac extended his arms and lurched forward like Frankenstein's creature. "Must have woman!"

Mary found the humor in Mac's joke and played along, giving a little scream, then running from him to shelter behind the couch. "Will no one save me?" she cried.

She pretended to swoon and fell backward into Mac's waiting arms. He caught her and held her tight as she lay in his steady grasp. Slowly she opened one eye then the other. She reached up, wrapping her arms around his neck, saying nothing; letting the embrace speak for her.

"I love you, Mary."

Before she could respond, there was a knock at the door. Knowing what it meant, the young couple quickly disengaged from each other, straightened up, and Mary wiped what was left of the happy tears from her face.

After a respectful moment, the door opened and Billy bounded in, followed closely by Reg. "I would have stayed out a little longer, but the bitter cold got to poor old Billy, and after he did his business, he wanted to come straight home." He rubbed the labrador's neck. "I'm going to have to trade you in, old boy, and get a new doggy that works better."

Mac and Mary laughed, and Billy looked up at his master with big eyes as he waited for the treat he knew would come soon.

"I am glad I got back before you left, Mac. I have something for you." Reg walked over to the fireplace and lifted down a small wooden box sitting there. "I thought you might want this. I was given it for surviving a battle."

Reg opened the lid of the sealed box. Inside, against a velvet background, was a gold cross attached to a purple ribbon.

"I don't have much use for it these days, with my soldiering long behind me, so I wanted to pass it on to you. It was my lucky charm and helped keep me safe, so it should do the same for you." He took it out from the box and held up the medal by its purple ribbon. "I know you can't wear it, being a Yank and all, but hopefully you can carry it with you. Maybe stick it in your pocket, for good luck."

Mac took the medal and stared at it, dumbstruck. "This is a Victoria Cross."

The old soldier reacted as if he was being told something he didn't know. "Well, I'll be. So it is!"

"This is the British Empire's highest award for valor." Mac searched his memory. "Not many have been given out. I think maybe only fifteen hundred have ever been awarded."

"Eleven hundred and sixty-one, actually. But who's counting?" answered Reg.

"I'm honored you'd want me to have your medal. But I really can't take it. It's too special to be a gift."

"Then look at it as a loan. Return it to me when the war's over and you've kicked Jerry's ass. That way, you'll have to come home here to my little girl."

Mac nodded. "That I'll do, and under those conditions I'll take it and carry it proudly. You'll get it back, I swear." He stared down at the precious medal lying in his hands. "This has been quite a night. I can't wait to see you both again in about a week when the exercises are over."

"Yes, but don't expect me to give you any more medals."

They both laughed at Reg's dry humor.

"Thank you, si –" Mac caught himself, "Reg. I have to go now. I can let myself out."

"Nonsense, boy. My granddaughter would never forgive me if she didn't have a final moment or two with you. Make sure you put your warmest coat on, my love, when you go outside with your suitor; it's cold enough to freeze the bollocks off a brass monkey."

Bundled up against the bitter nighttime temperature, Mac and Mary stood outside the cottage, inches apart, not wanting to say goodnight or goodbye.

"I'm going to miss you this week." Mary's sad eyes made her words ring true.

"I wish I could sneak out again and see you, but from what I hear, we'll be on the boats the whole time, night and day, and with this kind of chill in the air, it'll be tough for a lot of the boys who aren't used to the sea."

"Don't worry too much about them, I need you to try to stay warm. I don't want you coming down with pneumonia or anything like that."

"I won't."

"You better not. And thanks for the drawings of the boat-"

Mac interrupted her. "You should start by using her name, because one day you'll have her for your own, I promise."

"I do believe you, Mac. Thank you for the pictures of Mary's Dream. I love them."

"And Mary, I love you."

Mary stiffened, hearing those words. Mac picked up on her change of mood.

"Did I say something wrong?"

"No. Nothing wrong. Everything you said was perfect. I hope..." she struggled to find the right thing to say. "I hope you'll still love me."

"What do you mean, still love you? How could I not?"

"Because..." She held her hands to her face, covering her eyes, dreading this moment that she knew had to arrive. "Because I have something for you, but I don't know if you'll want it."

"I don't understand. What wouldn't I want that you could give me?"

She looked him straight in his eyes, both fear and excitement playing across her face. "I'm carrying our baby."

It was Mac's turn to fall silent. He stared at Mary in shock, and could only parrot her words back to her.

"You're carrying our baby?"

Mary nodded.

"Our baby?"

She hung her head in guilt.

"Our baby!"

Mac reached out, grabbing Mary, pulling her in tight against him.

"Our baby."

He kissed her again and again on her lips and cheeks.

"You're happy?"

Mac threw his head back and laughed aloud. "Happy is hardly the word I'd use. I'd need a dictionary to find the right one. Can we start with thrilled? Over the moon?" He kissed her again. "Thank you."

Mary sighed, and Mac felt her body relax in his arms. "I wasn't sure how you'd take it."

"I hope I didn't disappoint you." He smiled before becoming serious. "Have you told your grandpa yet?"

"I wanted to tell you first."

Mac's excitement built back up again. "Should we go inside and tell Reg now?"

Mary stiffened. "Now? Heavens no! Not tonight. I have to work up the courage to do that."

"Then we'll do it together as soon as I get back. Not a minute later."

Mary tilted her head, still uncertain how her crusty old granddad would take being told there would be a new addition to the household.

"Be strong, Mary, it'll be fine. And Mary's Dream will be a great wedding present for you."

"Wedding?" Mary hadn't expected to hear that word tonight. "Hold on, soldier, no need to rush things. We'll talk about that the next time I see you." She planted a firm kiss on his lips. "Now be off with you, and make sure you're careful, you've got two people waiting for your return." She patted her stomach.

Mac grinned. "I will, and don't worry, it's only more exercises. I can't wait to make plans with you afterwards."

With a spring in his step, the exhilarated father-to-be was swallowed by the night.

SUPREME HEADQUARTERS
ALLIED EXPEDITIONARY FORCE
G-3 DIVISION

SHAEF/23036/8/trg   19 April 1944

Subject: Exercise Tiger.
To:

       1. Exercise TIGER will involve the concentration, marshalling and embarkation of troops in the TORBAY - PLYMOUTH areas, and a short movement by sea under the control of the U.S. Navy, disembarkation with Naval and Air support at SLAPTON SANDS, a beach assault using service ammunition, the securing of a beachhead and a rapid advance inland.

       2. Major troop units are the VII Corps Troops, 4th Infantry Division, the 101st and 82nd Airborne Divisions, 1st Engineer Special Brigade, Force "U" and supporting Air Force units.

       3. During the period H-60 to H-45 minutes, fighter-bombers attack inland targets on call from the 101st AB Div and medium bombers attack three targets along the beach. Additional targets will be bombed by both fighter-bombers and medium bombers on call from ground units. Simulated missions will also be flown with the target areas marked by smoke pots.

       4. Naval vessels fire upon beach obstacles from H-50 to H-hour. Smoke may be used during the latter part of the naval bombardment both from naval craft by 4.2" chemical mortars and at H-hour by planes, if weather conditions are favourable. Naval fire ceases at H-hour.

       5. The schedule of the exercise is as follows:

	22 April	Move to marshalling area commences.
D-Day	27 April	101st AB Div simulates landing. Preparatory Bombardment by air and navy. Assault landing And advance of 4th Div.
	28-29 April	Advance of 4th Div & 101st AB Div continues. 82nd AB Div simulates landing, secure and holds Objective. (Exercise terminates on 29 April)

                                         W.R. Pierce
                                         Colonel, G.S.C.
                                         Chief, Training, Sub-section

TOP SECRET
This paper must not be taken out of this Headquarters except as Laid down in Para. 27, SHAEF Inter-Division Security Regulations Dated 9 February 1944.

Actual memo from SHAEF - Supreme Headquarters Allied Expeditionary Force – now declassified

CHAPTER FOURTEEN
Exercise Tiger

A public address system had been set up so the six thousand men; soldiers, sailors, and Rangers, could clearly hear the words of their base commander, Brigadier General Walters, as he addressed his assembled troops.

"At ease, men. This morning marks the start of a multi-day exercise and full combat live-fire rehearsal for the upcoming invasion. It will combine our air, land and sea forces, and those of the British Royal Navy who are adding their strength to protect our vessels. You will be spending several days on board our ships to prepare you for the channel crossing we will have to make and any prolonged delays we may encounter due to inclement weather. You might find this uncomfortable, but believe me, it is very important to get you ready so we can put an end to this war, drive the fascists from their occupation of Europe, and all go home. As to when and where the real battle will begin, we still do not know, but when it does start, I want you to be confident you can handle anything awaiting you. And after all this is over, you'll be able to finally speak of it to your families and say, I was there from the very beginning and took part in what has been designated Exercise Tiger, which got us ready to return to France and kick some Nazi ass."

April 26th, 1944 – 7pm GMT

The rain sliced down, driven by a bitter easterly wind pushing five-foot swells into the side of LST 289, rolling the huge ship.

Mac worked his way along the second level, passing where the troop transport trucks were stored, holding onto the siderails for safety, careful with every step to guard against the pitching deck. The smell of vomit mixing with salt water assailed his nostrils.

Ahead, a group of men struggled with the securing straps on one of the GMC Jimmys. Ricky oversaw their efforts.

"How is it down here?"

Ricky turned from the work to his friend. "How do you think it is? It sucks. Half my squad can't get out of their bunks, they're so sick. And they aren't faking it, you should see the color of their faces. If this keeps up, they'll be more puke on the decks than vehicles."

"There is some good news, Ricky. The latest MET report says the wind will be dropping and the swell starting to lay down by midnight."

"Great. Just another five hours of throwing up on the vomit vessel. And everyone is frozen. What with this damn rain and the constant spray from these waves, it's impossible to stay dry or warm."

Mac took in Ricky's heavy soaked overcoat. "When you're done with these trucks, have the men change out of their wet gear. I don't need pneumonia killing them or you." He tried putting on a brave face. "It'll be better later. I've got to make my report."

As Mac left, Ricky turned to his men. "You heard the supervising sergeant. The quicker we secure these trucks, the quicker we can get some warm clothes on. But no skimping your work. I want every one of these vehicles fueled, loaded, and ready to roll at a moment's notice."

Mac continued his cautious pace as he reached the steps leading up to the bridge at the stern of the pitching boat. Using both hands on the rails, he made his way into the control center of the LST. The glass enclosed wheelhouse glowed red from the overhead lighting, designed to assist the crew's night vision. Lieutenant Commander Rogers heard Mac enter and turned expectantly to him. "What's the word, sergeant?"

"The beachmaster reports that all support units are ready, sir. The transport squad is rechecking the securing restraints on the Jimmys, because of this swell."

"As they should. With these kinds of seas, even the tanks will be pulling against their holding chains and shifting position below decks. But we've got good men doing a good job. However, I need more than that from you, sergeant. We've been standing offshore, freezing on this rust bucket for two days and nights. Going nowhere, doing nothing, just eating, shitting, and trying to get a few hours sleep. And judging by the smell, puking everywhere. How are they holding up? That's what I want to hear."

Mac drew in a deep breath. "They're uncomfortable, sir, but they understand."

"So, no bitching or moaning?"

"Oh yes, sir. Plenty of that, but really, no more than usual. They're not sailors, they're soldiers. They want to know when they're going to be back on land and seeing some action."

"Then I have good news for them. While you were making your rounds, we received a dispatch from base command. The unified exercises are ready. The landings start tomorrow at O-six-thirty to secure the beach. Then the next day it'll be our turn to go ashore with the trucks and tanks for armored support. That means only two more nights on LST 289."

"That's good news indeed, sir. The landing exercises will take their minds off the cold, and the prospect of getting off the boat is all they need to know."

Lieutenant Commander Rogers grunted in approval. "I thought that would improve morale. I'm putting you in charge of sounding general quarters at O-six-hundred. I want everyone up for the initial beach landings. If the info HQ sent is correct, it should be a sight to see."

The first rays of the morning sun hit the LST, transforming its steel gray hull into a vivid gold, as the boat's klaxon unleashed an ear-splitting blast, signaling general quarters.

The ship exploded into action as men rushed to their assigned posts, many still pulling on their uniforms, but not allowing their disheveled dress to slow them from getting to their stations. As the klaxon's wail faded, a roar of engines took its place, causing the soldiers on deck turn their eyes upward to find where the sound was coming from. It didn't take long to locate the source. Above, the sky was blackened by countless aircraft, led by a series of protective squadrons of fighters and then followed by the planes they were there to escort, troop carriers, all crossing over the nearby shore. As they moved across the land, it seemed the larger planes were throwing out their cargo, as hundreds of black dots appeared from the side of the transports and dropped through the air. But then, each of those seeming dots had a stream appear behind it which snapped open into a circular shape. The 101st Airborne descended from above, drifting down as if suspended by silk mushrooms, ready to embark on their mission of freeing Europe.

Mac and Ricky stood on the upper deck taking in the action. Ricky shook his head, amazed. "We didn't have this much air support when we went into Sicily, and Tiger is only an exercise."

"You're right." Mac tried absorbing the amount of military force being brought into play. "When the real thing comes, it'll be even bigger. And not just-"

The thunder of naval guns drowned out Mac's words. He swiveled his eyes seaward and saw smoke rising from the huge guns of the six US destroyers and the Royal Navy cruiser floating halfway out to the horizon.

The shells screamed overhead, and Mac found himself holding his breath waiting for them to impact. Moments later, the center of Slapton Sands beach, almost a half mile of the shingled shoreline, erupted in plumes of red, white and blue smoke as they found their target.

Ricky yelled to be heard over the second volley. "Thank God they're only firing markers, or there would be nothing left for us to land on tomorrow."

More columns of smoke exploded across the beach, as the accuracy of the naval bombardment became evident. All around Ricky and Mac the watching soldiers cheered, hoping those same naval gunners would be there to support them when the day of the actual invasion arrived.

Ricky grinned. "The men are happy. This is better than the fourth of July. What with all these fireworks and the sea finally laying down, it's going to be a good day."

The navy guns fell silent, and in their absence another sound took over, the rumble of diesel engines being pushed to their limit. Fifty small landing craft, each carrying their full complement of thirty-six men, raced toward the pummeled shore. The fast-moving craft barreled through the waves, their blunt bows sending cascades of spray into the air, drenching the men huddled together inside the open boats. Six of the landing craft peeled away from the main body heading for the center of Slapton Sands, and instead set their course for the eastern edge of the beach, and the narrow strip of shingles below the cliffs.

"There go the Rangers." Ricky shook his head. "They must be freezing; they're getting soaked through. That could have been us, Mac."

Ricky's words resonated with him, causing Mac to involuntarily turn his eyes to his scarred hands. "Yes, it should have been."

He tore his gaze from his healing burns and watched as the Rangers stormed ashore under a hail of fire, launched their grappling hooks, and scrambled up the sheer face, disappearing over the top. Mac said nothing, but began counting slowly. He was about to reach two minutes when a tall column of yellow smoke appeared above the cliff.

"They've taken the guns."

"Already?" Ricky found their speed hard to believe.

"Already." Mac had no way to mask the disappointment ringing through his voice. "With the German guns neutralized, the center of the beach will be open. It'll be safe for the rest to go in."

He wasn't the only one to make that decision. Another eighty landing craft raced past their LST, heading to the shore, the men onboard knowing the deadly heavy machine guns entrenched in this part of Hitler's dreaded Atlantic Wall, guns which had the entire beach pre-sighted, leaving any attacking troops nowhere to find cover or safety, had been eliminated.

The two friends stood shoulder to shoulder and watched as the landing craft unloaded their human cargo and spun back around to get more assault squads who would make up the second wave.

The landed soldiers met limited resistance thanks to the naval shelling and the skill and courage of the Rangers, and fought hard to quickly mop up the pockets of fighters remaining. As they overwhelmed the surviving gun emplacements and groups of German soldiers along the beach, they too set off yellow flares. Soon, the entire shoreline was a mass of unbroken yellow smoke.

Ricky checked his watch. "It's not even eight. They took the whole damn thing in less than ninety minutes. If the real invasion goes like that, they'll land on the beaches after breakfast and be done in time for lunch."

The horns of the accompanying naval warships interrupted the friends' conversation again, signaling their victory salute to the American soldiers celebrating on the beach. And with that acknowledgement, the massive ships steered into a long turn to steam back to the shelter of Plymouth Naval Dockyard.

Photograph from April 27th, 1944. Observing the shelling at Slapton Sands

As the sirens marked the end of the exercise, a miraculous resurrection occurred and the GIs playing the thankless roles of the German defenders returned to life. They joined in on the celebration, knowing they had accomplished most of their work for the day, and after a detailed debriefing, good food, and possibly a beer or two, awaited them in the mess tents.

Mac was not in a celebratory mood. "They're done. Just us left out here to clean up and bring in the reinforcements when we go ashore tomorrow."

"You don't think they'll move everything ahead and let us off this damn boat today?"

He shook his head at Ricky's question. "That won't happen. When we do this for real, they need to be certain they can hold the beaches before the supplies and heavy equipment goes ashore. They'll have to rig a defensive line to make sure the Germans can't mount a successful counter attack. If they push us off the beaches and back into the sea, we're in big trouble."

"So, we wait here?"

"That's about it."

"Look on the bright side, we might be sick, cold and bored, but at least we're safer on this tub."

"Yes, safer." Mac reached into his pocket and took out Reg's Victoria Cross. "I guess I won't be needing this good luck charm for a while."

Ricky stared at the medal. "What is that?"

"It's something Mary's grandfather gave me. He said it would keep me safe. But the navy and Rangers are taking care of that, with me stuck out here, away from the action."

Ricky moved closer, his eyes widening. "Shit, Mac, that's a Victoria Cross. I've heard about them but never seen one before. Can I hold it?"

"Sure." Mac handed it to his buddy.

Ricky took it, and at first simply stared at the famous medal resting in his palm, then, with a grin, he snapped to attention as if on a parade ground, and held the medal to his chest. He deepened his voice as he attempted to adopt the manner of an officer. "Awarded to Sergeant Ricky Esposito for valor above the call-"

His medal presentation ceremony was abruptly ended by the blare of the LST's loudspeaker. "Sergeant Harper, report to the bridge."

"Got to go. Sorry, buddy." Mac held out his hand.

Ricky reluctantly passed him the Victoria Cross. "Hey, can't blame a guy for dreaming."

"You'll get some more medals one day." Mac carefully put Britain's highest award for courage into his chest pocket and buttoned it up.

"Hopefully not posthumously."

Mac laughed as he took off to answer his summons.

Lieutenant Commander Rogers was briefing his radio operator as Mac entered the bridge. He met his commanding officer with a salute.

"You called for me, sir?"

"Yes. At ease, sergeant. HQ is happy with the completion of day one of our live-fire exercises and wants to step things up. Later tonight, all eight LSTs from Force U have been ordered to form a convoy, designated T-4, and leave Slapton Sands and steam to Torbay where we will rendezvous with two Royal Navy warships who will then sail with us and act as our protective screen. At that point, we'll be in Lyme Bay. There, we'll continue on twenty-four more miles before turning around and returning to Slapton. This is to simulate our sixty-mile channel crossing for the big day. When we get back, we will beach and disembark the trucks and tanks as scheduled, to complete day number two of the invasion. Once the ships are empty and the remaining troops and vehicles are ashore, that will conclude Exercise Tiger."

"Sounds straightforward, sir. Shall I tell the men this so they'll know what's happening when the engines fire up?"

"Exactly, sergeant. And one other thing. Along with the orders for the convoy, word came in from the top brass that they are changing our radio frequencies at O-twenty-two hundred hours tonight, so make sure all radios in the trucks and tanks are switched otherwise no one will be able to communicate when they disembark, and we'll have a real mess on our hands."

"O-twenty-two hundred hours, sir? We normally set the new frequencies at O-five-thirty hours. That's seven and a half hours early."

"When the invasion comes, nothing will be normal. Maybe Ike and Winston think the Nazis know when we do our frequency change so they're switching it up to keep them guessing. I don't know why, it's above my pay grade. But whatever the reason, it's O-twenty-two hundred hours, tonight."

"Yes, sir."

Rogers took out a manilla envelope and pulled a sheet of paper from it containing a series of numbers. "These are the new frequencies they came up with. Make sure all the appropriate radio operators have them, and they are aware of the start time to initiate them."

"Will do, sir."

"And Sergeant Harper, I'd like you on the bridge tonight by twenty-three hundred hours." His tone became warmer. "It would be good to have another sailor beside me as we start our long steam. At the speed these floating bricks move, it's going to take us the best part of eight hours to complete the sixty miles."

"I'll be here, sir." Mac saluted and left the bridge holding the paper.

It was an hour before midnight, and the soldiers assigned to LST 289 were sleeping, or trying to sleep. After three full days on the boat, exhaustion had set in, and they were sprawled wherever they could find space, wrapped in sleeping bags for protection against the cold. Meanwhile, on the lower decks, others huddled in the back of trucks, attempting to ignore the uncomfortable wood planks making up the base of the GMC Jimmys' cargo area.

Mac was not sleeping, he'd caught a few hours of quiet time that afternoon, but he had an appointment with his commanding officer who'd called him a sailor. He could not ignore the invitation or the flattering comment which had stayed with him throughout the day. He entered the bridge a few minutes before his prearranged time.

APRIL 27th – 11 pm GMT

"Glad to see you, son. We could use your young eyes about now."

Mac looked at the LST's captain curiously. "What for, sir?"

"We can't locate our escort. The Brits sent us a message about three hours ago that one of their two ships, the destroyer, wouldn't be making the rendezvous with us. Apparently, it sustained some kind of damage in port. Another boat collided with it when they were leaving dock and they had to return for repairs."

"How about the other ship, sir? You said there'd be two."

"That's the thing, Sergeant Harper, it's not out there. We left on schedule and were expecting them to meet us between Torquay and Slapton, and accompany us from there on, but nothing. Since then, we've been going back and forth, stalling for time and hailing the Brits on the radio but getting no response. We can't keep going nowhere if we are to meet our schedule and be back for the beach landings in the morning."

The concern in Lieutenant Commander Rogers' voice was obvious, and Mac had to ask. "Will we be continuing on without the Royal Navy's shield?"

"We have to. This is the final night of the exercise. Everybody else has done their part; marines, infantry, airborne, rangers, and now it's our turn, and if we screw up, we'll be the laughingstock of the armed forces. So, we're changing plans slightly and staying closer to land and not steaming as far in one direction. Just going back and forth between Torbay and Slapton a few times; it'll still give us the same distance we need to simulate a crossing. But we have to find that damn boat, without naval cover we're naked out here. You're looking for a Corvette Class ship, the H.M.S. Azalea. How the limeys came up with a name like that for a warship is beyond me; it sounds like a goddamn floating flower. Grab a pair of glasses and sweep the horizon, there's a two-day pass waiting for you if you can spot her before our radio operators can raise the Azalea."

"Yes, sir!" Mac found it hard to conceal his excitement. It had been five days since he'd last seen Mary; to have two full days with her after he returned from the exercise would be an unexpected gift. A pass was all the motivation he needed to begin his scanning of the dark ocean to try to find the missing escort.

Mac was unaware there were two pairs of distant eyes already trained on him. Six miles away, on top of the cliffs at Slapton's north-eastern edge, Mary and Mrs. Northcott stared out at the convoy of the eight massive LSTs.

"I think they're leaving now," said Mary.

"Goodness gracious, it's about time. They've been going around in circles for the last two hours. It must be bloody freezing out there. Can you make out which ship your lover boy's on?"

Mary couldn't help but smile at the old lady's words. "Yes, he's on the one marked 289. You can see the big white numbers on the side."

"With my eyes? Give me a minute." Mrs. Northcott reached for her own pair of binoculars on the small folding table between them and raised the glasses to her face. "Yes, I can see it now. Oh, and there he is. I think he's waving at you."

"You can see him?" Mary jolted upright and strained her eyes at the huge boat.

"Don't be daft. Of course I can't. Even with these binocs, it's all I can do to make out the blooming numbers."

"Well, Mac's out there on the ship, I know that."

"And you're up here, watching over him, like his guardian angel."

On board the watched ship, calls continued to go out for the missing escort. "H.M.S. Azalea, this is Force U. Come in. H.M.S. Azalea, this is Force U with convoy T-4. Come in please." The sailor making the pleas shook his head as his transmission remained unanswered.

Unknown to the persistent radio operator, although he was getting no reply, his words were not going unheard. However, the recipient of the ongoing broadcast was not the British radio operator on the Azalea he was trying to reach, but a communication specialist crouched over a large receiver, carefully moving his rotary dial up and down, looking for traffic on the Allies' frequency bands. As he locked in on LST 289's signal, he sat up abruptly and increased the volume in his headphones to confirm what he was hearing. He listened as the words rang out again, noting the urgency in the operator's voice, and realized their importance.

The transmission repeated a third time and he knew this was what they had been looking for, and perhaps even more than they had hoped to come across. He straightened his grey uniform, creased from hours of being hunched in his cramped quarters, searching the radio dial for contacts, and checked his collar was done up and his iron cross in place. It was important to look good, because if this proved to be as momentous as he thought, it could earn him a long overdue leave to return to see his family in Berlin.

"Mein Kapitän," he called out, his shouted words grabbing the attention of the three other occupants of the E-Boat's crowded bridge, "Komm schnell her – *come here quickly*."

The captain of the hunter-killer warship spun around, annoyed at the tone of voice a junior officer had used to address him. To be spoken to like that, especially in front of other crew members, was a violation of protocol and swift disciplinary action should be taken. "Was ist es? – *What is it?*" he barked.

"Kapitän, ich habe einen Funkkontakt – *I have a radio contact.*"

"Was? Ist es Deutch oder englisch? – *Is it German or English?*"

"Hören Sie. Der Funkspruch kommt von einem amerikanischen Schiff, aber sie suchen nach einem britischen Kriegsschiff. – *Listen. The radio broadcast is from an American ship, they are looking for a British warship.*"

"Das Boot hat keinen Schutz? – *The boat has no protection?*"

"Kapitän, es ist nicht nur ein Boot und sie haben einen Namen: Force U, Konvoi T-4. – *Captain, it's not just one boat and they have a name: Force U, convoy T-4.*"

The German captain jerked forward, grabbing the headphones from the radio operator and pulling them on to listen to the broadcast repeating. After seconds, he slammed down the headphones. "Mein Gott! Es ist ein amerikanischer Konvoi! – *My God! It's an American convoy!*" He fixed his burning gaze on the radio operator, excitement raising his voice almost to a yell. "Finden Sie den Standort der Signale. – *Find the location of the signal!*"

"Jawohl, Kapitän. – *Yes, captain.*"

Sensing what could be awaiting them, the captain called to the other two men on the bridge, "Alarmieren Sie die Besatzung. Laden Sie die Torpedorohre. Motoren auf Höchstgeschwindigkeit vorbereiten. Alle Mann auf Gefechtsstation. Alle Schiffe werden jetzt zur englischen Küste auslaufen! – *Alert the crew. Load the torpedo tubes. Prepare the motors for maximum speed. All hands to battle stations. All ships will leave for the English coast now!*"

The captain's orders were passed to the other waiting E-Boats in the attack fleet hungrily patrolling the waters off of Cherbourg, France. The battle-hardened crews, used to their nightly missions of intercepting and sinking unwary ships in the English Channel, took their positions and readied for combat.

Moving as one, the flotilla of the nine E-Boats set course toward the English coast, only fifty miles away, hoping to quickly lock in the exact location of the unprotected American convoy.

The Kapitän's voice blasted through on the radio to all boats. "Volle Kraft voraus, flankieren! – *Full speed ahead, flank!*"

As their highly tuned engines roared to maximum revs, generating a top speed of fifty-five miles per hour, the bows of the one hundred and fourteen foot, heavily armed boats, painted steel grey to camouflage them against the murky sea, leaped from the water and the boats raced north, as they began their mission to search and destroy.

Onboard the flagship, *Schnellboot S-136*, the kapitän checked the gauges and controls; everything showed green. He nodded in satisfaction at the incredible German engineering and intricate machinery which made his boat one of the most dangerous and effective weapons of the war. At this speed, they should be across the channel and closing in on their unsuspecting targets in less than sixty minutes.

He knew the British and Americans called them E-Boats, but never understood the designation. Did *E* stand for enemy? Stupid, he thought, they should have kept our German name for these amazing ships, *Schnellboot – Fast*

Boat – after all, there was nothing faster than his flotilla on any ocean, anywhere in the world. And after tonight, the Americans would know there was nothing deadlier either, not after he had sunk their ships with his torpedoes and his deck guns, the devastating forty mm Bofors cannon at the stern and the thirty-seven mm on the bow. He had seen many times how effective that armament was, and the combination of exploding flak rounds and armor-piercing shells had sent numerous cargo ships to their final resting places on the sea floor without even having to waste a torpedo. What would be his weapon of choice tonight, he wondered? With a grin, he thought he should delay his decision until the mysterious, unprotected American convoy came into sight; maybe he would start with a torpedo then strafe the enemy decks with the Bofors as the ship sank. Whatever he chose, he knew the results would be the same; triumph for the Fatherland and death for the Americans.

The movement of the truck bed woke Ricky from his restless dreams. He stirred in his sleeping bag and stared at the intruder. "Where have you been?"

"On the bridge," answered Mac.

Ricky checked his watch. "It's after one. They needed you up there all this time? I thought we were just sailing back and forth?"

"We are. They had me looking for some British boat that's not there."

"What's that mean?"

"Our escort. The Brits are meant to be giving our LST convoy protection, but we can't find them, or maybe they can't find us. Either way, I couldn't spot them and the radio operator couldn't raise them."

"Perhaps they're sleeping, like I was before you woke me."

"That's a good idea. If you'll move over, I'll grab some shuteye. We'll all need to be alert for the beaching and unloading in the morning."

With those words, Mac unrolled his waiting blankets and stretched out next to his friend.

"I see them!" Mary's excited voice rang out, shattering the quiet night. She turned the central focus dial on her binoculars hoping to get a better look at the ships and spot the one carrying Mac. "They're coming back into the bay."

"I see them too." Mrs. Northcott was happy for her companion, remembering how the thrill of young love felt.

Mary lowered her binoculars and saw the elderly woman staring out to sea. "You don't have to humor me, Mrs. Northcott."

"What do you mean, love?"

"You're looking the wrong way, to the south. They're coming from over there, from the east."

"East, west. I never know which is which."

"From your left, Mrs. Northcott. They must have passed Brixham and Dartmouth and now they are heading back to Slapton."

"Well, if that's them over there, what boats am I looking at?" She pointed straight out to the channel.

Mary sat up straight, her instincts telling her something was very wrong. She swung her binoculars in the direction Mrs. Northcott indicated and saw the heavy white foam kicked up by the fast-moving flotilla. She estimated they were eight miles out, due south, on the far side of the bay. Mary strained her eyes trying to make out any names, numbers or details, then gasped as she focused in on the red, black and white ensign flying in the wind behind the boats, the swastika in the center of the flag telling her all she needed to know. "My God, they're German E-Boats!"

"They can't be, my love. The Yanks wouldn't keep sailing toward them if they were."

"But they don't know they're coming." Panic riddled Mary's voice. "They are too far away on the other side of the bay and can't see them from sea level. We can see them because we're between them and so high up here. By the time the Americans spot the German boats they'll be so close..." Her words trailed off.

"But the Yanks should be fine. Their ships are much bigger than the Krauts. They wouldn't dare attack them."

"No. Don't you understand? The American ships don't have any real guns. They're troop transports, not battleships. It doesn't matter how big they are if they can't fight back."

"Then who'll protect them if the Germans attack?"

Mary grabbed the battery powered signal light lying between them and flipped it on.

"What are you doing, love?"

"My job." Mary shook with fear. "I pray I can remember my morse code."

"I'll get the book out." Mrs. Northcott reached into her bag for the code guide. By the time she had located the little red book, Mary was already flashing her light.

"Come on, come on. Please see it." She beamed the flashes down the coast. "Please, please."

"There's a return light, Mary." Mrs. Northcott pointed at a hilltop six miles further down. "That's the Coastal Watch at Start Point."

"They see us. All right. I have to think. Enemy ships approaching. German E-Boats. Send help." She worked the shutters on the light, sending out the coded message. "I hope they understand and relay it quickly. I'll keep repeating it so they know it's urgent."

Standing watch at the edge of Slapton Sands' long beach, a sentry on duty spotted the light flashing on the hill and turned to his partner.

"See that?"

"Yes. Someone's signaling. Can you understand what they're saying?"

"A little. I haven't done morse code since the boy scouts, but I think it says something about *enemy ships*. Go get a couple of men and send them up there to check what's going on; I'll alert the captain of the watch."

"But he'll be sleeping."

"Then I'll wake him up. Snap to it."

The two soldiers hurried to carry out their individual tasks.

On the hilltop, Mary paused her signals as she tried deciphering the return flashes. She scrawled down the sequence of dots and dashes she was seeing, then turned to the codebook to check her findings.

"Come on, luvey. What does it say?" Mary's urgency had infiltrated Mrs. Northcott's words.

"They got our message. Now they'll pass it on to the watch at Bigbury, because they have radios there. They'll probably call the naval base in Plymouth."

"And they'll be able to send help?"

"Yes. Our whole navy is there. I'll keep signaling just in case."

The sentry raced along the narrow street leading into the village and the stone buildings housing the officers, and without waiting to catch his breath, pounded on the old wooden door again and again. Finally, it creaked open and the annoyed captain of the watch stood there, fuming at being woken from his sleep.

"Do you know what time it is?"

"Yes, sir. Almost two in the morning. That's why I'm here. There's signaling happening on top of the cliffs."

The captain stepped through the door and saw the flashing light. "It's freezing out here. Who's sending the signals?"

"The Coastal Watch civilians, I think. I've sent some men to make sure."

"Good. See what they find out, and put it in your report in the morning." He turned to go back inside.

"Sir, it's what the flashes are saying that's concerning. It's why I came here now and didn't wait."

"And what does it say?"

"My morse code is rusty, sir, but I'm pretty sure the message says there are German ships approaching."

"And did you look for German ships?"

"Yes, sir."

"Did you see any?"

"No, sir. But...."

The captain took two steps from his requisitioned home and stared across Slapton's long bay. Four miles away he could see the unmistakable dark shapes of the first of the massive LSTs returning from their night time voyage. "Those are our boats out there completing Exercise Tiger. Jerry doesn't have anything like an LST. Typical limeys, they don't know their ass from their face. A ship goes sailing by at night and they panic. It's nothing."

"Shall I have the radar sweep the bay for enemy boats in case there is anything we're not seeing?"

"Corporal, the nearest German port is sixty miles from here, on the other side of the channel. We need our radar to watch for planes not imaginary ships. Keep it skyward, that's where the enemy would come from. Look what happened in Plymouth a couple of months ago." He stared again at the insistent signals continuing from the clifftop and scoffed. "Good job we're here to save these scared Brits, or they'd all be eating sauerkraut by Christmas. I'm going back to bed to try to get warm." He turned on his heels and went inside his comfortable house, shutting the door on the troubled sentry.

ROYAL NAVAL HEADQUARTERS - PLYMOUTH
APRIL 28th, 1:51 a.m.

Even in the early hours of that Friday morning in 1944, the regional headquarters of the British Royal Navy overseeing Devonport Dockyard and the Allied fleets sheltering in Plymouth's vast natural harbor was a hive of activity. Four officers hovered around a large glass table representing the positions of the warships of the fleets, while two other naval personnel and six assistants checked the status of military and naval ports stretching across the south coast of England, including Southampton, Portsmouth, and Dover.

The entry door into this secured area opened, and a breathless runner was escorted inside by a burly armed guard who kept one hand firmly gripping the messenger's shoulder and his other ready on his holstered pistol.

"I need to speak with the commander." The messenger's voice shattered the concentration of the officers in the top-secret room and tore their attention away from their jobs to this unexpected intruder.

A white-haired man in his late fifties, with a kaleidoscope of medals across his chest, stepped from the planning table. "I'm the officer in command of the room. Do you have an appointment here?"

"I didn't have time to go through channels or appointments. I have an urgent message for you."

The guard pulled on the man's arm. "That's '*sir*', to you."

"No, go ahead, let him speak," the ranking officer ordered.

"Thank you. I'm with Coastal Watch. We've received a message from up the coast. They've spotted German E-Boats, and they are approaching an American convoy off of Slapton Sands."

"E-Boats? Do we have any confirmation on this?" The commander looked around the room and was met with blank stares. "And what American ships are sailing off Slapton at this time of night?"

A junior lieutenant stepped forward. "That would be convoy T-4 carrying Force U. Eight LSTs make up the main body of the convoy. They're part of-"

"Right, Exercise Tiger. They're bringing the support troops and transport ashore. It's scheduled for later this morning, correct?"

The lieutenant nodded in agreement.

"Have the Yanks been notified about the E-Boats?" The commander was now fully aware of the seriousness of what was unfolding.

"I have no way of knowing, sir. Coastal Watch are not allowed radios in the occupied area of South Hams the Americans are using as their base. This came in by signal light and morse code." The concern in the messenger's voice almost overwhelmed his words.

"Then we had better take over now and hail them as quickly as we can. They might be out there thinking the E-Boats are part of the live-fire exercises they've been going through the past two days."

"That's a problem, sir."

The base commander stared at his junior aide. "What is? Spit it out, lieutenant."

"We've been trying to raise the Americans aboard T-4 for almost four hours. They haven't responded to any of our messages."

"Are they running under radio silence?"

"We don't think so. We were in constant communication with them until O-twenty-two hundred hours, then nothing."

"Nothing? What do you mean by that?"

"It was as if they switched their radios off."

"Could they have changed frequencies early?"

"It's possible, sir, but we have no way of knowing."

"Can't we try the new frequencies; see if they are on them already?"

"No, because the frequency change isn't scheduled until O-five-thirty, another three and a half hours from now. We won't receive the new frequencies until O-five hundred, when they are sent by messenger pouch from Whitehall. The Americans get their frequencies from Ike's headquarters in London, completely separate to our boys. If they took it on themselves to switch early, then we have no way of knowing what they are or how to reach them, and we'll remain in the dark for a few more hours."

"Damn it. There must be something we can do. Aren't we running a protective screen for them? I remember at least two escorts being designated for Force U."

"Correct, sir, but unfortunately there was a problem with one of the boats this afternoon, before you came on duty. H.M.S. Scimitar was putting to sea and collided with another vessel and sustained considerable damage to her bow, so she had to return to dock."

"Was a substitute sent to replace the Scimitar?"

"No, sir. It wasn't deemed necessary. There's only the Azalea out there."

"I know that boat. Her pennant number is…" The commander searched his memory, "K-25. I've met her captain, George Geddes. He came to my son's wedding, he's a good man. Radio the Azalea, tell them to stay close to Force U and expect contact from the E-Boats anytime now."

The lieutenant stuttered as he again had to break more bad news to his superior officer. "We can tell the Azalea about the E-Boats but she can't stay close to the convoy, sir."

"For God's sake, why not?"

"She hasn't been able to find them. They should have rendezvoused off of Berry Head and continued sailing on past Torquay into Lyme Bay, but they weren't there. She's been searching for them ever since. After three hours, the Azalea widened her search pattern and began to backtrack. Right now, we have her position as halfway between Start Point and Plymouth. About twenty-two miles from the eastern side of Slapton Sands."

"Jesus H. Christ, when will this end?" The commander paced back and forth, collecting his thoughts. "Radio the Azalea, bring them up to date on the situation. Tell them to go to battle stations right now and find the Americans at all costs. Start sending up flares to get the convoy's attention. If they see anything that looks like an E-Boat attack happening, to steam for it at flank speed and engage the enemy immediately. And let Commander Geddes know if he doesn't blow at least one of his boilers getting there, he'll have me to answer to. Do we have any other ships we can send to help?"

"H.M.S. Saladin is patrolling the eastern end of Lyme Bay, near Poole in Dorset. We could order her in, but it would be a good two hours before she reaches Slapton, sir."

"Send her anyway; we have to do something. And get me RAF Exeter on the line now. We need to scramble a squadron of Hurricanes and have them in the air. Someone's got to get to the Yanks and help those poor bastards before it's too late."

Mary stood on her tiptoes, hoping to gain an extra few inches and find a better vantage point as she strained her eyes through the binoculars pressed tightly to her face. "They're still sailing toward the Germans. They should have spotted them by now, unless they think it's part of their exercise."

Mrs. Northcott lowered her glasses and put her arm around the young girl in a gesture of support. "Perhaps it's because the Jerries have turned their engines off and are just floating out there. They won't be able to hear them or see their white wake anymore. Maybe they're thinking about going back to France and not doing anything."

"That won't happen." Mary shook her head. "When have the Germans not attacked when they had the chance? Never! I think they're planning which of the ships to go after first, and letting our boys come to them."

Two distant flares appeared in the sky, interrupting Mrs. Northcott's reply, and both women swung their glasses toward the burning lights.

"There's a battleship out there, right on the horizon. But it's so far away. It'll take forever to get here."

"But at least they're coming, my love, at least they're coming." She hugged Mary. "They got your signal."

The bridge of the H.M.S. Azalea was crammed with uniformed personnel, their naval whites turned crimson by the red night-time running lights.

"We've passed the headland and we're picking up convoy T-4 on our radar now, sir. I'm showing eight confirmed contacts, but there's also a number of smaller vessels about a mile from them that aren't moving, they seem to be just floating out there, observing."

Lieutenant Commander Geddes kept his eyes trained on the radar screen as he replied to the first lieutenant. "The big ones will be the American LSTs, and the smaller contacts, probably the damned E-Boats waiting and plotting their attack. The Yanks are sailing toward them in a straight line, one after the other, no zig-zagging, no attempt at evasion. They have no idea what's about to happen. They're sitting ducks. How long until we reach them?"

"We're fourteen miles from Start Point, and seven miles east-"

"I know our position, Goddamnit! I asked you how long until we're in a position to help the convoy and use our guns to engage the Germans?"

"At least an hour, sir, possibly longer with this headwind-"

"It won't be longer than an hour or I'll see that you and everyone in engineering is busted back to shore duty. Push her, lieutenant, push her. And send up more flares. Let them know we are coming."

APRIL 28th, 2:02 a.m.

A distant glow flickered across Mac's face, disturbing his short sleep. He sat up in the truck bed, staring at the fading flares.

Ricky felt his movement and reluctantly stirred. "What is it? Can't you sleep?"

"There are flares on the horizon. Looks like we may be starting the live-fire exercises early."

"Great." Ricky's voice told Mac it was anything but. He dug his head back into the rolled towel being used as a pillow. "They won't need the beachmaster until it's time to unload. Goodnight."

"Goodnight, Ricky." Mac started to lay back down but thought better of it and continued staring out to sea where a second set of flares arched skyward.

Onboard the lead E-Boat, S-136, Kapitän Bernard Mirbach also saw the flares on the horizon, but for him they instilled a new confidence, knowing their distance gave him time to execute his mission. "Es ist gut, dass die Briten uns wissen lassen, dass sie kommen, aber sie werden erst in einer Stunde oder später hier sein. Wir müssen unseren Angriff jetzt starten. – *It's good of the British to let us know they are coming, but they won't be here for an hour or more. We must start our attack now.*"

He looked at his men; they were as excited as he was to bring the war to the unsuspecting American convoy. "Funken Sie die Boote an, sagen Sie ihnen, dass ich den Angriff leiten und das erste Schiff einnehmen werde. Kampfstationen! – *Radio the boats, tell them I will lead the attack and take the first ship. Battle stations!*"

His crew of twenty-four sailors, hardened by four years of raids and battles in the English Channel and attacking exhausted convoys returning from their North Sea crossings, rechecked their life jackets and dimmed the cabin lights further. They knew what was expected of them and never failed to deliver. This was one of the reasons their flotilla was the pride of Germany's Kriegsmarine.

The massive engines of the E-Boat S-136 roared back to life, their pounding sending a familiar and welcome vibration through the floor of the bridge. Kapitän Mirbach rested his hand on the controls and grinned. "Die Amerikaner haben ein Sprichwort – *The Americans have a saying,*" He switched his words and spoke in heavily accented English to show off his language skills, "Who let the fox in with the chickens?" He returned to his native German as he slammed the throttle forward. "Ich bin der Fuchs! – *I am the Fox!*"

The bow of the E-Boat rose out of the water as it raced toward the unprotected convoy, reaching torpedo launch speed and bearing down on the side of the lead ship.

S-136 was four hundred yards from LST 507 and lined up dead amidships when the kapitän threw the pair of red *fire* switches.

There were two loud thuds as the twin twelve-foot-long torpedoes launched from the lethal craft toward the barely moving LST.

The kapitän wrenched the boat's wheel hard to the starboard and accelerated away to avoid the expected blast.

Onboard the crowded LST, the night watches heard the E-Boats but thought nothing of it, as they were back off of Slapton now, and expected to hear boat traffic in the bay as part of Exercise Tiger, and those speeding engines were fading and almost drowned out by the continuous heavy, low thump of the big inboard diesel drives pushing the landing ship's blunt bow through the cold waters. Instead, they carried out their duty of making sure there were no collisions between the American craft as the convoy kept their line consistent and evenly spaced. This was only a training maneuver after all, and they had been briefed the worst thing that could occur would be two of the ships running into each other. To prevent this, there were two lookouts with radios and warning lanterns posted at the bow, and two placed at the LST's stern watching aft, making sure the other ships kept to their assigned positions. On the morning hours of April 28th, none had been assigned to monitor the starboard or port beams on any of the LSTs.

Had there been a lookout there on duty, he would have noticed the two phosphorescent wakes cutting through the calm waters at sixty knots. However, due to the speed of their approach, there would have only been seconds for him to have reacted; barely time to shout a warning. Instead, the unseen torpedoes, running fifteen feet apart, each carrying eight hundred pounds of high explosive, slammed into the side of the unprepared vessel, detonating on contact, and sending flames, smoke and shards of twisted red-hot metal hundreds of feet into the air.

For the purposes of Exercise Tiger, LST 507 had been designated for troop and truck transport rather than tank support, the honor of carrying the heavy armored vehicles being given to two other LSTs in the convoy, LST 499 and LST 289.

As a result, 507's two lower decks were packed with GMC Jimmy trucks, all fully fueled and loaded for beach evac, their wooden sides and stretched canvas tops, a known fire risk. Because of this, smoking was forbidden on these decks, as it was thought just a spark could start a serious blaze. The torpedoes provided more than just a spark.

The blast hurled the trucks across the decks, crashing into each other, crushing any men trying to find a place to sleep there that night. As the wooden sides and tailgates splintered and gas tanks ripped open, the flames of the incendiary charges reached them and a second, even bigger explosion rocked the almost four-hundred-foot landing ship.

Before there was a chance to even sound an alarm, the six hundred and fifty soldiers on the upper, outside deck were thrown into the air as the boat heaved and convulsed, and came crashing down onto the unforgiving metal decks. Smoke and flames shot from the eight stairwells leading to the lower decks, making access impossible and graphically spelling out that anyone in those lower quarters was either already dead or being roasted alive with no chance of help or rescue getting to them.

As the shocked and stunned GIs tried to find their footing, the first announcement blared from the ship's P.A. system.

"Abandon ship. Grab your gear and abandon ship. This is not a drill."

Another series of explosions rang out from below decks stressing the urgency of the message, LST 507 was doomed, she was burning up and it was too late to fight or even slow down the fires consuming her.

The young soldiers heard the order but stood there, momentarily confused and unsure. They had been trained for combat, to expertly use guns, knives, and explosives. They had followed orders and learned how to fearlessly engage and attack their enemy, but one thing they had zero instruction on was what to do in the case of a sinking ship. How could they get off the boat when the aft decks were inaccessible because of the rapidly spreading blaze, and the sheer metal walls surrounding them on the forward part of the cavernous top deck reached up ten feet on either side?

The men followed the order that continued screaming from the P.A. speakers. They fought to remain calm as they pulled on their helmets, fastening the straps tightly under their chins as they had been shown how to do, slipped their backpacks into position, and slung their carbines over their shoulders.

A big sergeant flung rope webbing up and over the deck's wall and secured it quickly in place. Two more NCOs followed his lead and did the same on the other side. Now they had a way to climb up and get off the ship; they weren't trapped rats any longer.

"Life belts! Don't jump without them!" yelled the sergeant as he pulled open the waterproof chests running along the edge of the boat's hull. The men hurriedly lined up, and each took one of the solid rings, quickly realizing they had to put it on, rather than carry it, before attempting to climb the webbing and abandon the sinking LST. For all of these soldiers, it was their first time using a solid life ring and there were no instructions on how it should be used correctly.

With their backpacks in place, it was impossible to slip the ring over their heads, so the first of the boys stepped into it and pulled it up around his waist. It fit snugly against his bulging, gear-filled backpack, seemingly perfect. And it was perfect; the seemingly perfect way to drown.

With the life rings in position, the men climbed awkwardly but quickly up the rope meshing to the top of the hull's enclosing wall. They balanced there for a moment, nervous of the forty-three-foot vertical drop to the burning ocean below; a sea set on fire by gasoline pouring from the ruptured fuel tanks of the GMC Jimmys. But it was their only choice, and at least it was water waiting for them between the flames, and it gave them a chance to live. Staying onboard meant one of two certainties; they would either die in the rapidly approaching blaze or be dragged to the bottom with the ship when it sank, which they knew was coming in minutes.

The men jumped, one after another, into the darkness, trying to avoid the spreading patches of burning oil. But it wasn't the flaming sea that killed so many, dozens died immediately upon hitting the surface of the water; the impact from the wrenching fall forcing their tightly fastened metal helmets up and backwards so violently, the chin straps snapped their necks like a child breaking a pencil.

Those that survived the drop found themselves flipped upside down by the very thing they had pulled on to save them; their life ring. The ring was meant to be worn around the chests and under their shoulders to support the upper body and keep their heads out of the water. Pinned against the backpack, around their waists and lower body, it made them top heavy, a fact exasperated by the weight of the pack itself and the carbines slung over their shoulders. This off-balance teeter-totter flipped them backward, pushing their heads underwater and their legs into the air.

Many struggled in the dark, freezing water, trying to get the deadly ring off of them before it was too late. Some succeeded, two-hundred and two did not, and either drowned or died from hypothermia within ten minutes.

From four miles away, the heavily listing ship was lit by the fuel-fed flames consuming it from within and the blazing ocean surrounding its hull. Bodies filled the burning water, some fighting to stay afloat while others struggled in their death throes, as an evil twist of fate meant they either died from being burned alive or from cold water shock caused by the freezing sea temperature. It was a scene of such horror, even Dante could not have imagined it. For the two civilians watching, it rendered them dumbstruck.

Shattering their silence, they saw, in the glow of the fires, the E-Boat flotilla reforming, and two of the deadly ships accelerating forward to carry out their next coordinated attack.

Mary managed to breathe three terrified words, "Oh, my God!"

Kapitän Mirbach led the two craft toward the convoy for their second strike. He called instructions on the radio to the other *Schnellboot*. "Ich habe vier Torpedos übrig. Ich werde das erste amerikanische Schiff mit meiner Bofors-Kanone angreifen, Sie nehmen das nächste mit Ihren Torpedos. – *I have four torpedoes left. I will attack the first American ship with my Bofors cannon, you take the next with your torpedoes.*"

"Ja, Kapitän," came the unquestioning reply.

The two E-Boats veered apart as they raced to find their targets.

Mac and Ricky crowded on the starboard gunwale of the deck with thirty other soldiers, staring open-mouthed at the catastrophe happening just half a mile from them.

"This isn't part of the exercise, not unless someone's fucked up big time."

Mac agreed with Ricky's words and added, "We have to launch our lifeboats and get ready to help the men in the water. If we don't get to them quickly, they'll die from the cold."

"If they're not dead already. What do you think it was, a sub or a mine?"

Mac saw the approaching wakes in the distance and knew the answer instantly. "E-Boats. And we're next."

Ricky saw them too, as did the rest of the GIs stretched along the deck's edge. At that moment the klaxon sounded for General Quarters.

"Spread the word. This is real, Ricky. Some of the men might still be thinking it's part of the live-fire exercises." Mac saw several of the soldiers hesitantly retrieving their carbines and raising them to a firing position. "We should get our rifles."

"What about the forty mils?" Ricky pointed to the heavy guns mounted at the bow and stern.

"They're anti-aircraft. Our gunners won't be able to angle them down low enough to use against a small, fast boat."

"Fubar, man, fubar."

"That's why we're gonna need our guns."

"Let's go get 'em, Mac."

The two friends spun around from the gunwale and ran back to the truck Ricky had used as an impromptu bed, to grab their M1s, stored there with the rest of their gear.

They didn't see the two E-Boats veer apart as S-124 continued down the long straight line of the convoy of LSTs looking for its victim, while Kapitän Mirbach turned his boat broadside on to LST 289 and slowed to twelve knots to allow his gunners the opportunity to pick their targets.

The E-Boat began its killing spree at the bow of the LST, the forward thirty-seven millimeter spraying the upper deck while the stern-mounted forty-mil Bofors cannon directed its armor-piercing shells at the side of the vessel, the heavy rounds tearing through the hull, shredding metal, hoping to cripple machinery and engines within the helpless boat.

As the shells hit, every seventh round a green tracer lighting up the darkness, the carnage began. A group of soldiers formed up on the starboard side, returning fire with their M1 carbines, a brave but almost useless attempt at defense, as the German gunners on the E-Boat had fifteen-millimeter molded, curved metal shields protecting them.

The American bullets ricocheted harmlessly from the defensive armor, not one finding its mark. Instead, the gunners used the rifle flashes for targeting and trained their automatic fire on the young GIs lining the deck. In seconds, virtually every soldier was hit and the volleys from the LST stopped as the men fell to the now bloody deck, dead or critically wounded by the heavy shells.

S-136 continued around the lumbering vessel, crossing its wake as it passed the stern. Kapitän Mirbach slowed even more at this point, knowing this was where the American bridge was, and where the ship's captain would be. The previous few seconds had only been target practice, he thought, now they were in position where the real prize awaited.

In his raised bridge, the highest point on the LST, almost sixty feet above the water, Lieutenant Commander Rogers was at the controls. His ship was under attack and no one else, not even the helmsman, could be trusted to get his vessel and his men out of harm's way. It fell to him.

"They're behind us now," warned the young midshipman.

"Understand. We have to move it. Increasing th-"

The dedicated career sailor never got to finish his words as the wheelhouse erupted in a rain of lead exploding around them. The combination of fire from the two heavy guns on the E-Boat tore apart everyone in that small area. In less than two seconds, shells designed to shred metal and sink merchant ships ripped apart the six officers, leaving behind a bloody pile of body parts and flesh.

Fire broke out as the wires on the radio panel shorted, and heavy black smoke began pouring from the shattered windows, trailing out behind the barely moving landing ship, marking its dying passage.

Kapitän Mirbach saw the blaze start and the thick smoke streaming from the bridge, and knew how effective his gunners had been. With its control center gone and the fire spreading, this American ship is doomed, he thought, and he broke from the attack in search of his next victim.

High on the clifftop overlooking Slapton Sands and its sheltering waters, Mary saw the smoke billowing from the stern of the LST. There was no mistaking the eight-foot-high letters on the vessel, 289. She dropped the binoculars from her eyes, too shocked to shed a tear. She was barely able to gasp a single word, "Mac!"

Onboard the crippled LST, Mac and Ricky, carbines in hand, returned to the gunwale and saw the horror show awaiting. Men who had cracked jokes with them, played poker, shared pictures of sweethearts and talked about their plans of what they would do back home when the war was over, lay dead at their feet, the deck awash with their young blood.

"Jesus, Mac, if we hadn't gone for our rifles…" Ricky's words trailed off.

Pungent smoke wafted across the LST, rising from a stairwell leading down to the lower decks.

"The German guns started a fire at the stern, below decks. Isn't that where our munitions are, Ricky?"

"No, not any more. Only a few are left back there, still in storage. I had most of them loaded on the trucks. They were ready to move out in the morning when we beached."

"Thank God for that. If they'd all been stacked there and one of those shells hit them…" Mac didn't need to complete his sentence, instead he let those words hang as he shifted his focus to more urgent matters. "We need medics up here now to take care of any of these poor souls who are still alive."

"And then?"

Mac looked back at the shattered bridge spewing black smoke. "Get this boat to shore before the fire spreads and we end up like 507."

Ricky stared across the dark waters at the E-boats' first target, LST 507. She was fully ablaze and sinking fast. "But if it's as bad on the bridge as it is down here, everyone could be shot up."

"Then we'll have to do something about it ourselves. Let's get the medics here, then follow me to the bridge."

"Okay, Mac, let's do this."

The two friends ran through the smoke, searching for medical aid for the fallen wounded.

A fist pounded against the old wooden door, not stopping until its demand was answered. Finally, it creaked open, the bleary-eyed captain of the watch standing there, annoyed.

"You again, corporal!" he barked to the sentry. "This better be good. What is it this time?"

"You should have changed the fucking radar." The sentry spat out his words, not deeming to include a '*sir*'; his friends were dying out there. He swiveled and pointed to the sprawling bay.

The sight shocked the captain awake. Flames and explosions filled the quiet waters of Slapton Sands. War had broken out in his backyard, and he could have been the one to help stop it.

E-Boat, S-124, was lining up its target when a second boat joined it. The kapitän flashed a quick signal acknowledging its welcome presence, and S-100, now became a part of the chase. The two hunter/killer vessels prepped their torpedo bays as the crew of their intended prey, the sailors onboard

LST 531, ran to line the decks and opened fire with their M1 carbines.

In the wheelhouse, the captain sent a distress message to any ship who could pick it up asking for aid and support.

The following LST, designated 469, operating on the same frequency, received the call and responded instantly. The captain increased his ship's speed from six knots to nine, and sounded General Quarters a second time. He opened the P.A. and called out to his deck gunners. "This is your captain speaking. We have two German boats approaching off our port bow. I want fire concentrated on them now. Bring our forty millimeters to their lowest elevation and blow those Nazis out of the water. We only have a few seconds before they attack. Do it now."

The three-man gunnery crew, already in place after receiving the earlier call to General Quarters, cranked the elevation wheel forward. This was an unusual move for them. Normally, during their training exercises, they would pull hard back on the wheel to elevate the guns for use against aircraft; lowering them was a first, and trying to fire downwards from their upper deck perch forty-eight feet above the water in the dark at a small, speeding target, was stranger still, but orders were orders, and this was no training exercise any longer, this was life or death.

Even as they cranked the wheel forward, dropping the barrels of the forty-mill guns, the German E-Boats started their engines, initiating their torpedo run. Knowing time had run out, the crew of the bow mounted anti-aircraft gun opened fire, hoping they had achieved their goal.

Tragically, their best efforts had not been able to over-ride the built-in safety design of the gun's mechanism, and the barrels had not depressed enough. The gunners commenced their desperate automatic fire, but the barrels kicked upwards and the shells flew harmlessly above the two racing E-Boats – harmlessly, until they hit another, unintended target, one of their own boats, LST 511.

The armor-piercing shells slammed into the hull of the ship, ripping through the metal, driving deep into the LST, killing seventeen American servicemen instantly, victims of the most contradictory of phrases, *friendly fire*.

"Cease firing!" screamed the gunners' mate as he realized what had happened, and as the smoking forty-millimeter fell silent so did the three-man crew who sat speechless, praying one day they would be able to forgive themselves for what they had done.

The men of LST 531 sent unrelenting volleys of rifle fire at the two German E-Boats, even though they knew they were at the very limit of their range. Unconcerned by the small arms fire, they continued their coordinated attack, racing together at the vessel nicknamed a *Large Slow Target*.

Four hundred yards from the ship, they each fired a pair of torpedoes in unison, and with their lethal packages discharged, they broke from their approach, S-100 veering port and S-124 turning hard to the starboard and speeding into the protection of the night.

As their targets disappeared in the darkness, the soldiers stopped firing and watched in terror at the burning white wakes of the four torpedoes streaking toward them at sixty knots. Some men ran from the side, trying to find shelter in the center of the ship while others were struck motionless and froze in place, their eyes locked on the incoming death. One young soldier dropped to his knees and pulled a crucifix from around his neck, which he kissed and held up to his face.

The four torpedoes hit simultaneously, squarely amidships, sending a wall of flame hundreds of feet skyward, turning night into day. The immense force of the blast lifted the three thousand eight hundred ton vessel out of the water, ripping the great ship in two.

A series of secondary explosions from within LST 531's shattered hull blew what remained of the vital transport ship apart, sending a shockwave radiating miles outward, shaking

SLAPTON SANDS

the rest of the convoy, knocking men from their feet on the following boats.

Seven miles away, the H.M.S. Azalea, approaching at flank speed, felt the power of the blast and saw the pillar of flames stretching upward.

"Jesus Christ. That's at least two ships gone now. There's going to be no one left when we get there." Captain Geddes pulled his eyes from the distant horrors and turned to his radar operator. "Do we have any contacts for our guns yet?"

"We do, sir. But it's too dark for our gunners to target them visually, and the E-Boats are too small and fast to pinpoint by radar from this far out. And they're in amongst the Americans."

"But we have a good lock on the Yanks?"

"Yes, sir."

"Then I want two salvos. All guns. First salvo, one mile past the convoy, then the second between us and their ships. We're going to let the Americans and Jerry know we're coming. But make bloody sure we don't hit the Yanks."

"Will do, sir."

Keeping at flank speed, the Corvette Class warship swung its two forward one hundred-and twenty-millimeter guns toward Slapton Sands and convoy T-4. The four barrels moved upward, then spit flame and smoke as the guns fired. Moments later, the elevation of the barrels changed a second time and the guns fired again.

Watching on the clifftop, Mary saw the flashes from the British Corvette's large guns. "The navy's here!" she called out.

The first shells flew over the burning American ships, exploding in a series of two-hundred-foot-high columns of water.

"All this time waiting, and they bloody well missed." exclaimed Mrs. Northcott.

"They just want them to know they're here," said Mary. "Hold on, Mac."

The second set of shells impacted the other side of the embattled convoy, reinforcing her words.

"Stay safe, my love. It won't be long now." She stared out at Mac's ship, made unmistakable by the trail of smoke and flames pouring from its stern.

Onboard LST 289, Mac and Ricky fought their way back through the heavy smoke. Both boys had towels wrapped around their mouths to help them breathe.

They grabbed the handrails of the stairway leading to the bridge and instantly let go. They were red hot, heated by the blaze below deck, as fire continued spreading through the lower levels of the stern. Treading carefully, and nearly blinded by the suffocating smoke, they continued up the metal stairs made treacherous by oil and blood.

The heavy bridge door offered no barrier as it hung down at an angle, the top hinges blown apart. The two friends entered the smoke-filled cabin, carefully stepping over the broken glass and contorted bodies.

Flames poured from the bullet-riddled radio console, burning the wires within, creating a toxic, acrid smoke.

Mac pulled a fire extinguisher from its mounting clips against the wall and sprayed the blaze, smothering it with the heavy white chemical foam, stemming the smoke.

"Holy shit, I didn't think it would be this bad. Everyone's dead here, the whole crew." Ricky's eyes panned around the wrecked control room. "And it's all shot up. Do you think anything is still working?"

"We have to clear the smoke first before we can find out." Mac moved forward to check the only pane of glass not shattered by the German's strafing. It was the main windshield at the front of the bridge, reinforced to take the brunt of the vicious wind gusts that swept in from the North Sea.

"Stand back, Ricky," he warned.

Mac pulled his Colt M1911 and pointed it at the center of the glass. He covered his eyes with his left arm to protect them from any flying fragments and pulled the trigger. He fired six times before lowering the gun, and was rewarded by seeing most of the glass broken away.

"I can't believe you did that." Ricky was stunned at his friend's actions. "You'd be arrested if there was an MP here."

"If there was an MP on the bridge, he'd be dead along with all the others. I'm going to try to bring what's left of her in. It's the only way." He lifted the fire extinguisher again. "Stay back."

Using the butt end of the heavy metal cylinder, he leaned forward over the console and broke away the rest of the remaining glass, leaving the bridge open to the outside, and allowing the breeze, caused by the ship's forward movement, to clear the smoke away.

Now they could see the damage the German guns had inflicted on the LST's control center. Ricky stared at the riddled radio and navigation controls. "It looked better with the smoke in here. There's nothing left."

"Maybe. Let me try something." Mac ignored all the secondary control systems and pushed on the throttle arms. There was a vibration from deep below deck as the big diesels increased their revs. "The shells didn't touch the engines, they're okay. We can get her to shore."

"But everything else is broke?"

"Probably, but I don't need any of that. The radar, radio, navigation controls aren't necessary to beach her. It's all visual. We're in the bay and there's enough moonlight to see the coastline. I'll use my eyes to take her in."

"You make it sound so simple."

"Let's hope it is."

"If you can do it, Mac, how long before we reach land?"

He paused as he considered Ricky's question, and answered by thinking out loud. "We're about five miles from the beach. If the pumps are still working and I dump her ballast now and get her riding higher so there's not as much drag, and really push her, less than twenty-five minutes."

"How will you know if the pumps work?"

"We'll try them."

Mac flipped the ballast pump switches and a rumble began, drowning out the throb of the engines. He peered from the smashed starboard bridge window and saw an immense bubbling around the hull's waterline. He looked back at Ricky. "They're working. The water's being forced out. The shallow draft will give us an extra two knots." He pushed the throttle levers fully forward. They both felt the enormous ship starting to speed up. "Okay, you have less than twenty minutes to organize everything. I'll bring her in, you get the men ready for immediate beach evac as soon as we make contact and the ramp's down."

"Mac, you can't stay up here that long. The stern got the worst of it and the fire below is spreading. I can feel the heat through my shoes. If the floor's getting that hot, you won't have twenty minutes. The smoke will be back and so will the rest of the shit that comes with it."

"We've got no choice. The boat can't beach herself, Ricky. I'll bring her in before it's too late, I promise. Have I ever lied to you?"

"No, and don't make today a first. I'll ready the men." With that, he disappeared from the bridge, leaving Mac in sole control of the crippled ship.

Standing alone at the damaged controls, the bridge became a stark and lonely place. Mac stared at the bodies strewn across the floor, and the man who had given him the chance to pilot this ship the first time, lying face down, his right arm severed by the impact of the heavy German fire, and wished he could be anywhere but here, now. But he had no choice, this is where he found himself and he had to step up and keep himself together if he was to get the men of 289 to safety.

He whispered a silent prayer for the fallen crew then focused his attention on what remained of the control console. He could feel the boat's momentum and checked her speed; a pointless attempt as that dial along with the fuel gauges, engine monitors, exhaust valve indicators, were all destroyed by the intense strafing the E-Boat had inflicted on the LST's bridge. And now, despite the cold, eleven-knot wind blowing through the broken windows, smoke was building up again. That meant the fires Ricky had warned him about in the lower sections of the stern were spreading. If they intensified, they could interfere or even melt the cables running to the steering and control mechanisms, leaving the ship, and all aboard, helpless.

Mac knew these negative scenarios were pointless and pushed them aside; he had no time for them. There was only one job to do, get this boat to the land without any further delay. He pulled back slightly on the starboard engine, allowing the port motor to continue at maximum revs. This imbalance of thrust would turn the ship and put them on the shortest, most direct heading for the beach at Slapton Sands.

He felt the boat beginning to swing, and stared at the distant shoreline. Nineteen minutes, he estimated, and began the countdown in his head. If she could hold together, if the engines didn't fail, and if the fires below didn't spread too quickly, they might make it. Too many *ifs*, he thought; they had to make it, there were six hundred men on board counting on him; he had no other option.

LST 289 broke from the line of ships in convoy T-4 and maxing out at its top speed of eleven knots, it pushed through the burning waters, set on fire by spilled oil and gasoline from the two blazing LSTs, and turned its blunted bow toward Slapton Sands and the promise of safety.

"Isn't that your boy's boat?" Mrs. Northcott pointed to the LST leaving the line of ships in the convoy.

Mary already had her binoculars locked on it, and replied simply, "Yes."

"It's getting away from the others. But it's on fire."

"At least it's still moving," answered Mary. "Mac told me he's been in the bridge with the captain the past few weeks, and has sailed it himself a few times."

"Then maybe he's in there now with him. It would probably be the safest place to be, at the back of the boat."

"Normally, it would be, but that's where most of the flames are."

"Where do you think the boat is going?" asked Mrs. Northcott.

"My guess is they're trying to come straight in to the beach. That'll take them right past us." She fought through her tears. "Hurry, Mac, hurry."

There was a momentary pause in the fighting as Kapitän Mirbach sent a radio message to the other German captains, warning them of the approaching British warship, and relieving six of *S-Boot Flottille* E-Boats from the attack and ordering them back to Cherbourg. As they raced away across the channel, he saw Mac's LST breaking from the convoy, trailing a heavy column of smoke, making for the shore.

He pounded his boat's console in anger; he had been certain his earlier attack had finished the giant vessel with his automatic fire on its bow, the decks, and by obliterating the stern and bridge, but now he was being proven wrong. The ship had not been crippled; it was under power and heading for land.

Furious, the kapitän shoved his helmsman away from the controls of S-136 and seized them himself, thrusting both throttles to full without warning, spinning the wheel hard right. As the one hundred and ten-foot boat leaped forward in a sharp starboard turn, the men on board were thrown around by the sudden unexpected, violent acceleration.

The displaced helmsman grabbed for a rail to stabilize himself and looked questioningly at his kapitän, as did the three other surprised officers in the E-Boat's tight bridge.

Mirbach felt their stares but kept his eyes locked on LST 289. He shouted, not only to his men but also because he was unable to control his rage, "Das Boot gehört mir!! – *That boat is mine!*"

He knew this would be no foot race; his E-Boat would be on the slow American ship in less than three minutes, and then he would finish it for good.

The huge wake the speeding E-Boat kicked up was not going unnoticed. As both the lumbering LST and the German hunter raced in toward Slapton Sands, they gave Mary a clear but unwanted vision of what was happening. She sat motionless, watching the chase unfold. Mrs. Northcott saw it too, and reached out, squeezing her companion's arm in the hope of calming her.

The old lady heard a strange sound coming from Mary's mouth. She realized it was a word repeated over and over, but muffled and made almost unintelligible by the sobbing wracking her body. "Mac, Mac, Mac."

H.M.S. Azalea's crew stood by for imminent combat. They were less than five miles from the embattled convoy and closing fast.

The radar operator shouted across the bridge to his captain. "I can confirm it now. Six of the E-Boats have fled. Only three remain, sir, and we're almost in range of them."

"Then let's get rid of those animals as well. Give them another warning volley and see if we can make them run."

On his command the corvette's enormous guns fired again, letting both the American convoy and the last three E-Boats know the Royal Navy was almost upon them.

Though the shells landed over a mile from the racing S-136, the crew on the bridge could not fail to hear the explosions of the one hundred and twenty-millimeter shells and the mammoth wall of water they unleashed into the air.

The displaced helmsmen called to warn his kapitän who continued to man the controls. "Kapitän, das englische Kriegsschiff ist eingetroffen. – *The English warship is here.*"

"Ja, ja. Schicken Sie die anderen beiden Boote nach Hause. Ich brauche noch eine Minute. – *Yes, yes. Send the other two boats home. I need one minute more.*"

The radio operator jumped on his gear, and understanding the urgency, relayed the message. He had barely finished his transmission when the two recipient E-Boats gratefully broke from their attack and to avoid being intercepted by the British corvette, turned southeast at maximum speed, heading to the shelter of their harbor in France.

Mac was unaware of this turn of events and continued with his primary duty of getting LST 289 to shore. Fourteen minutes to go, he thought. He scanned the shoreline, then, as a good sailor does, he looked all around to make sure there were no unseen obstacles nearby. It was then he saw the lone E-Boat racing up behind him.

"Shit!" he breathed through clenched teeth, and instinctively pushed harder on the throttles, even though he knew they were already at full and there was no more power available. For the first time in his life, he felt truly helpless.

Mary had the same reaction to the one-sided chase she watched play out, and as the torpedo boat bore down on Mac's ship, she pleaded, "Please, you're almost home to me, Mac, just a little faster."

Word of what had happened to the E-Boat flotilla reached H.M.S. Azalea, and the radar officer brought the captain final confirmation of the welcome news. "Eight of the Jerrys have broken off, sir."

"And that last German?"

"It looks like he's in pursuit of one of the American ships."

"Damn it. Can we target him directly yet?"

"Yes, sir. He's away from the main body of the convoy, and I have a clear radar fix, plus we can now get a visual for the gunners as the landing ship he's after is burning at the stern and the flames are lighting him up. If Jerry plans to use his torpedoes, he'll have to slow down to launch speed, and that will give us our best chance."

"Good job, radar. Have all guns lock on that E-Boat and ready to fire on my command."

The men in the warship's crowded bridge were veterans of guarding convoys during hazardous Atlantic crossings and went about their well-rehearsed roles as they prepared for the upcoming engagement with the enemy.

Mac remained alone in the bridge, his sole company the six mangled bodies scattered on the floor. But he was fully aware of the threat behind him. The attack could come at any moment, and with it, sudden death.

He glanced over his shoulder and watched as the E-Boat began changing course. It was no longer right on his tail, it was pulling out of his wake and racing away from him. For the briefest of moments, Mac allowed the tenseness in his shoulders to relax; the Germans had given up, his boat and his men were safe. Then the fear returned. The E-Boat was not leaving, but setting up for a torpedo run, and to do that he would not attack from behind, which would only give him a comparatively small, narrow target, but launch from amidships, where it would be virtually impossible to miss such a massive boat.

The E-Boat maneuvered parallel to LST 289, standing five hundred yards out, and slowing to fifteen knots as it prepared its bow-launched torpedoes.

The kapitän waited impatiently as his torpedo crew double checked the weapons were loaded correctly and the trigger mechanisms set. With everything in place below deck, they flicked the switch which lit a green light in the bridge, signifying to their captain that all was on track to launch.

Kapitän Mirbach grinned to himself; finish this boat then return home to great acclaim. He personally would be rewarded for sinking two of the American ships and disrupting whatever it was their convoy had been doing. It meant another medal, at least. Possibly a promotion even higher in the Kriegsmarine.

"Bereit zum Abschuss der Torpedos–*Ready the torpedoes*."

The bow of S-136 was lined up perfectly with the center of the American ship. Now they would see the power of a *Schnellboote* under the control of a great kapitän. He would launch the torpedoes at three hundred yards; closer than normal, but he wanted to rule out any possibility of missing.

He accelerated to the optimum speed of twenty-five knots and began his run.

Mac's eyes had been locked on the maneuvering E-Boat for the past three minutes and knew what was about to happen. He grabbed the cabin microphone and clicked on the P.A. system, hoping against hope it still worked. He tried controlling the fear and apprehension running through him, and not allow it to show in his voice. "We are under attack again. There is an incoming German boat on the starboard beam. If you have a carbine or are with a rifle company, fire at will."

The soldiers onboard the embattled LST grabbed their weapons and ran to the side of the ship, taking their positions. For many, the idea of slingshots against armor came to mind, as three hundred modern day Davids bravely prepared to battle the charging Goliath.

"Sir, she's turned toward the LST, slowed to twenty-five knots, and is beginning her torpedo run."

The captain of H.M.S. Azalea replied instantly. "Is she in the clear and targeted?'

"Yes, sir. There are no other boats near the Germans."

"Then open fire."

On his order, the heavy forward guns blazed and the huge shells shot into the air on their deadly mission.

Kapitän Mirbach held steady at the helm as the E-Boat raced toward LST 289 and passed the four hundred yard mark, the distance where the torpedoes would normally be launched. He dismissed the quizzical stares from the officers in the bridge; this was his target, his kill.

At three hundred and fifty yards the gunnery *feidwebel* pleaded, "Mein Kapitän. wir müssen… *Captain, we must…*"

The first of the rounds from the soldiers onboard 289 began hitting the E-Boat as it sped in closer. Kapitän Mirbach ignored the small arms fire as well as the question. "Nein. Warte, warte. – *No. Wait, wait.*" His anger dictated that he would not be denied his prize.

The sea around S-136 erupted in immense towers of spray as shells from the British corvette hit the water either side of the E-Boat, rocking it violently with gigantic swells generated by the explosions, and throwing it off its course toward the LST. The German crew grabbed for handrails to stabilize themselves, and the kapitän was forced to back off the throttle to allow the boat to settle.

"Das Kriegsschiff- *The warship-*"

"Das Kriegsschiff verfehite. Das werde ich nicht. – *The warship missed. I won't.*"

Kapitän Mirbach curved his boat around to once again line up with his target and restart the torpedo run, as he readied to complete his deadly task.

"Did we get him? Did we sink Jerry?" The Azalea's captain strained his eyes through the darkness, hoping for the answer he sought.

"No, sir. But it was close."

"Close! What damn good is close? Have the guns reload and next time, tell the gunners it's either a direct hit or they walk the plank."

"Sir, the E-Boat is already going back in." The radar operator gave his warning as he looked up from the images playing out on the green cathode-ray screen.

"Can we-"

"No, sir. They are on a new track and going too fast. There's no time to retarget them."

"Then God help the Yanks, because we can't."

Again, the relentless German E-Boat sped at LST 289, enduring a hail of desperate volley fire from the servicemen spaced along the upper deck. At three hundred yards, Kapitän Mirbach finally gave the command his crew had been waiting for, "Feuer! – *Fire!*" and with no delay, the twin silver fish carrying sixteen hundred pounds of high explosive launched from the torpedo tubes.

As they hit the water, there was no hesitation from the kapitän as he expertly steered into a sharp turn and accelerated to maximum speed to take his boat as far away as possible from what would inevitably be a huge explosion.

Mac saw the twin wakes approaching fast and knew they only had seconds before the impact. He yelled into the ship's P.A. "Torpedoes in the water. Brace yourselves." He watched helplessly as the two harbingers of death raced at his boat.

On deck, the soldiers ceased firing and stared down at the dark sea and the incoming tracks. There was nothing they could do, nowhere they could go to avoid their fate as the torpedoes, perfectly aimed, rushed at them, only yards away.

The twin wakes reached the LST but there was no explosion. The only sound was the thumping of the engines continuing to push the big boat toward the shore, a sound almost drowned out by the pounding of the heartbeats of the soldiers waiting for the blast that would end their lives.

A voice rang out from the port side of the ship. "The torpedoes are still going. The Krauts missed!"

From his eagle's nest vantage point in the bridge, Mac watched the gleaming wakes continuing on across the bay, and realized what had happened. The LST, now ready for a beach landing with its ballast pumped out, was running at its shallowest draft, less than twenty-six inches. The torpedoes, primed for larger vessels in convoys, ran much deeper than that to cause maximum damage when they impacted below the waterline. As a result, they had gone under the LST without hitting anything, and would keep going until their engines ran out of power and they sank harmlessly to the bottom.

This fact was not missed by the furious kapitän of S-136. "Scheisse! Mehr torpedos. – *Shit! More torpedoes.*"

His crew looked at him in horror. The shells from the Azalea had fallen only a few meters from them. They were lucky to still be alive, and now the English ship was even closer. To try again would be madness.

The Chief Petty Officer – the *Strabsfeldwebel* - felt compelled to speak up. "Kapitän, das Englische kriegsschiff ist zu nah. Wir mussen jetzt hier raus. – *Captain, the English warship is too close now. We must get out of here.*"

"Nien! Wir gehen, wenn ich es sage. Wir haben zwei Torpedos übrig. – *No! We leave when I say. We have two torpedoes left.*"

Kapitän Mirbach seized the boat's microphone and shouted his order down to the forward torpedo crew. "Passen Sie die Tiefe an. Ich möchte, dass sie an der Oberfläche laufen. – *Adjust the depth. I want them to run on the surface.*"

H.M.S. Azalea was three miles from the stricken convoy and readying to lower lifeboats to rescue any survivors still alive in the freezing waters. The captain's attention was pulled from this task when his first officer gave him the news.

"Sir, it looks like Jerry's going back in a third time to have another go at the landing ship."

"What?" The captain grabbed his binoculars and swept the sea until he saw S-136 speeding into position to line up with the LST. "Is he insane? With us right upon him, he should be running back home with his tail between his legs after missing at point blank range."

"That's what we thought, but he did a wide turn which made it look like he was leaving. Maybe he had to buy some time to do something on the boat or had a problem reloading his torpedoes. Either way, he's setting up to attack again."

"Damn it, I thought we were done. All right, lock in the guns. Tell the chaps to be bloody accurate this time. If that German wants to commit suicide, let's help him meet his maker. And tell our boys if I see a direct hit and we blow those bastards out of the water, I'll have a week's leave waiting for them."

Mac saw the E-Boat positioning itself for another run. He took the microphone, quickly thinking through his words. "Men, we're only minutes from the shore, but the Germans are coming back. This time they won't miss. They're on our starboard side again. Give them everything you've got."

Tired, cold, and exhausted, the heroic soldiers reached deep inside themselves to draw on their reserves as they returned to their firing positions along the deck, praying for a miracle.

S-136 lined up with the LST. The kapitän knew there would be no mistakes this time, and there had better not be, because these were the last two torpedoes his boat carried, but they would be more than enough to blow the already damaged American ship to pieces. With that satisfying thought in mind, he pushed the throttles forward and began his run.

"I'm getting a thumbs up from the gunners, sir," reported the Azalea's first officer. "They have the E-Boat targeted."

"Then give the fire order. Send those buggers back to their Fatherland in boxes."

There was no hesitation as the first officer hit the com to the gunners. "All guns, FIRE!"

The warship shook as the big guns roared, sending death skyward.

Kapitän Mirbach held his course true. The LST had a large outline of a sealed doorway almost in the center of the midships position. It was probably used when they were in harbor, pulled up along a dock, he thought. They would run a gangplank to it so the crew could disembark through it and go home to their loved ones. He smirked to himself; they would never use that doorway again, or see any loved ones, not after his torpedoes hit. And it gave him the perfect target to line up with. So convenient of the Americans to put a bullseye right in the middle of the hull.

Knowing the British warship was bearing down on them, and confident with his positioning, he hit the first of the red FIRE buttons at four hundred and fifty yards out, then five seconds later, at four hundred yards, punched the second. Space the torpedoes this time, just in case. Let the men onboard feel the fear as they watched the torpedoes hurtling toward them; especially now, while on the surface. There, the wakes would be bigger, more prominent, more terrifying. Two unstoppable metal sharks, ready to bite deep and rip them apart.

One after the other, the two torpedoes flew from the forward tubes and splashed into the water, both set on a perfect track to do most damage. He smiled with satisfaction, and turned to tell his crew it was time to break from the attack and go home, but he never completed his head movement.

Six shells from the Azalea rained down on the E-Boat, two hitting it directly and flinging it into the air as it exploded into a million fragments. Body parts, engine fittings, equipment and gun mountings scattered wide across the ocean, and a series of secondary explosions rang out as the unused ammunition on board ignited and brought the 4th of July to Slapton Sands on that chilly early morning in April.

Mac saw the E-Boat explode in flames but felt no desire to celebrate. The torpedoes were already in the water and unaffected by its destruction. They were next, unless...

He threw the starboard engine into reverse and held the port throttle fully open, knowing he needed every rev from it he could muster. He could turn his father's tugboats on a dime, with this monster, he would have to see what could be done.

The LST began swinging to the right, slowly at first, then more rapidly as momentum kicked in. But would it be fast enough? The lead torpedo was less than two hundred yards out now, and closing fast. It was all he could do, that and pray.

Riding high in the water, with considerably less drag than with a full ballast, the boat continued to pivot, almost on its access, and with a hundred yards left to cover, Mac knew now the torpedoes wouldn't impact amidships, a strike that would have been a fatal blow.

"Come on, come on," he urged. "Just like back home."

The soldiers on deck felt the LST's rapid turn and realized what the captain was attempting to do. Ricky stared up at the wheelhouse where he knew his friend was controlling the gigantic transport, "You got it, Mac, you got it."

The first torpedo was only yards from them now, and Mac held his breath as he watched it pass harmlessly behind him, missing the boat's stern by inches. If he could just keep the turn going...

A huge explosion threw him from his feet, headfirst into the control board and dropped him to the floor where he landed on the pile of bloody corpses lying there. The second torpedo had impacted into the already damaged stern, tearing open a gaping hole in the lower deck where the heavy transports were stored.

The blast shattered the chains securing the positioning of the Sherman tank closest to the hull wall, blowing it from its mountings. As the ship lurched into a sudden tilt from the violent explosion, the unattached tank skidded across the transport deck to the very edge of the storage area, where it balanced precariously against the jagged opening ripped apart by the torpedo strike. It stopped and hung there, but after a few seconds its weight proved too much for the already weakened steel deck, damaged by the earlier raging fire, and the metal sheeting collapsed beneath the forty-ton fighting vehicle, and the tank slid and fell from LST 289, plummeting into the ocean, creating a huge splash before disappearing below the dark waters.

Less than two miles away on the clifftop, Mary watched it happen through her binoculars, and as the tank sank out of sight and flames roared upward around the stern, she lowered the glasses and stared with her bare eyes at the blaze threatening to engulf the rear of the struggling ship. She had no more words, only tears.

Mac struggled to his feet, slipping on the blood pooled on the floor. His uniform was soaked red, and he added to the blood of the earlier victims with a vicious cut on his forehead torn open when he was blown into the metal edge of the console as he fell.

He wiped his eyes to clear his vision, and pulled the starboard throttle from reverse, pushing it forward. The LST shuddered as the motor and props changed direction, but they were still working. Mac uttered a sigh of relief; had the torpedo hit only a few feet further back, it would have wiped out both the engine and the propellor shafts. He searched his pockets and found a handkerchief and wrapped it around his nose and mouth. Smoke poured back into the bridge, so thick and heavy with oil, that even the wind generated by the ship's forward movement wasn't enough to dissipate it. But it was coming from below and behind, which meant he could still see ahead and make out the beach beckoning to him, only minutes away.

A hunched figure pushed its way through the smoke onto the bridge, a jacket covering their head to protect them from the acrid fumes. Mac turned to see who it was, and though his bloody, burning eyes had a tough time making him out, the voice gave the identity away.

"You're alive. I thought the torpedo got you for sure."

"It almost did. We were lucky."

"Lucky, my ass." Ricky reached out and put his hand on his friend's shoulder. "If it wasn't for your fancy sailing, we'd all be dead now." As he spoke, he saw the jagged gash on Mac's forehead and the blood streaked across his face. "Jesus, you look like you went ten rounds with Joe Louis. You need medical attention and fast!"

"It'll have to wait until we reach the beach. We're nearly there now. How is it on the decks?"

"It's not good there either. The explosion pushed the fires forward, and started a bunch more, and they're heading toward the trucks, and they're filled with gas and ammo."

"How long before the flames reach them?"

"Maybe fifteen to twenty minutes. I have two fire teams with hoses doing their best to slow it down, but there's a lot to burn. But Mac, as bad as it is below decks, you've got it so much worse up here. The main fires are right below you and intensifying rapidly. And there's still some of our munitions back there, I couldn't get them all loaded. If the fire reaches them…"

"I can handle it. I won't be up here much longer. We'll be beached in less than ten minutes. Can you move the men off quickly?"

"Yeah." Ricky had no doubt about this. "That's what they've been training for, a quick evac. They'll do it even faster now it's for real."

"There's nothing blocking the ramp or the trucks?"

"We've got some debris there from when the Nazis sprayed us the first time around with their heavy guns; a few holes in the side and shit, but the ramp's solid and looks like it's in one piece, and the Jimmys are pretty much untouched and ready to roll."

"Okay." Mac needed to hear some good news. "Go back down and load all the men in the trucks. Have the fire teams prepared to bail at a moment's notice once the rest are out-"

Ricky cut him off. "Are you sure I should load the men? If they're below deck in the trucks and we go down, they'll have no chance to get out. And any that do won't last five minutes in the freezing water."

"Ricky, we're not going down; I won't let her sink. I'm going to get her in, I promise."

"You and your promises, man." Ricky forced a smile. "Okay, you land us on the beach, I'll do the rest and get everyone off."

"I know you will."

Ricky turned to leave but Mac reached through the smoke, grabbing his arm to stop him.

"I have something I need you to look after for me, Ricky, just in case." He reached into his chest pocket and took out Reg's cherished Victoria Cross. "I promised Mary's grandfather I would return it to him. Take it."

"Mac..." Ricky understood what his closest friend was saying, but didn't want to hear it. "You keep it and give it to him."

"We don't have time to argue. I'll get it back from you as soon as we reach the shore. All right?"

Ricky continued to hesitate.

"Please." Mac knew what he was asking of him. "I have to stay here to bring us in. There's no other way. I can't leave the bridge."

Ricky took the medal from Mac's hand and slipped it into his pocket. He snapped to attention and saluted his dear friend. "My honor to serve with you, Sergeant Harper."

Mac returned the salute. "The honor was all mine, Sergeant Esposito. Now get going, beachmaster, your men need you."

Ricky nodded and hurried out from the devastated, smoke-filled bridge.

With less than five hundred yards to go before reaching the beach, the LST looked enormous in Mary's binoculars. The ship's dire situation was too obvious to all who could see it; smoke and flames streamed from the lower decks, leaving an incendiary trail behind; it had become a floating dragon breathing fire in its wake. But for all the damage it had suffered, the LST kept going as if it refused to stop until it found the safety of the shore.

Mary reached out her arm to the crippled transport vessel, creating an optical illusion that she could touch the burning landing ship with her fingers. "Come on, my love," she whispered. "You're almost there."

They were barely a hundred feet from the beach when Mac finally cut the engines. He didn't put them into reverse to slow the LST, but allowed her drifting speed to take her further up the sloping shore even though it meant the keel would scrape badly against the hard shingles. Regulations be damned, he thought. Any dents and scratches would be the least of the damages she'd already suffered. Mac wanted her as far up as she would go to ensure a fast and safe evac.

He called into the ship's microphone. "All hands brace for beach landing."

Seconds later, the burning LST shook as she contacted the round rocks and slid noisily up the beach, before grinding to a stop.

For a second there was silence, then a huge cheer erupted from below decks as the men realized they were back on land, the fighting and fear behind them.

Mac threw the bow release switch and breathed a sigh of relief as he heard the satisfying sound of the double bow doors slowly swinging apart. A moment later a loud metallic clunk rang out, signifying the doors were fully opened and locked, and the ramp was now ready to deploy. Mac hit the ramp release lever but now there was silence.

Something was wrong. Mac sensed it right away. Even in the bridge, at the opposite end of the ship, he should be able to hear the heavy chains releasing and the five-ton ramp lowering, but there was nothing. The forty-foot-high metal ramp was stuck in place, not only stopping the planned evacuation but trapping everyone inside the burning ship. With the fire spreading rapidly, Mac knew what would happen when the flames reached the fuel tanks of the line of trucks waiting to drive off the ship. Trapped below deck, with all the gasoline fumes, and the Jimmys carrying not only the men but many of them also loaded with ammunition, the blast would make the torpedo's payload look miniscule.

Mac pumped the lever again and again, but still the metal ramp remained locked in place, a towering prison door refusing to free its captives.

Ricky, standing, waiting for the ramp's deployment, heard the grinding noise from the gears trying to move forty feet above him and knew it meant something was jamming the release. He hit the forward ramp release, hoping that would free it, but still nothing. With both the bridge and the forward release inoperative, there had to be a major problem. He stared up at the towering metal ramp to see if he could locate what was locking it in place.

A young private jumped from the cab of the first truck and ran to him, panicked. "You're the beachmaster. If we don't get out of here, we're all going to die." He pointed to the fire crew valiantly trying to hold back the flames spreading rapidly at the rear of the immense transport bay.

"No one's going to die. Everyone's getting off."

Ricky's words did not console the teenage soldier. "But if it won't open-"

"I'll get it open. There has to be something blocking the chain."

Ricky pushed the scared private aside and started climbing the sheer ramp. Every six inches, ridges protruded outward, designed to stop the vehicles from slipping and to give them traction when the ramp was deployed and usually wet. Ricky used these for hand holds and to drive his feet against to help push him upwards. But they were hot, burning hot. A secondary fire at the bow on the upper deck had heated the metal ramp to a point where even a touch could blister skin, and to climb it, Ricky had to do more than touch the ramp; he had to grip it tightly to avoid falling the forty feet to the unforgiving deck.

He felt the skin peeling from his fingertips and his palms blistering, but kept going. He had no choice; it was climb or leave these men to die. As he neared the top he saw the source of the problem, across the length of the ramp release chain there were several large fragments of metal sticking through it, blown in there when the Germans attacked with their Bofors cannon, fragments from the ship's hull that were now blocking the mechanism. They had to be removed or there was no chance of lowering the ramp.

He pulled the first jagged metal shard out, and with a warning call, let it drop to the deck below. Then he made his way hand over hand, dangling from the scorching chain, wrenching out each fragment as he came to it, and flinging them down. Finally, he reached the far side of the ramp, and exhausted, wrapped his hand around the last piece. He knew what would happen when he freed the chain, and yelled the alert to the watching men below. "She's going to open now. Stand back, and as soon as the ramp's down, move out!"

With a last, hard tug, he freed the blockage, and the chain unwound rapidly, the ramp dropping forward. Ricky grabbed the chain and driving his feet into one of the serrated ridges, rode the ramp down, where it contacted with the shingled beach of Slapton Sands.

"Go, go, go!" he yelled to the waiting drivers. And one after another, the fully loaded GMC Jimmys rolled past him as he waved them on and up the beach.

High up in the bridge, Mac watched with satisfaction as he saw the line of trucks carrying the soldiers to the shoreline road and away from danger. The boat was beached, the men were off. His job was done, he could leave now.

He stepped carefully over the bodies still lying scattered across the bridge floor and moved through the smoke to the shattered door. As he reached it, a wall of flames burst up from the stairway and into the cabin itself, singeing Mac's hair and clothes, and driving him backward.

And the fire didn't die down; as Ricky had warned him, the lower decks had become an out-of-control inferno. With the ramp down, a breeze was now blowing the length of the ship below decks, fanning the flames. That's why the flare up had happened, blocking his exit, and he knew this would make the stairs impassable, and that was the only door and the only passage down. He'd have to find another way off the bridge.

Thinking quickly, he climbed onto the console, his boots cracking the few glass-covered gauges remaining unbroken after the German attack, and crawled through the shattered window. He grabbed the edge of the roof, pulling himself up and onto it. Free and outside of the bridge, Mac stood on the highest point of the LST, over sixty feet from the shallow water below. With the bow on the beach, he figured the stern rested in perhaps four or five feet of water, not deep, but enough to jump into and cushion some of the impact. He only had to clear the roof's rails to make it.

"I see him!" Mary yelled at the top of her voice, fear and relief mingling in her words. "He's on top of the bridge."
"What's he doing up there?" asked Mrs. Northcott.
"It was probably Mac's only way out because of the fire."
"Then how's he going to get off the boat?"

"I think he's going to jump. But he has to make it over the rail and not hit the back of the ship. He's going to have to run to clear it all and reach the water. I know you can do it, Mac. Run, my love, run."

Almost as if he had heard Mary's plea, he tensed, then sprinted across the roof. Mac had taken two fast steps when the flames on the second deck reached the remaining ammunition storage. The shells and charges boxed there were already scorching hot from the fires burning since the attack, and were a literal powder keg waiting to be ignited. Those naked flames provided the ignition.
A massive explosion engulfed the entire stern which disappeared in an enormous fireball that blew up and out across the dark sea, lighting what remained of the night with a terrifying orange glow as the burning cloud and fragments of molten metal sprayed hundreds of feet into the star-filled sky.
Ricky was walking up the beach, following the last of the trucks, when the shockwave from the blast hit, blowing his feet out from underneath him, knocking him face first into the rough sand and pebbles. He rolled over, trying to collect his thoughts and understand what had happened. It was then he saw the twisted metal that had been the bridge, and watched as raging thirty-foot-high flames consumed the entire rear of the once proud ship. His head dropped forward as he realized what it meant, and a sea of emotions washed over him, knowing he would never see his best friend again.
He pulled the Victoria Cross from his pocket and stared at it, understanding what he would have to do, and dreaded being that awful messenger. He turned his eyes to the clifftop, fearing the effects his unwanted words would have.
Ricky was unaware he would not have to deliver the terrible news. Mary stood on her rocky perch, shaking, her eyes locked on the burning ship, only a hundred yards from her. She had seen the boy she loved, the person who had

given her back her happiness, and that she had hoped to spend her life with, disappear in the mass of flames that swallowed the entire stern of the LST. There was no doubt in her heart, that her love, her young American, was dead.

She dropped to her knees, crying uncontrollably. Her body shook and she made no attempt to wipe away the tears pouring down. It was too much pain, too much loss to endure, and she let herself fall forward onto the wet grass she had laid on with him; laughing, talking, planning, blowing bubbles together and making wishes, in what seemed to be a lifetime ago. She sobbed the same word over and over, knowing he would never hear her say it again, "Mac, Mac, Mac."

The tears continued to run over Mary's cheeks, as they had almost four decades before, so much so that Fred inched closer and put his arm around her for consolation.

She lifted her head and looked at him. "That, Fred, is how your tank got there."

"I'm so sorry," he said, knowing his words would mean nothing to appease such a loss.

"I've had to live with this all these years. And not being able to share the truth made me feel like I was going crazy."

"And no one knows this story?"

"Only the people who were there and survived. But they were sworn not to talk, and the military had it classified Top Secret immediately to protect D-Day, which was less than six weeks away. And after the invasion was over, the generals never lifted the order and denied the terrible night ever happened to avoid getting blamed for all the mistakes that were made, in case they found themselves being held responsible."

"What about everyone who was killed? What happened to them, and their families?"

"It got worse. The families were told they died in accidents on the base, like falling off a ladder or being hit by a truck.

As they came from all over America and the families didn't know each other, they had no way of finding out how many had been killed. These men were heroes who died fighting and should have gotten medals; instead, they were forgotten."

"But the bodies? They must have been everywhere."

"There were hundreds of them, Fred, hundreds. Some were fished out of the sea, and others kept washing up on the beach for more than a week. It was awful, like driftwood after a big storm. They buried most of them in mass graves at Newland's Field and on the local farms. We saw the bulldozers digging huge holes in the fields, then all the bodies they pulled out of the water being loaded onto trucks. Those brave boys should have been sent home to America with honors, not stuck in the ground here, covered in lime to disguise the smell, and left in unmarked graves."

"And you never told anyone this?"

"I tried to talk to their officers but they wouldn't listen to me. When I kept coming back, they threatened me and then my grandfather. After Mrs. Northcott passed away, I was the only civilian witness left. That's when they said no one would believe me without proof, and they'd have me locked away if I spoke about it or went to the newspapers."

"But you're telling me, now. Why?"

"Because, Fred, for the first time, I have proof. I'm no longer a nutty as a fruitcake old lady ranting about some crazy story. Now, we have a tank! How will they be able to deny that? And if I have to mortgage everything I've got, I'm going to help you bring it up. When the world sees the tank, then what will they say?"

JUNE 12th, 1984

Two sturdy tugs whose hulls showed the evidence of many years of salvage, floated off of Slapton Sands. Both had heavy steel cables deployed from their winches, running down and disappearing into the green water. Onboard, the crews of both boats stood silently with Mary and Fred as they anxiously waited, focusing their stares over the side at the calm sea. They were all hoping to get an idea of what was happening below, and locked their gaze on the four sets of bubbles marking the progress of the SCUBA divers slowly ascending. After several anxious minutes, a large white shape over twenty feet across, rising like some monstrous jellyfish, came into view through the murky water, sparking a relieved gasp from the watchers above.

The first of the three air-filled lift bags broke the surface, followed quickly by two more. This is what the tugs' captains had been waiting for, and together, working as a well-rehearsed team, they turned on their winches to tighten the metal cables and secure the precious cargo the bags had finally, after hundreds of dives and years of work, been able to bring up from the sea bottom, sixty feet below.

The top of the tank was first to appear from the water, and at the sight of the enormous oval-shaped armored turret and long protruding gun barrel, a huge cheer erupted from both boats.

Mary spun around and hugged Fred. "Thank you for making this happen."

"It took four years, so many people, and such a lot of money; I hope it was worth it for you."

Her eyes filled with gratitude as she answered. "This wasn't for me." She gazed across the bay that forty years before had been filled with carnage and death. "It was for all of them."

NOVEMBER 23rd, 1987

Hordes of TV cameras and reporters pressed forward trying to get their own exclusive interview with Fred and Mary, to obtain a story about the restored American tank now sitting proudly in the parking lot of The Slapton Arms, and why it rested there, surrounded by seven hundred and forty-nine stones set firmly into place.

The pack of reporters broke apart as an even more newsworthy target appeared, a convoy of black limousines cresting over the hill, escorted by six British police cars, their blue lights rotating. The man of the hour was on hand, the Vice President of the United States, George H. W. Bush, coming in person to Slapton Sands, to dedicate the tank as a permanent memorial to the American servicemen who died fighting the flotilla of German E-Boats during Exercise Tiger, as they trained for their landing at Utah Beach in Normandy. Ironically, four times as many young American soldiers died that night than would be killed during the actual landing on Utah Beach.

The honor guard snapped to attention as the Vice President stepped from his protective limousine, and the crowd hushed as he walked up and stood beside the recovered Sherman tank, proudly bedecked with the Stars and Stripes and the Union Jack, and resting on a bed of seven hundred and forty-nine stones, one for each man lost that terrible night. He asked for a moment of silence before delivering his speech about the heroism of those who lost their lives in the battle against fascism and how they would never be forgotten. After he finished, he presented the villagers with a grateful letter signed by President Ronald Reagan, then revealed his own military background as a lieutenant in the United States Navy during World War II by snapping to attention, and staying ramrod straight while a lone bugler played Taps.

As the haunting, mournful sound drifted across the empty beach and eerily still waters, the crowd sobbed softly at the loss of so many young lives, and the unveiled memorial, finally standing to remember their sacrifice after forty-three years.

The Sherman Tank memorial, Slapton Sands.

Evening was drawing in, as two miles off of Slapton Sands, Mary stood on the deck of a boat, holding onto the polished railing, looking out over the calm ocean as the rays of the late afternoon sun painted the bay a burnt orange.

Even though she was alone on the boat, apart from the young man who expertly held the wheel at the stern of the yacht, she spoke aloud to let her words carry across the haunted sea. "A plaque was dedicated to you today, my love. People stood there and said kind words about the boys who died fighting to save their country and the world. They called you heroes, and asked us to remember those who had sacrificed everything."

She choked as emotions swelled up, but forced herself to continue. "As if I could ever forget you. You are my first thought when I wake up, and my last before I fall asleep. But I have something for you today."

Mary reached into her purse and pulled out the Victoria Cross. "Reg wanted you to have this. Even when your friend returned it to him, my grandfather never really wanted it back. He spoke about you many times after that dreadful night, and what you did, and said it should have been yours, for valor above and beyond the call of duty."

She tensed her arm. "I've waited so many years to give this back to you, and I think today is the right day to do it. I know you're here somewhere, I feel it in me, so until we meet again, my dearest love, this is for you."

Mary flung the treasured medal far out across the glowing water and watched it splash into the sea.

"God bless you, and thank you for touching my life with your love and your passion."

She turned from the rail and walked back along the yacht's deck to the man at the boat's wheel, the bartender from her pub. He wrapped his arms around her affectionately.

"You still miss him so much, don't you, Mum?"

She looked at her son and rubbed her hand softly across his cheek. "Every day; but he gave me you, and you're so like him; your smile, your eyes, even your laugh."

"I wish I'd had a chance to know him."

"Your father would have been so proud of you, and of this boat you built."

"Dad made it easy. All I had to do was follow his plans; he had everything there." He looked at the sky. "The sun is almost gone. We should be getting back; we'll lose the light soon."

"You're right, Mac. Let's go home."

Mac set the sail and spun the wheel to turn the yacht, laying in a heading for their berth in Dartmouth Harbor. A slight wind filled the spinnaker and the boat trimmed into its new course, moving toward the headland and leaving Slapton Sands behind. The last rays of the sun lit the stern, causing the boat's name to glow against the coming darkness, *Mary's Dream*.

THE END

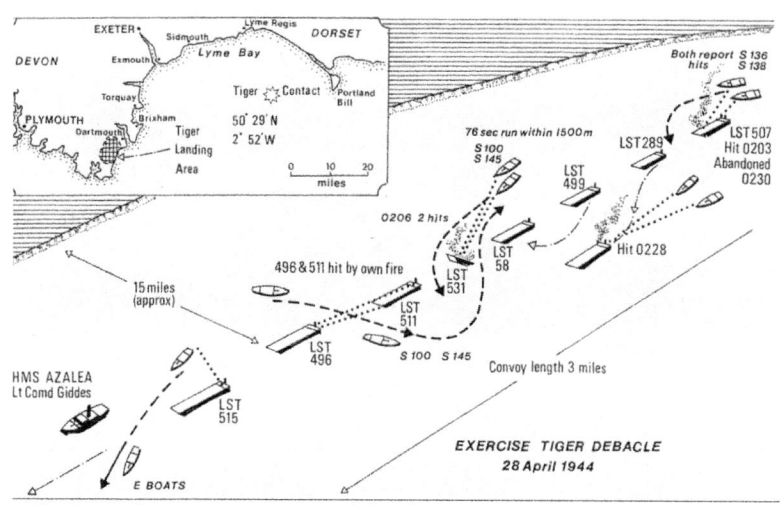

Defense Department map of the E-Boat attack on convoy T-4

Marshalling plan for D-Day, six weeks after Exercise Tiger

LST 289 being towed to Dartmouth Harbor with extensive stern damage from the torpedo attack

Close up of the stern damage caused by the torpedo strike and subsequent explosion aboard LST 289

Another angle of the massive stern damage to LST 289 – in Dartmouth Harbor

The following photographs are screenshots, courtesy the US National Archives, of movie footage shot by military cameramen at Slapton Sands between December 1943 and April 29th 1944.

Civilians being moved out - Slapton Sands, December 1943

3

Officers being moved in – Slapton Sands, January 1944

Troops in GMC Jimmys, in convoy to Slapton Sands

Aerial shot showing Slapton Sands and Slapton Ley, LSTs beached and maneuvers, days before Exercise Tiger, April, 1944

LSTs & LCAs maneuvering at Slapton Sands, April 1944

Lowering the LST's massive ramp

Driving off a beached LST onto Slapton Sands

Heading through the bow doors and down the LST's ramp

Sherman tank leaving an LST onto Slapton Sands beach

Soldiers on Slapton Sands loading supplies for Exercise Tiger

Aerial shot taken on April 27th, 1944 of LSTs massed off of Slapton Sands for Exercise Tiger

Classified document obtained from the National Archives
From the Ship's Diary – LST 499 – Exercise Tiger

MOST SECRET

125.11.4) of the Follow-Up Convoy Group (Task Group 125.11).

"The Convoy proceeded in accordance with sailing directions contained in Annex F, Appendix 3, to operation order 2-44, following the convoy route as shown in Minesweeping Overlay (Appendix 1 to Annex F). At 1930B, on reaching point F, convoy was joined by the Brixham section, Green LST Unit No. 3 (Task Unit 125.11.3) consisting of LSTs 499, 289, 507, 508. It is believed that LST 508 did not join convoy as scheduled.

"At 0100B, 28 April 1944, the situation was as follows: Convoy was proceeding via searched channel between points G and H on course 145 T. at about 4 knots, in the following order -- HMS _____ (escort), LSTs 515, 496, 511, 531, 58, 499, 289, 507. Distance between ships was 5-800 yards.

"At 0135B LST 507 was observed firing anti-surface from her starboard battery. (see sketch 1) We went to General Quarters but were unable to pick up any target on radar. At 0150B, on reaching point H, we changed course to 206 T., following in wake of guide. At Approximately 0215B, LST 507 was torpedoed. (see sketch 2) Convoy maintained course and speed. At about 0218B an unidentified LST in the vicinity of Point H opened fire with her starboard battery at target bearing about 080 relative, from her. Fire was returned from low in the water with blue tracer. At approximately 0221 LSTs 289 and 531 were torpedoed within a few seconds of each other. We made a 090 degree turn to port, went ahead flank and gave the order to open fire with after battery on radar target bearing 180 relative, distance about one and one-quarter miles. Cease fire and commenced zigzagging, endeavoring to present our stern to radar targets. At 0225B Escort radioed Portmouth that convoy was under E-Boat Attack in a position 16 miles bearing 250 T. from the Bill of Portland. At about 0228B we sighted target slightly abaft starboard beam and opened fire with starboard 40mm. battery. Put helm over and swung to port in order to present stern to target and gave order to cease fire. At 0230B Escort repeate transmission to Portland. We laid a course for Bill of Portland and proceeded at flank speed. At 0235B airline parted on port motor. Motor was repaired in five minutes, and adjusted our course by radar fixes, we proceeded to Chesil Cove, West Bay, Bill of Portland, dropping anchor about 1000 yards offshore at 0415. LSTs 511, 58 and 499 arrived in Chesil Cove shortly thereafter.

"At 0700B secured from General Quarters and endeavored to contact LST 515 for instructions. At 1030B, being unable to contact LST 515 sent following message CTG 125.11, aboard LST 491: "Unable contact LST 515 for instructions. Am proceeding with LSTs 511, 58, 499 from West Bay Portland ill to transport area. Weighed anchor at 1113B, proceeded to Transport Area off Slapton Sands, arriving at 1545B. Thence

-5-

MOST SECRET

continued with landing exercises as scheduled.

"Chronological sequence of events follows -- all times Baker:

0945 Under way from Plymouth
1930 Green LST Unit No. 3 joins convoy off Brixham
0100 Proceeding via searched channel between points G and H on course 140 T. at 4 knots.
0135 LST 507 observed firing anti-surface from starboard battery. No radar targets picked up.
0150 Arrived at point H and changed course to 206 T.
0215 LST 507 torpedoed.
0218 Unidentified LST at Point H opened fire with Starboard Battery. Fire returned from low in water with blue tracer.
0221 LSTs 289 and 513 torpedoed. We go ahead flank, make 90 degree turn to port and open fire with after battery at radar target bearing 180 relative, distance one and one-quarter miles.
0222 Cease fire and commenced zigzagging.
0225 Escort radios we are under E-Boat Attack
0228 Target sighted slightly abaft starboard beam. We open fire with Starboard 40mm battery. Helm put hard aport in order to present stern to E-Boat and order to cease fire.
0230 Escort repeats radio transmission
0235 Port motor cut out
0240 Port motor repaired
0415 Anchored in Chesil Cove, West Bay, Bill of Portland
0700 Endeavor to contact LST 515 --(by radio to request instruction) --unable to contact LST 515, inform CTG 125.11 aboard LST 491 we areproceeding to Transport area with LSTs 511, 58, 499.
1100 Three HMS escort ships arrive
1113 Anchor aweigh
1545 Arrive at Transport Area off Slapton Sands.

"Rounds expended: 40mm. -- 156; 20mm. -- 500.

"Ordinance casualties: Two misfires, one due to insufficient magazine pressure, the other to a short blowback. One runaway. No 40mm. casualties."

28 April 1944

1745 -- in accordance with directions from traffic control boat anchored 1000 yards off red beach and commenced unloading over LCT. At 1915 moved to new anchorage off Sugar Red Beach and continued unloading. In pulling away from bow, LCT damaged port bow door to point where it would not close (buckled worm gear). At 2120, on orders from SOPA, ceased unloading. In endeavoring to close ramp, wires pulled out of

-6-

From Ship's Diary – LST 499 – Exercise Tiger

The following pages may be a little disturbing, but need to be shown so that the sacrifice of those brave American servicemen is never forgotten.

From the Department of Defense, I obtained the first list that was put out internally of those killed during Exercise Tiger. At the time it was not available to the public and ruled Secret and Restricted. Sadly, another five hundred names would later be added to this list, including those of seventeen servicemen on LST 511 killed by friendly fire.

RESTRICTED

QMC Form
No. 2-ORS

2. 314.6 Q-ORS (Trans).

SUBJECT: QMC Form No. 2 ORS
Weekly Report of Burials. No. 85.

	NAME	SOLDIERS NO.	RANK	ORGANIZATION	DATE OF BURIAL D, M, Yr	CEMETERY
72.	CANADY, Allen J.	16161656	Sgt.	72nd T.C.Sq.	6 May 44	Brookwood
73.	HILL, James H.	311-68-74	Sea. 1/c.	11th Amph.Base U.S.Navy.	13 May 44	"
74.	KOHLER, Walter F.	36121880	PFC	H & S Co. 393 Engr.Regt.	13 May 44	"
75.	JUDD, Edward M.	35308031	PFC	Co."L" 18th Inf	13 May 44	"
76.	NIEMIEC, Julius J.	33439509	T/5	Co."A" 295 Engr Combat Bn.	13 May 44	"
77.	PARIS, Robert M.	Z-411442	AB	U.S.Merchant Marine.	13 May 44	"
78.	WOLF, William A.	312-48-17	S 1/c	U.S.S. Lst 280 U.S.Navy.	13 May 44	"
79.	CARLISLE, Lewis S.	806-73-49	G.M. 3/c.	U.S.S. Lst 280 U.S.Navy.	13 May 44	"
80.	GAINES, Warren W.	38416573	Sgt.	Co."C" 300th Engr. Bn.	13 May 44	"
81.	GENTRY, Homer S. Jr.	O-733456	1st Lt	705 Bomb Sq. 446 Bomb Gp.	13 Apr 44	Cambridge
82.	HACKES, Mike G.	712-01-76	S 2/c	L S T 289 U.S.Navy.	2 May 44	Brookwood
83.	HARVIE, James H.	806-02-82	S 2/c	L S T 289 U.S.Navy.	2 May 44	"
84.	KORTENHORN, Herman H.	868-31-11	F 1/c	L S T 289 U.S.Navy.	2 May 44	"
85.	BROSKE, Mitchell	807-27-14	GM 3/c	L S T 289 U.S.Navy	3 May 44	"
86.	MAY, Robert M.	657-87-98	S 2/c	LST 289,U S Navy	3 May 44	"
87.	MOODY, K. G.	V-22874		U. S. Navy	2 May 44	"
88.	HILL, John H.	363-969	Lt(JG) NVS.	LST 531,U S Navy	2 May 44	"
89.	HURLEY, James W.	834-88-54	HA 2/c	" "	2 May 44	"
90.	COYLE, Michael J.	245-67-29	HKR 3/c	" "	2 May 44	"
91.	BROCK, Norris G.	825-08-32	S 1/c	" "	2 May 44	"
92.	KESSINGER, Mark F.	895-33-32	S 2/c	" "	2 May 44	"
93.	LAND, Charles G.	867-76-58	S 2/c	" "	2 May 44	"

RESTRICTED

RESTRICTED

QMC Form
No.2-GRS

QM 314.5 Q-GRS (Trans).

8 JUN 1944

SUBJECT: QMC Form No.2 GRS
Weekly Report of Burials. No. 85.

	NAME	SOLDIERS NO.	RANK	ORGANIZATION	DATE OF BURIAL Dy M. Yr	CEMETERY
94.	LOCKLEAR, Melvin L.	341-72-16	CCS	LST 531 U.S.Navy	2 May44	Brookwood
95.	HAYTH, Eugene N.	612-46-06	SF 2/c	" "	2 May44	"
96.	EDSON, Richard W.	800-88-96	S 2/c	" "	2 May44	"
97.	KUHNS, Harold D.	805-57-59	S 2/c	" "	3 May44	"
98.	PEAR, William	647-48-20	EM 3/c	" "	3 May44	"
99.	KIRKWOOD, R.	855-93-04	F 2/c	" "	3 May44	"
100.	KRIZANOSKY, A.	249-52-60	F 2/c	" "	3 May44	"
101.	HOLMES, Samuel D.	83-27-30	MOMM 2/c.	" "	3 May44	"
102.	PARKER, Cornelius J.	843-60-94	MOMM 2/c.	" "	3 May44	"
103.	UNGER, A.C.	621-30-84	SK 3/c	" "	3 May44	"
104.	BOLLING, Floyd H.	832-77-43	S 2/c	" "	3 May44	"
105.	HAUBER, Bernard A.	629-00-91	EM 2/c	" "	3 May44	"
106.	MONTGOMERY, Doyle D.	656-18-11	Y 1/c	" "	3 May44	"
107.	VENDELAND, Albert J.	857-79-69	S 1/c	" "	3 May44	"
108.	GALLAGHER, J. J.	313847	Ensign DVG	" "	3 May44	"
109.	JACKMAN, Walter P.	267-163	Ens. NVG.	" "	3 May44	"
110.	LEVY, L.H.	247575	Lt DVS	" "	3 May44	"
111.	MANNING, Tiffany V.	132268	Lt (G) MC	" "	3 May44	"
112.	PETCAVAGE, William J.	820-95-96	S 1/c	" "	3 May44	"
113.	ACHEY, Allen O. Jr.	832-41-77	MOMM 3/c.	LST 531,U.S.Navy	2 May44	"
114.	JACQUES, Edmond J.	823-92-33	S 2/c	" "	2 May44	"
115.	KELLY, Ford H.	851-79-75	S 2/c	" "	2 May44	"
116.	MILLER, Ralph R.	249-87-62	Cox.	" "	2 May44	"
117.	SOLOMON, William	872-58-77	HA 1/c	" "	2 May44	"
118.	BAUGHER, Ellis W.	864-47-68	HA 2/c	" "	3 May44	"
119.	DAWSON, Glenn H.	263-66-86	HA 1/c	" "	3 May44	"

RESTRICTED

QMC Form
No. 2-GRS

QM 314.6 Q-GRG (Trans).

2 JUN 1944

SUBJECT: QMC Form No.2 GRS
Weekly Report of Burials. No. 85.

	NAME	SOLDIERS NO.	RANK	ORGANIZATION	DATE OF BURIAL Dy M Yr	CEMETERY
120.	COWAN, Eugene R.	892-91-68	S 1/c	LST 531, U.S.Army	3 May 44	Brookwood
121.	SHEPPARD, Thannel V.	534-44-49	"	" "	3 May 44	"
122.	SCHIMANSKE, Daniel R.	623-34-64	GM 3/c	" "	3 May 44	"
123.	CARR, Fredrick C.	627-94-66	Cox.	" "	3 May 44	"
124.	LACEY, Burtil E.	868-18-94	S 2/c	" "	3 May 44	"
125.	PETERS, James D.	819-11-09	Cox.	" "	3 May 44	"
126.	SHOWERS, Lyle F.	312-51-92	Ph.M. 3/c	" "	3 May 44	"
127.	HARRELL, Charles	556-93-72	HA 1/c	" "	3 May 44	"
128.	WITTEN, Lloyd L.	355-93-60	C Ph.M	" "	3 May 44	"
129.	LEVINE, Harry	812-86-95	Hq 1/c	" "	3 May 44	"
130.	DENTON, H.	807-58-00	SM 3/c	" "	3 May 44	"
131.	CALLAS, Vincent M.	811-88-95	S 1/c	" "	3 May 44	"
132.	BENTON, Elmer C.	601-54-00	S 2/c	" "	3 May 44	"
133.	SOCHACKI, Edward A.	312-57-81	Ph.M. 2/c.	" "	3 May 44	"
134.	LEEMAN, Hollace H.	846-06-42	HA 2/c	" "	3 May 44	"
135.	STEMATS, Steve J.	807-54-30	RM 3/c	" "	3 May 44	"
136.	SAUCIER, Henry Q.	188-420	Lt(JG)	LST 507, U.S.Navy	2 May 44	"
137.	KARASINSKI, Louis F.	710-92-02	S 1/c	" "	2 May 44	"
138.	WOODS, Deward W.	295-80-67	GM 1/c	" "	2 May 44	"
139.	CUSACK, Vincent P.	709-32-53	S 2/c	" "	2 May 44	"
140.	GARLOCK, Charles W.	621-75-50	QM 2/c	" "	2 May 44	"
141.	LEDBETTER, Alvin L.	834-01-50	S 2/c	" "	2 May 44	"
142.	FIELD, Paul R.	225-40-59	SM 3/c	" "	2 May 44	"
143.	BAILEY, James	725-84-44	Y 2/c	" "	2 May 44	"
144.	BENNER, Charles D.	821-05-26	RM 2/c	" "	2 May 44	"
145.	KING, Phillip E.	655-80-45	F 2/c	" "	2 May 44	"
146.	SCHREIBER, William H.	653-88-83	S 2/c	" "	2 May 44	"

-7-

RESTRICTED

QMC Form
No. 2-GRS

QM 314.6 Q-GRS (Trans).

SUBJECT: QMC Form No. 2 GRS
Weekly Report of Burials. No. 85.

2 JUN 1944

	NAME	SOLDIERS NO.	RANK	ORGANIZATION	DATE OF BURIAL Dy M. Yr	CEMETERY
147.	MARTIN, Howard A.	819-60-30	S 2/c	LST 507, U.S. Navy	2 May44	Brookwood
148.	GRIFFIN, Jimmie W.	892-95-16	SC 3/c	" "	2 May44	"
149.	MORANCY, Edgar F.	573-26-25	S 2/c	" "	2 May44	"
150.	GAMBREL, Jake	856-34-86	S 2/c	" "	2 May44	"
151.	MOORE, Joseph M.	818-74-58	S 2/c	" "	2 May44	"
152.	GOLDSMITH, Leonard	818-30-04	S 2/c	" "	2 May44	"
153.	HAMPTON, Jerry P.	828-36-37	S 2/c	" "	2 May44	"
154.	DURRAM, J.W.	634-39-33	S 1/c	" "	3 May44	"
155.	KOSKI, Theodore J.	610-61-07	MOMM 2/c	" "	3 May44	"
156.	SQUIRES, Lawrance P.	666-98-33	MOMM 2/c	" "	3 May44	"
157.	GULLEDGE, William T.	833-86-48	S 2/c	" "	3 May44	"
158.	GIBSON, Richard M.	667-20-00	S 1/c	" "	3 May44	"
159.	CLEARY, James F.	802-34-93	HA 2/c	" "	3 May44	"
160.	EISENBACH, Harold E.	865-63-87	S 2/c	" "	3 May44	"
161.	SULLIVAN, George A.	853-87-80	S 2/c	" "	3 May44	"
162.	GEEHAN, Raymond R.	667-12-94	GM 3/c	" "	3 May44	"
163.	SWARTS, J.S.	96231	Lt DVG	" "	3 May44	"
164.	SMITH, Dennan H.	236354	Lt EVS	" "	3 May44	"
165.	COLLINS, Conner D. Jr.	313-728	ENS	" "	3 May44	"
166.	HOFMANN, Bruce B.	190-360	Lt(JG)	" "	3 May44	"
167.	CLARK, James J.	211-310	ENS SC VG	" "	3 May44	"
168.	WRIGHT, Curtis M.	836-61-51	HA 2/c	" "	2 May44	"
169.	DINNEEN, Joseph M.	404-73-59	BM 1/c	" "	2 May44	"
170.	MALOTT, Robert J.	820-99-58	Ph.M 3/c	" "	2 May44	"
171.	MATHEWS, John E.	643-19-62	S 2/c	" "	2 May44	"
172.	BETTENCOURT, John J.	205-45-59	MOMM 2/c	" "	2 May44	"

RESTRICTED

Best Possible Image   DECLASSIFIED AUTHORITY - NND 785095

RESTRICTED

Q.C Form
No. 2-GRS

QM 314.6 Q-GRS (Trans).

SUBJECT: QMC Form No.2 GRS
Weekly Report of Burials. No. 85.

	NAME	SOLDIERS NO.	RANK	ORGANIZATION	DATE OF BURIAL Dy M. Yr	CEMETERY
173.	GROWN, James T. Jr.	265-57-39	MOMM 2/c	LST 507, U.S. Navy	2 May 44	Brookwood
174.	O'CONNELL, Michael J.	338-30-32	MOMM 2/c	" "	2 May 44	"
175.	DICKERSON, William W.	619-15-80	SK 2/c	" "	2 May 44	"
176.	MACKEY, Robert C.	285-04-07	Cox.	" "	2 May 44	"
177.	STANESIC, John L.	822-89-22	HA 2/c	" "	2 May 44	"
178.	SUTHERLAND, Pete J.	966-13-83	S 2/c	" "	2 May 44	"
179.	RAGUSO, Paul M.	642-34-34	Ph.M. 3/c	" "	2 May 44	"
180.	STAUDT, Charles J. Jr.	809-02-98	MOMM 1/c	" "	2 May 44	"
181.	DAILEY, Carl W.	630-82-19	Ph.M. 2/c	" "	2 May 44	"
182.	DELDUCA, Thomas	810-17-78	Cox.	" "	2 May 44	"
183.	HOFFMAN, Russell W.	819-11-25	S 1/c	" "	2 May 44	"
184.	BLACKIE, Henry A.	209-08-71	S 2/c	" "	3 May 44	"
185.	MILLER, John H.	813-84-35	S 2/c	" "	3 May 44	"
186.	DOBSON, Henry R.	641-45-73	Ph.M. 2/c	" "	3 May 44	"
187.	GREECO, Joseph G.	809-42-85	S 1/c	" "	3 May 44	"
188.	RYAN, James P.	601-17-55	SM 5/c	" "	3 May 44	"
189.	MAGGARD, Daniel W. Jr.	835-67-34	S 2/c	" "	3 May 44	"
190.	RAPTIS, Charles G.	805-70-65	THM 3/c	" "	3 May 44	"
191.	FITTS, Felton T.	269-12-88	GM 2/c	" "	3 May 44	"
192.	ROGERS, William L.	837-41-73	HA 2/c	" "	3 May 44	"
193.	MEYERS, L.A.	653-83-15	F 2/c	" "	3 May 44	"
194.	JOSLYN, Leonard L.	32735944	T/5	984 M.P. Co.	12 May 44	Lisnabreeny
195.	LEATHERBERRY, J.C.	34472451	Pvt	2913 Disciplinary Tng. Center	15 May 44	Brookwood
196.	CUNNINGHAM, Robert R.	33390426	Pvt	Co. "A" 851 Eng. Bn. (AVN)	16 May 44	"

RESTRICTED

May their sacrifice never be forgotten

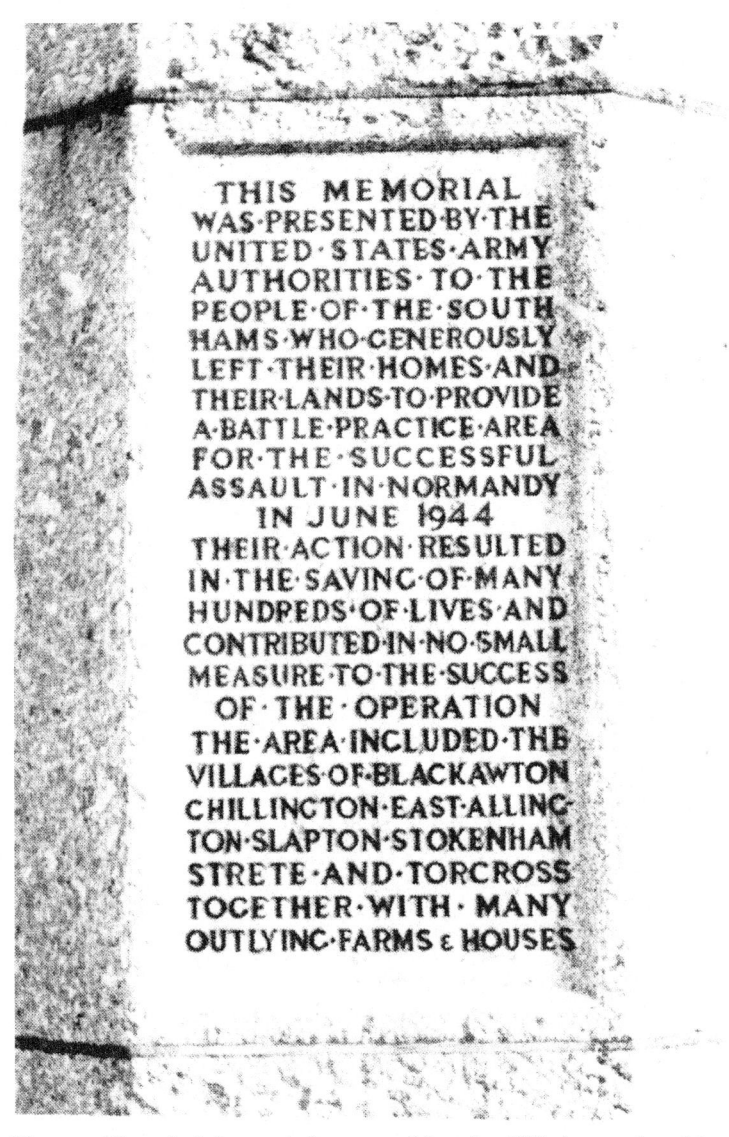

> THIS MEMORIAL
> WAS PRESENTED BY THE
> UNITED STATES ARMY
> AUTHORITIES TO THE
> PEOPLE OF THE SOUTH
> HAMS WHO GENEROUSLY
> LEFT THEIR HOMES AND
> THEIR LANDS TO PROVIDE
> A BATTLE PRACTICE AREA
> FOR THE SUCCESSFUL
> ASSAULT IN NORMANDY
> IN JUNE 1944
> THEIR ACTION RESULTED
> IN THE SAVING OF MANY
> HUNDREDS OF LIVES AND
> CONTRIBUTED IN NO SMALL
> MEASURE TO THE SUCCESS
> OF THE OPERATION
> THE AREA INCLUDED THE
> VILLAGES OF BLACKAWTON
> CHILLINGTON EAST ALLINGTON SLAPTON STOKENHAM
> STRETE AND TORCROSS
> TOGETHER WITH MANY
> OUTLYING FARMS & HOUSES

Slapton Sands Memorial erected by the US Army thanking the villagers for their help and sacrifice in allowing the training exercises to take place prior to D-Day

US Army memorial at Slapton Sands

In France, at Utah Beach, this memorial to the young Americans who died fighting during Exercise Tiger, was erected in June of 2012

SPECIAL THANKS

To the United States National Archives for permission to research and use the photographs and documents within this book.

To the late Ken Small, for all you did in raising the tank and bringing to light the forty-year cover-up. Thanks to you, the true story has come to light. Read more about his struggle in his book, *The Forgotten Dead*.

To Historic England for having the two sunken LSTs, 507 and 531 placed on the National Heritage List in May of 2020. This means that divers can visit the vessels but nothing can be removed and all contents will be protected, including the remains of the many young soldiers who went down with those ships. Their final resting place will not be disturbed.

To Simon Lewis for the use of several of your photographs of Slapton Sands and Torcross. Simon's work can be found at www.westcountryviews.co.uk

To Romy Vrana for your help with the German translation, it's so appreciated.

ABOUT THE AUTHOR

Richard Blade is the best-selling author of *World In My Eyes*, his autobiography, the novels *SPQR, Birthright, Imposters, Ghosts of the Congo,* and *The Lockdown Interviews* and *The Unlocked Interviews* with some of music's biggest stars. He is also one of the most popular and best-known DJs in America, hosting a daily radio show on SiriusXM 1st Wave, and on KCBS.

Richard was born in England, educated at Oxford, toured Europe for two years as a DJ then came to the USA. In the 1980s he was the #1 morning drive DJ on KROQ, Los Angeles, and hosted and directed numerous TV shows including *MV3, Video One* and *VideoBeat.*

He has been honored with a star on the Hollywood Walk of Fame, been given Richard Blade Day (*June 9th*) in Los Angeles by the City Council, nominated for the Radio Hall of Fame, and has won multiple awards including the Golden Microphone, California's Best DJ, Brit of the Year, and the American DJ Association's Lifetime Achievement Award. Richard has starred or co-starred in many TV shows and movies including *Girls Just Want To Have Fun, Spellcaster,* and *Long Lost Son* which he also wrote.

Richard lives in L.A. with his wife, Krista, and two dogs. He travels extensively as he continues to DJ live and is in high demand as a speaker, MC and host at events around the world.

Facebook – Richard Blade Page, X and Threads @RichardBlade

Printed in Great Britain
by Amazon